PECOS SCHOOL LIBRARY
SAN DIEGO CA

FIC   Saver
SAV   Smu

D0442277

AP 24 '03			
SE 24 '03			
OC 14 '03			
DE -3 '03			
JA 5 '04			

BRODART, CO.   Cat. No. 23-233-003   Printed in U.S.A.

WITHDRAWN
La Jolla, CA 92093-0536

A PERFECT ARRANGEMENT

Thérèse placed the last bouquet in the center of the dining room table and stepped back to look at it. Leaning forward, she gave it a quarter turn and checked again. She nodded, turned, and found herself with her nose very nearly pressed against a waistcoat made up of a gray satin material with a narrow darker gray stripe. The buttons, she noted, were silver. Well-polished silver.

Miles lifted his hands slowly. Slowly he placed them, flat and open, against her upper arms. She didn't move. She didn't even look up. For a long moment they stood like that, neither moving, neither speaking. Then Miles put his fingers under her chin and lifted it. They stared into each other's eyes. . . .

Books by Jeanne Savery

THE WIDOW AND THE RAKE

A REFORMED RAKE

A CHRISTMAS TREASURE

A LADY'S DECEPTION

CUPID'S CHALLENGE

LADY STEPHANIE

A TIMELESS LOVE

A LADY'S LESSON

LORD GALVESTON AND THE GHOST

A LADY'S PROPOSAL

THE WIDOWED MISS MORDAUNT

A LOVE FOR LYDIA

TAMING LORD RENWICK

LADY SERENA'S SURRENDER

THE CHRISTMAS GIFT

THE PERFECT HUSBAND

A PERFECT MATCH

SMUGGLER'S HEART

Published by Zebra Books

SMUGGLER'S HEART

Jeanne Savery

ZEBRA BOOKS
Kensington Publishing Corp.
http://www.kensingtonbooks.com

Preuss School UCSD
9500 Gilman Drive
La Jolla, CA 92093-0536

ZEBRA BOOKS are published by

Kensington Publishing Corp.
850 Third Avenue
New York, NY 10022

Copyright © 2002 by Jeanne Savery Casstevens

All rights reserved. No part of this book may be reproduced in any form or by any means without the prior written consent of the Publisher, excepting brief quotes used in reviews.

If you purchased this book without a cover you should be aware that this book is stolen property. It was reported as "unsold and destroyed" to the Publisher and neither the Author nor the Publisher has received any payment for this "stripped book."

All Kensington titles, imprints, and distributed lines are available at special quantity discounts for bulk purchases for sales promotion, premiums, fund-raising, educational or institutional use.

Special book excerpts or customized printings can also be created to fit specific needs. For details, write or phone the office of the Kensington Special Sales Manager: Kensington Publishing Corp., 850 Third Avenue, New York, NY 10022. Attn. Special Sales Department. Phone: 1-800-221-2647.

Zebra and the Z logo Reg. U.S. Pat. & TM Off.

First Printing: April 2002
10 9 8 7 6 5 4 3 2 1

Printed in the United States of America

With special thanks to Professor James K. Kieswetter, Department of History, Eastern Washington University. With great patience, Dr. Kieswetter helped me with my abysmal French. Any errors made when editing after his help, are my fault entirely.

And in memory of my mother, who heard all about Sahib when I put him forward as part of a novella, and for my editor, John Scognamiglio, who suggested the tiger might work better as part of a novel. I doubt John guessed I'd sneak my favorite tiger into six books!

One

"Tiens! René, you cannot!" The words, spoken in French, burst from the young woman standing in René Laurent's parlor.

"But I *can, chérie,"* he replied, his voice soft. "I have. We are chartered as traders here in England, a business. We are legitimate and no longer hover on the verge of disaster."

Thérèse Marie Suzanne Laurent de Saint Omer stared at her father's cousin, her disgust obvious. "Make of us a business! And how will this business differ from what we have done for years—except that our costs increase?"

"The war is over, Thérèse," said René gently. "No longer is it necessary to go outside the law. No longer need we take chances." He smiled a sweet sad smile. "Or should I say *you?* You, *chérie,* have been exceedingly careful to assure that I am, in no way, associated with the dangerous side of things."

A muscle jumped in the younger Laurent's jaw and she turned away from him. "It would be stupid to involve you except in the most indirect fashion. Your work here in England is crucial, but if I am captured, you and my father could organize another crew and carry on. I do not see why we cannot continue as we were," she complained.

René's voice grew stern. "I have said: It is unnecessary. With the war ended the British Navy has more time to hunt for such as we. *You.* From now on we will stay within the law of both countries." He lifted the letter that Thérèse Marie had handed him some twenty minutes earlier. "Your father agrees."

She whirled around. "That packet I took with me when I last crossed the Channel! You proposed this then! That is why he went to Paris. It is to set up the French side of your stupid *business.*"

"The business, which is not stupid." René shrugged. It was an exceedingly French gesture, considering he had lived a great many years in England, exiled from a world that no longer existed. Still, in many ways, he had changed little. *"Mon cousin* agrees you must no longer risk your pretty neck!"

"Pretty!" Thérèse Marie felt heat in her throat. She raised a hand in a futile effort to cover the embarrassing expanse of bare skin above the neckline of her gown. "You perjure yourself, René!"

"Will you never learn to accept compliments gracefully?" he retorted.

Despite the chiding tone, Thérèse thought she saw a certain amount of compassion in his gaze. She swallowed hard, and turned away. She was *not* pretty. She had not been pretty when young and, at twenty-four, she hadn't even youth to compensate for strong features and lithe limbs, for weather-gilded skin. . . . No. Not pretty. Never pretty . . .

And it doesn't matter a jot, she told herself, twitching her skirts into place. *Not one jot.*

When visiting René, she changed to the gowns he'd had made for her. The first time he saw her in her trousers he'd been shocked beyond anything, truly appalled, even though her slim figure was well camouflaged by her male attire. Thérèse Marie hated skirts, which were a nuisance. They hung around her legs, and beyond the fact they got in the way, feminine fashion was, to Thérèse Marie's mind, far less modest than the trousers, shirt, cravat, and coat she wore by preference.

The only pieces of feminine finery she actually preferred

were the slippers. She found boots ugly and hard to care for, the saltwater ruining them if they were not cleaned and polished regularly. Her feet were long, narrow of heel and high of arch, and boots had to be made for her by an English cobbler who charged the earth for them. Thérèse Marie had more important things to do with her money than to buy boots.

"We also discussed your future, my dear," said René, interrupting her thoughts.

"*My* future?" Thérèse Marie turned, saw that he studied his fingernails rather than looking her in the face. What was he thinking? She blinked. Twice.

He looked up and his lips turned up at the corners, but his eyes did not reflect the implied humor. Was he laughing at her? Mildly seething irritation bubbled up and pushed aside her curiosity as to his thoughts about her future.

"Don't laugh at me!"

"I never laugh at you, *chérie.*"

"You do!" Thérèse Marie's lips firmed into a narrow line. "What business have you and Father discussing my future? This is not at all humorous that you do such a thing!"

"We *must* discuss it."

A certain stubborn expression, which her father called her mule-face, hardened Thérèse's features. "My future is what my past has been. What is there to discuss?"

"Your past is all wrong!" He became suddenly more brisk. "Thérèse Marie, you must be introduced to society. You must meet others of your station, enjoy yourself as you should have done for many years now. Most important, we must find you a husband!"

"A husband?" Thérèse scowled fiercely. "Who would wed such as I and why should I wish to marry? *Moi?*" She pointed to herself. "*Mon Dieu!* Wed a man who would confine me to womanly tasks? Who would demand that I stay at home in his house and manage it for him? While *he* goes where he wills? While *he* enjoys life? The devil I will," she finished, using one of the milder oaths from her large repertory.

René sighed. "My dear, when things were desperate, your father allowed you to behave in what is, you'll admit, an extremely unladylike fashion—"

"*Allowed* me!"

"—but—" René broke into her rampaging thoughts. "—we are no longer desperate."

"Father was never desperate," she muttered.

Her father had had no knowledge of what she did until the venture was organized and under way for some time. Only then did he stick his finger in the pot—and more to indulge his desire for a few luxuries than to further the work she'd begun at an age when girls did not yet put up their hair! Thérèse felt angry all over again with the self-pitying man who cared for nothing and no one beyond his own comfort. Or at least—Thérèse Marie tempered her wild exaggeration slightly—would see that his comfort was cared for *first*.

"Thérèse," said René, "there is no need for you to risk your neck ever again."

"No need?" she muttered.

"Can you not see we only wish the best for you?"

Thérèse Marie shook her fists in the air. "You wish me to pine away into my grave from boredom, that is what I see!"

"Nonsense. *Chérie,* you will enjoy an English Season. Or—" René looked a trifle doubtful. "—perhaps your father could take you to Paris. . . ."

"Where, stripped of his lands and his fortune, he has nothing but his title? Where he is nobody?"

"London, then. There, at my side, you will take your proper place in the world. You will wear proper gowns—" An expression of exquisite pain crossed his mobile features as his eyes tracked over the dress, long out of the mode, presently gracing her figure. "—and dance far into the night. You will attend plays and concerts, ride in the park, be invited to soirées, breakfasts, teas, all the parties which make the Season so delightful."

"You do that, do you not?" she asked, wondering what pleasure he found in such things.

"For two or three weeks only. Yes. Ah! How I wish it could be longer!"

"You have the *entrée* in the best houses?"

He nodded, a complacent expression making him look smug. "I no longer have wealth, but I have status and I have, hmm, friends from the old days who do not forget me."

"Then why," she asked, "have *you* not wed?" Her eyes narrowed. "You are a personable man even now." She studied him. Tall, wiry rather than thin, his thick hair whitening at the temples, his narrow dark brows accentuating dark deep sunk eyes over high cheekbones. Thérèse Marie was surprised to discover her offhand comment truer than she'd known. "You might have found yourself an heiress years ago. And not have scraped and pinched and starved yourself so that you might have that two or three weeks each spring!"

René turned away. After moment he said, "My dear Thérèse, has your father never told you?"

"Told me?" Thérèse Marie sobered, identifying an air of tragedy hanging around him like a nearly visible cloak. "You would say there was an *affaire de coeur* from which you never recovered?"

René turned back. A sweet sad smile graced his features. "You might say that. Your father and I fell in love with the same woman." His eyes watched for her reaction, his voice was gentle as he added, "Jean-Paul won her."

"I see." What she saw embarrassed her, although she hid it well. Her cousin had been kind to her all these years for her mother's sake, not her own as she had thought!

Embarrassment faded to be replaced by a sense of loss. She had, she realized, pretended René was her true father, the man her father should have been, instead of the lazy dreamer who had to be managed, prodded, protected, and who was *not* the strong arm she wanted and needed and had learned, at an early age, to do without.

Thérèse Marie wandered around her cousin's small dark parlor, picking up a piece of porcelain here, a framed miniature there, and finally an apple from the blue bowl centered on the highly polished round table from which her cousin took his meals.

"You gnaw that like a schoolboy! Here—" He drew a penknife from his pocket. "—allow me to peel it for you and core it!"

Thérèse Marie took another bite, grinned, and mopped juice from her chin with the back of her fist. "They taste better this way."

"You, Thérèse Marie Suzanne Laurent, are the complete hoyden!"

She shook her head, suddenly a trifle grim. "No, I am the boy I should have been, my father's heir, except, of course, he has no property other than what we—*I*—pretend is still ours. Which reminds me. Did you find that ram I need?"

René cast her a look pregnant with disgust. "Sheep breeding! What else will you attempt?"

"*Attempt?*" Her brows arched high and her chin jutted. "What have I tried that has *failed?*"

René was silenced. The orchards planted nearly ten years previously, her first effort, were producing well, as were the vegetable gardens. The poultry she transported across the Channel had multiplied to the point that the peasantry were selling eggs and, occasionally, a few extra cockerels or a brace of geese.

Some of the younger women had learned to embroider from an elderly and homesick Frenchwoman Thérèse talked into returning from exile in England for that purpose, and still another elderly lady taught lace-making. René sold the handwork in shops in several provincial English cities, providing the women a steady income.

"So?" she asked again. "My ram?"

He sighed. "I have procured a ram of the proper breed which, with luck, will improve the wool your peasants produce."

"Excellent. What else have you for me this time?"

"This *last* time," he said. He caught and held her gaze, a warning in his voice. When she responded with no more than an irritated twitch of her lips, he listed the few small luxuries he had bought for her and her father's use.

"I wish," she complained, "that you would not indulge my father with the cigarillos. It is a waste. And I have no need for ribbons and laces. Besides, I acquire far better lace in France."

"Which you bring to me and I sell." René frowned. "Thérèse Marie, have you *no* interest in feminine fripperies? None at all?'

"No." She noticed that her blunt response appeared to distress him, although she did not understand why. To lighten the atmosphere she added, "Now if you could purchase me a new sail, or find a really good varnish for the deck, which already needs it again, ah! That would delight me no end!"

René shook his head, laughing. "You are irrepressible, are you not?"

"Of course," she said pertly. "You would be unhappy if I were any other way. Now, about my next crossing . . ."

"Mais non!"

"René!"

"Non." He sighed when the mulish look returned, giving her features that hard expression he deplored. "Your sailing days have ended. When all is organized, we, your father and I, will do things with a proper captain and paying proper duties, honest and aboveboard." When her mouth thinned to the point it practically disappeared, he strode to her side and grasped her chin firmly. "Your days as a smuggler are finished. More, you are no longer captain to your crew. Accept it. You will no longer ply the lanes across the

Channel, carrying contraband. You will not smuggle it ashore in England, nor return with properly bought and receipted produce—"

"—which I then," she interrupted, "smuggle into France." She frowned. *"And no duties either side.* It is insane, René, to lose so much by paying duty. It is nonsense. Why can you not see that?'

"What I see is a young woman who should be playing with her babies! Instead, she risks her neck. You will return home, my dear, with a whole skin, *priez le bon Dieu,* and you will burn your boy's clothing. You will don skirts and you will remain in them!"

Thérèse Marie knew when it was a waste of time to argue. She merely shrugged, finished her apple, and threw the core into the empty grate before going to the window. Her legs straddled widely, much as they'd be if she were on her ship, her hands clasped behind her, she stood there, staring out into the pouring rain and deepening dusk.

Rain. It was likely she'd be stuck here for another day. Perhaps two. The storm was not so bad she could not make the crossing, but René was, she suspected, lonely. The weather gave him an excuse to demand that she extend her visit.

Or perhaps—the thought crossed her mind fleetingly—*he really does worry about me?*

The result was the same. She was *here* instead of facing into the good clean rain, the wind blowing away the cobwebs, the huge slow waves leaden in color, oily seeming, rolling high, fat and stodgy, under her bow—how she pined to be on the water! But no, she would sit, a demure and proper spinster, in her cousin's parlor and pour tea for English ladies.

The local ladies adored René and, through servants' gossip, would know she visited. She was their excuse, an opportunity to converse with the delightful Frenchman who graced their little dinners and their evening parties with panache, but whom it was indelicate to visit in his own home—except for when Thérèse Marie was there to act the chaperon!

Miles Seward stared morosely out into the pouring rain. It had rained for two days straight and he felt housebound as he never did when on board the *Nemesis*. The ship he had won—along with his life—from a pirate captain some years previously had become a home to him and a sanctuary from ennui, providing continuous change and, often, the excitement he craved.

Ian looked up from the paper he perused. "Bored, Miles?" he asked in his deep rumbling voice.

"To the point it would be a blessing to cut my throat and be done with it!"

Ian chuckled. "Surely we can find a better solution then that! I cannot beat you at billiards, so I'll not suggest *boring* you in that particular manner, but what of a game of chess?"

"No, for *I* cannot beat *you* at chess." Miles turned. "I need to be doing, Ian. I cannot enjoy parties as does Tony. I have no interest in politics as do Alex and Jack." He counted off two more friends on his fingers. "I've an excellent solicitor who watches my investments and does a better job by far than I could ever do—unlike you who prefers to handle your family's investments yourself." Holding up four fingers, he thought a moment and, grinning, opened out his thumb. "Can you see me sitting at a desk—" He threw up his hands. "—and *writing?* I cannot emulate Jason either, and, now, even the army has no use for me as it did before the war ended." His whole body seemed to collapse in on itself. "With Napoleon exiled to St. Helena I am as useless as seaweed washed up on the strand!"

"You must find another comparison," said Ian. He grinned when Miles tipped his head, questioningly. "Seaweed is *not* useless. When gathered by our farmers and spread on their fields it makes an excellent fertilizer."

Miles grimaced and shoved his hands into his pockets. "I have been thinking of taking off for . . . oh, I don't know. East of India, perhaps?" A spark lit his eyes. "There are islands yet to be explored, full of beauty and wonders never before seen, exotic beyond belief . . ."

Reluctantly, Ian said, "I suppose you might collect exotic plants for collectors." He didn't want Miles disappearing to who-knew-where as he'd done soon after the six friends went up to University. Miles had disappeared and stayed away far too many years. "Collecting is being done by more and more explorers of odd corners of our world."

"I could." But it was obvious Miles had no interest in exotic plants. He turned suddenly, his decision made. "Ian, thank you for your hospitality. Tell Lady Serena that I will enjoy it again when next I make land."

"You are returning to the *Nemesis*?" asked Ian, who had been expecting just that for several days. After all, Miles had stayed with them for very nearly a month, which was nearly twice as long as he'd ever done before.

"I am. I haven't a notion where I'll go or what I'll do, but, I'll not be wearing a path in your carpet!"

"Carpets can be replaced. We will miss you," said Ian.

"Will you?" Miles smiled crookedly. "I always find it surprising that you say that."

"You find it surprising because you have never learned to value yourself as others value you."

Miles's shoulders hunched, a movement denoting discomfort. Soul-searching and the capacity for self-analysis were *not* to be found among his virtues!

Miles's few orders to his first mate, Toby White, were accomplished expeditiously, and, since the *Nemesis* was always in excellent trim and well stocked, he and his crew sailed down the Thames on the very next tide.

"Where are we off to, Captain?" asked Toby, glancing down at the top of Miles's head. They had left behind the worst of the congestion below the East India basin and Greenwich and it was nearing time to set a course.

Miles grinned, already feeling more the thing. He rested a hand on a spar and stared straight ahead. "I haven't a notion. Except I would take us away from land and out where a man may breathe."

Toby's teeth flashed against the well-weathered skin of his face. Crinkles appeared at the corners of his eyes. He lifted his beret, brushed back his thinning hair, and resettled his preferred headgear, pulling it down tight so the wind would not carry it away. "That is good. We have all felt like beached fish. A good sea wind will blow away the blue-devils," he finished.

Miles's humor had improved with every mile down river. He glanced up at the scudding clouds. The rain, which had become a drizzle as he'd left Ian's London house, had stopped altogether as they'd weighed anchor. He said as much.

"An omen, Captain! An omen!" crowed Toby, grinning like an oversized monkey.

"Ha! Omen indeed! For a start we cross the Channel. Perhaps we will take a peek into the cove into which we watched that smuggler's ship ease itself."

"We couldn't get through the rocks. Besides, can't do anything when it is moored."

"No. I can't, can I?"

Toby cast his revered captain a quick knowing glance. "Still burning, are you, that we never brought those smugglers to book?"

Miles grinned a quick hard grin. "Maybe I am."

"So?" The knowing grin broadened.

"So? We will pay the cove a visit and see if the thieving bastard is sleeping like the innocent he is not or if he's out of his bed and away.

"And if he is sleeping?"

"We leave him to his slumbers, of course. And if he is not? Why, maybe we'll see if we can find him!" Miles's most wolfish smile surfaced. "I doubt the leopard changed his spots just because the war ended!" He laughed, throwing back his head and enjoying the wind in his hair. Free! He was free and doing what he loved best! He was standing near the helm of his own ship and could go where he wanted and do what he wanted and be what he wanted. . . .

. . . and the blue-devils, as Toby called them, were tucked right back where they belonged, somewhere deep inside where he need not admit to their existence!

Two

"Easy, *mon ami*," whispered Thérèse Marie. "Easy now." She watched closely as her first mate brought the yacht into the hidden cove. It was a difficult approach and not made carelessly. At one place, a hand's breadth either way and they'd scrape the sides of the *Ange Blanc* on rocks hidden below the water's surface. "Easy . . ."

A shout from the third person on board drew her attention. She looked aft and her eyes widened. *"Sacre bleu!* That dratted man!"

"Mam'zelle?"

"Don't call me that!"

Her first mate grinned at her. "But your cousin insists I am no longer to call you "captain," so what am I to call you?"

"You'll call me captain and like it." She continued to stare aft where her nemesis—named the *Nemesis!*—followed her smaller swifter boat into the cove. Her eyes narrowed. "He will catch on the rocks."

"Should we not warn him?"

"Why? He has someone at the prow watching. On his head be it if he holes her."

"You do not like the master of the *Nemesis*?"

"The *Nemesis* and her captain came close to cooking our goose on more than one occasion, as you well know. Once we outran him. Once dark fell and we escaped, but that last time, if it were not for that fog bank rolling in, you and I would be fish bait hanging in chains. You think I like the man who came so near to drawing down disaster on our heads?"

"We are through."

Thérèse Marie turned and scanned the cove in which she regularly moored the sleek yacht. She sighed. *One more problem,* she thought, a grim look tightening her features. *Not only must I fight Father to allow me to continue my work, but now I will need a new mooring. One the idiot captain of the* Nemesis *cannot find.*

"Captain!" called the youth who had warned her before, "they are putting down boats."

"So?"

"So—" He turned wide frightened eyes toward her. "—do we fight them?"

Thérèse Marie glanced at the two dories rapidly filling with the enemy crew. "I think not," she said, her voice as dry as dust. Then her eyes narrowed and her mouth tightened into a hint of a grin her crew knew well.

"What devilment plan you now?" asked the youngest sailor, his fear vanishing in youthful curiosity.

"Devilment? Why none at all. Henri, my lad," she said to the not-quite-a-man at her elbow, "go into the cabin and set out the best brandy and—" She checked the men in the lead boat. "—five glasses."

"Five?" asked Armand. There were three men in the first and four more in the second boat.

"Do you think I would meet this strange captain and you not present?" The grin grew, widening until white teeth shone in her sun-gilded skin. "Ahoy," she called, her natural contralto voice deepened to the gruff cheerful tones that were part of her disguise. "Come aboard and join us in a glass of wine!"

Miles Seward noted that the French captain spoke surprisingly upperclass French. He responded in English. "Wine, is it? And who would say no to a Frenchman's good wine?" *Let the man think I know little French,* he thought.

Thérèse Marie was no more a fool than Miles. She pretended to look perplexed. Then shrugged as if to say it was unimportant. Armand gave their visitors a hand over the rail and Henri pulled in the boat's painter and tied it and grinned at the men in the second boat, caught the rope they tossed him, and tied it as well. Thérèse Marie's younger crewman gestured to where he'd set a pitcher, crooked his fingers, and as he'd expected, was followed to where a cheap wine awaited him and the four English seamen from the other ship.

Thérèse Marie opened the cabin door and bowed in the more important of her guests. She noticed that the foreign captain ducked under the lintel and felt her eyes widening. She had not thought him so tall. The English mate following his captain had to bend low and she realized why she'd assumed the captain a smallish man. Next to his first mate, he *was*.

Miles was an old hand at an odd form of French used between French and English seamen mingling in various channel ports. He addressed his hosts in this argot, using English where he might be expected to be ignorant of the French. "I am Seward," he said. "And you?"

"Captain Antoine-Clair," said Thérèse Marie, bowing. "My first mate, Armand Mouton." Armand bowed.

The five looked at each other.

"Toby White," said Miles, gesturing, "and his son, Johnny."

Toby nodded but Johnny grinned. He stepped forward and, with panache, lifted Thérèse Marie's hand and kissed it. Miles, taking a better look at his "host" swore. Violently.

Thérèse Marie turned her eyes on Armand, who stiffened into a rigidity that boded ill for someone. Recovering her aplomb, she put her hand on her first mate's arm, squeezing. Pinching, actually. "Pour for these gentlemen," she suggested.

"They . . ." began the mate.

". . . have guessed my little secret. But why not?" The

sound of a rousing good song drifted through the door. Thérèse Marie grinned. "Go assure yourself that no one takes it into his head to go swimming." She glanced at Miles. "The rock is not confined to the passage into this cove. I would not wish anyone to break his pate diving overboard."

Miles pretended to look confused. Armand translated into the sailor jargon Miles had admitted to and, reluctantly, left the salon. Miles sent Toby and Johnny after him.

Thérèse Marie blinked. It had not occurred to her that she would be left alone with this exceedingly dangerous English captain. She set down her wineglass, reluctant to muddle her head with even so much as another sip. "Do you sail these waters often?" she asked, speaking the French words slowly, attempting to make her words clear, unwilling to allow her enemy to know she spoke his language.

Miles pretended to mull over her words. "Sail these waters. Often. Yes." He nodded. "I have seen you. Your lovely yacht. You too sail these waters. Often."

Thérèse Marie gave him points for referring in such a bland way to the fact he had come far too close to capturing her on more than one occasion. "I have business across the channel," she said. Her features, too, were totally under control.

Miles had not expected her to come so close to admitting to her smuggling and the sip of wine he'd just taken went down the wrong way. When he ceased coughing, he gave her a long look of respect. "The war is over now," he said, suggestively.

She nodded. "My business will be different now, it is true."

"I saw a crated sheep on deck," said Miles after a moment. Blandly, he added, "It belongs, perhaps, to Armand?"

It was Thérèse Marie's turn to swallow wrong. In between sieges of coughing she caught Miles's eye and struggled between laughter and the attempt to clear her windpipe.

"Armand carries the *name* but he is *not* a sheep. Besides, the creature in the crate is a ram. A very good ram."

"You had a special order from a farmer near here?" asked Miles politely.

She shrugged, pretended to sip, and set aside her glass. A rollicking ditty drifted into the salon and she got up, opening the door. The men sprawled on the aft deck, each singing louder than the next, their glasses waving in time to the lilt. She shook her head, frowning. "They will be good for nothing for hours!"

"You fear you'll—"

She almost jumped out of her skin at the sound of his voice so near her ear.

"—not be rid of us before the wine runs out?"

"More likely, not before they sleep it off!" She tried to pretend she could not feel the heat of his body against her back and shoulder. He stood leaning in her direction, very nearly touching her, one arm raised to the lintel.

"I will order my men back to my ship." He straightened. "In fact we will all go." Seemingly with no effort, he set her aside, exited, then turned back. "I invite you and your crew to join us for dinner." Miles caught her eye and held it, a dare in his, wondering if he had judged her rightly. "Will you come?" He grinned an only slightly wolfish grin.

Thérèse Marie's chin rose a notch. "We would be rather late. The ram must be delivered."

"And the other things you bought unloaded?"

"The ram is the total of my business this day," she said coldly.

"Hmm."

"You do not believe me?"

He chuckled. "My dear Captain Antoine-Clair! Or is that Antoinette Claire?"

She didn't respond.

"But why would I doubt you?" he finished when even her expression told him nothing.

Thérèse Marie felt her temper climbing. If there was any-

thing in the world she disliked, it was to be taken for a liar.
"Search." She gestured broadly. "Search where and how
you will. *There is nothing to find.*"

She stalked forward, pulled Henri's hair until she had his
attention, jerked her thumb toward the crated ram, and went
on to Armand. She had to speak to him twice before he
dropped out of the chorus of the current song. *"Ma capitaine?"*

She rolled her eyes at his giving *mon capitaine* a feminine form, but all she said was, "Help Henri."

"Help . . ." He looked toward where the slender youth
was attempting to drag the crate nearer the port side of the
yacht. "What is it?"

"We are leaving. Leaving that . . . that . . ."

"Careful, *mon ange!*" said Armand in a soft voice.

Thérèse Marie drew in a deep breath. ". . . and we return
to have dinner on board his *Nemesis*." When Armand hesitated, she added, "Move!"

Armand moved. He and Henri affixed a davit where it
could be used to haul the crate over the side and into a
dory. They had the crate ready to be lifted when Toby came
to their side and, without asking, laid a hand on the crank.
The Frenchmen, startled, saw the load rise and jumped to
guide it. The job completed, Armand turned to Toby, nodded, and held out his hand. Toby glanced from hand to man
and back. He held out his. The two men shook hands.

Miles, jesting with his crew, noticed and frowned. It was
not part of his plans for friendship to sprout between his
men and his enemies! Once they were back on board the
Nemesis he said as much.

"Armand is a good man. Henri is still unfledged. And
your *enemy* has turned out to be a lady!" One of his brows
arched. "And that being so, I'd guess your plans must
change."

Miles had been watching the *Ange Blanc* and his eyes
gleamed at what he saw. "Plans? But I *have* no plans."

"If you do not it will be the first time!"

Miles chuckled. "As soon as that trio has disappeared, put the dory back into the water. You and I will return to the yacht and search it. Thoroughly. And—" He grinned at his mate's disapproving look "—before you say what is on the tip of your tongue, allow me to inform you that the charming captain gave me permission."

"She did *what?*"

"Well," said Miles, pretending to doubt, "I cannot be absolutely certain she believed I'd take her up on it." He turned on his heel and went to inform Piggy, the *Nemesis's* cook, there would be company for dinner. "French company," he said, a warning in his tone.

"French, hmm?" The cook's eyes narrowed until he looked still more like the pig that was his nickname. "So do I show off or do I insult their palates in the worst way possible?"

Miles was about to tell the man to do his worst when he realized he was saying the exact opposite. ". . . The best wine, too."

"Aye. That means the last bottle of the . . ."

Miles shook his head, alarmed at the thought of serving up the last of one of the finest burgundies he had ever drunk. "No! Not that. I'll not waste that on someone who very likely has no palate. You know exactly what will suit, so do not tease me!"

Miles returned to where, unhappy and disapproving, Toby awaited him. "Well? Ready?"

"You are making a mistake."

"Do I?" Miles thought about it for a moment. He shook his head. "The *Ange Blanc* is a smuggler's ship. We *know* it has been smuggling. That the captain is other than we expected does not change that."

Nor, he told himself firmly, *does the way I feel when close to her! Although,* he added, *perhaps it might be interesting to explore those hints of how it could be between us?*

He dropped gently into the dory, held it steady for Toby,

Three

Thérèse Marie, confronting confusing emotions, rose to her feet and followed Armand and Henri across the field to the lane. "How dare he!" she said softly . . . but at the same time she remembered the heat of him standing close to her, the sight of his lithe frame moving easily, freely, the feel of the raw silk of his voice rubbing her nerves raw . . . and, again, just now, the boyish braggadocio when he rowed toward her yacht. . . .

"Why," she asked Armand when she'd caught up with him, "did I say I'd join him for dinner?"

Armand had a notion about that, but not one he'd the courage to put into words. Instead of suggesting she found Captain Seward intriguing, perhaps more, he asked, "Because he dared you to join him and you are incapable of turning down a dare?"

"Am I so foolish?"

"It is your temper. It takes so little to rouse it and when roused, you lose control of your good sense."

Thérèse Marie could not deny it. "Perhaps I will send a message with you. Perhaps I will say that I forgot a prior engagement."

Armand chuckled. "And perhaps, *ma chère capitaine*, you will don your hated skirts and show him what a woman you truly are!"

Thérèse glanced his way and took note of the twinkle in his eye. She sighed and discarded the notion she'd had of doing just that. "No. I may be foolish, but I am not stupid. They search the *Ange*," she added, knowing it would upset her mate.

He stopped short. "They *what?*"

"There is nothing to find."

"This time!'

"And there will be no next time. For them. This is their only chance." She ignored Armand's snort. "Can you not make that beast walk faster?" she called, lengthening her stride to catch up with Henri. "Perhaps I will leave you to finish this job while I return home. I want a bath and . . ."

"What," called Armand, hands on hips, "should we do about those . . . those . . ."

She turned, walking backward. "Englishmen?"

"I will not have it. Searching the *Ange*! How dare they?"

Thérèse Marie cast him a look of mischief. "Well, I rather fear it is my fault."

Armand's expression did not lighten. "How?"

"As you would say, my temper."

Armand caught up and grasped her arm, stopping her. "What have you done?"

She lifted her hands in such a way he was forced to drop his if he were not to hurt her. "I suggested it."

Armand struck his brow with his fist. "You . . . You . . ."

"Earlier I was your dear captain," she teased. Her mood lightened still more as she felt chills of anticipation running up her spine. Suddenly, she was excited about the evening ahead. "You loved me."

"Any man who would take you for his love would be out of his mind," said Armand only a trifle harshly. He stopped. "I will return and rout them from the *Ange*."

"You will do no such thing. Let them search. They will find nothing. Then they will admit we have done nothing more than cross the Channel for honest trading. And," she said triumphantly, "they will leave us be!" *And best of all,* she thought, *I need not worry about finding another mooring!*

Armand trudged along in silence, thinking about her words. "As you say, *ma capitaine*. You are not stupid."

"Captain! Look at these . . ." Toby's voice trailed off as he read the items listed on yet another receipt, one finger holding his place in a modest ledger.

Miles turned from where he tapped the bulkhead, seeking secret compartments. "What have you found?"

"Records. Very neat and concise records and—" Toby touched a pile of papers ranging in size from smaller than his palm to full-sized sheets of paper "—the receipts to back up every entry!"

"I don't believe it." Miles turned to the table and sat down. He pulled the ledger and receipts toward him and began checking each item as he came to it. In the end he *had* to believe. "But this is nonsense. If they do legitimate trading, then why did they run from us?"

Toby pursed his lips. "It *was* wartime. And we are English. They could have feared they'd be impressed into the British Navy. Or merely that we were pirates who would steal their goods."

But Miles ignored him, having already gone beyond that question. "Did you note how odd their cargos are? Why, for instance, does it include six well-rooted chestnut trees?"

"The grain is understandable." Toby pointed to an entry dated during the previous winter. "Last winter was bad. The people of this region may have been starving. She could have made a huge profit on that."

"But trees? A milk cow in calf? In fact, very nearly every item appears to be of an agricultural nature, one way or another. Toby, I don't understand it."

Toby grinned. "Roused the beast in you, did she not?"

"Nonsense." Miles frowned. "Have you ever known a woman to catch my interest?" He held up a hand when it looked as if Toby would count off several and chuckled. "All right! But you must admit that none *held* my interest so if the fact I find her attractive is part of it, then she too will soon pall." The frown returned. "Still, I think it is more that I do not like it when I do not understand. I want to know what is going on. I *need* to know . . ."

"Curiosity killed the cat."

Miles grinned. "Hasn't killed this cat. Not yet anyway, even if it has taken me into some very odd situations!"

"You mean tight corners. Death came too close for comfort any number of times!" Toby had been in some of those corners with Miles. He shuddered at certain memories. "At least your neck shouldn't be at risk this time. I wonder how Johnny managed to tumble to the fact she was a female. I noticed nothing."

"I asked him." Miles's eyes sparkled and his mouth compressed into an oddly suggestive grin.

"So?"

"So she leaned over to pick up something, her coat fell away from her rear end, and it didn't look like any man's ass Johnny ever saw."

Toby's neck and ears turned red. "That whippersnapper! What's he about, looking at a woman's backside!"

Miles ducked his head to hide his reaction to his first mate's outrage. A snort of laughter escaped despite his efforts to control it. "He's young, your Johnny, but not *that* young! However that may be, he watched her until she twisted in such a way he caught a glimpse of the swell of a breast under her shirt. Then he was certain."

"I'm going to have a word with that boy!"

"Toby, accept it. Whatever you *want* to believe, Johnny hasn't been a boy for several years."

Toby did a quick calculation. His eyes widened. "Now how the devil did that happen?"

"What?" asked Miles a trifle absently. He'd just found a receipt for a sow and her litter. He frowned at it.

"How did the dratted boy manage to grow up and I not notice?"

"Probably because you didn't want to notice," said Miles, sifting through the pile of receipts until he found the other one for a sow and her litter. He compared the dates and nodded and wondered if a boar was the next thing on the saucy captain's shopping list and if so, why? "None of us wants to admit to growing older," he added absently, his mind on Antoine-Clair of the *Ange Blanc*. He had never met anyone less fitted to be a farmer. She *couldn't* be doing this for herself, for her own benefit—except for the profits.

But why livestock? Trees? Why not things that would bring her a good profit?

Why did none of it make sense?

Thérèse Marie sat in her bath, reveling in the warm water, the heady scent of the lavender oil she'd dropped into it. She recalled her cousin's question concerning feminine fripperies and wondered if her collection of bath oils qualified. She had learned from an old woman living on the estate how to make them and had been doing so ever since.

She held a handful of water to her nose and sniffed. Such oils might be another private source of income for any peasant willing to work for it. She made a mental note to discuss it with Jacques Rabaut, who oversaw what had, before the revolution, been her grandfather's estate. Lazily, she ran a well-soaped cloth over a lifted leg and wondered what would happen if the absentee owner ever decided to visit Saint Omer. Then she shrugged, making the water ripple across her breasts. Let that particular reckoning come when it may.

And then—a thought that crossed her mind more often than she cared to admit—she wondered if there was any chance in the world that Saint Omer could be returned to her father, to whom it rightfully belonged.

To whom did it belong? Jacques would know. He, after all, was responsible for taking the books to Paris each year. And the profits. She chuckled softly as she recalled Jacques grumbling that what they demanded as a yearly income was far beyond what any estate in France could provide.

They didn't get it, of course. Old Jacques made the journey each year toting the estate ledgers and explaining why he could not provide anything like what was demanded. Thérèse Marie grinned at the old man's duplicity, but the broad smile faded into a frown as she rubbed lavender-scented soap up the other leg. The war was ended. Would Jacques continue to find excuses? Could he continue to give the absentee owner only a portion of what was demanded?

Or—horrid thought—would Jacques be removed and a new man installed as agent? A man who would come, see how productive the estate was *despite* the war, and tell the owner how he had been cheated?

Thérèse Marie shrugged, a few bubbles sliding over her shoulder and down to rest against her breast. She'd worry about that when the day came—if then. She lay back and allowed the maid to rub her hair dry, the heat of the fire doing more to effect the desired result than the child's busy hands and soft towel.

Soon she must rise and dress. And *not* in the skirts she'd been tempted to wear. Why, she wondered, had the hated gowns crossed her mind at all? Toby's unsubtle hint that she might be attracted to the Englishman was nonsense. She wouldn't even think about it.

Forcibly, she put the notion from her mind and glanced at her best coat and trousers the maid had laid across the bed. Her eyes fell on the tall leather, newly polished boots. She *glared* at them. She truly did not like boots—big ugly things that clumped and clomped and nevertheless were necessary to her costume!

Armand was talking to her father when she came down. Saint Omer took one look at his daughter and, dramatically, winced. "René is correct. Why did I not notice you had grown far too old for such games?"

"You didn't notice because you did not wish to notice."

Her father winced again, but this time it was a true reaction and not an affectation. He sighed softly. "You are very likely correct, Thérèse. You put me to shame."

Thérèse Marie studied her father thoughtfully. "I wonder if it is that you were just a little too old when your parents . . . hmm—" Embarrassed to have reminded him that her grandparents were guillotined during the Terror, she hurried on. "—er, what I mean to say is that you remember the life you *should* live and I never knew it so I have made a different sort of life for myself while you yearn for the past."

It was the first time Thérèse had ever wondered *why* her father was the sort of man he was, why he had so little interest in his people, in the estate and how they and it fared. It occurred to her that, if he could only have given orders, seen the work done, then he might have been a very good *comte,* as was his father before him. It had not, however, been bred into him to do the work himself!

"Yes," she continued, "I think I finally understand."

Saint Omer's thin lips tipped at the corners. "You do not like it, but you understand it?"

Thérèse Marie shrugged. *"Mais oui.* How could it be else?"

A muscle jumped in Saint Omer's jaw. "As you say, I was not bred to this life, but to one of ease, of ceremony. I went up to the chateau last night," he added rather abruptly.

"And?"

"I am always amazed how the outside gives one the impression the whole will fall about the foundations at any moment while the inside seems very much as I remember it."

"It is a tricky business, that sham, and I do not know why we bother, but it has seemed the proper thing to do," said Thérèse Marie.

She'd explored the old house when a mere child, played there, pretended to own it, and eventually cleaned a room or two. When Jacques saw what she did, he found several peasants to do the work and had, as a surprise for the lonely young girl, brought back much of the old grandeur in one large suite of rooms.

She remembered the day Jacques had taken her by the hand and led her up the grand staircase and down a hall to those rooms, telling her they would have been hers if her father still owned the chateau. As he should do. She had been enthralled and she and others continued the work of restoring the inside of the building.

Her first voyages across the Channel had been to acquire things she needed for that restoration. She was very young and had had to mature a year or so before she realized how such jaunts could benefit those living on the estate.

"Armand. We must go," she said, pushing aside the memories of those first journeys, the fear, the hope, the pleasure of being on the water and free. . . .

"*Oui*, mam'zelle. We go." His eyes met the *comte's* and he nodded before turning to hold the door for Thérèse Marie—and then, when she asked, refused to explain what that exchange of looks had meant.

Thérèse Marie was furious that the two would go behind her back for any reason, although, in this case, she was nearly certain she knew. Very likely Armand had promised to protect her from the English captain's evil designs—as if anyone need protect her! She tipped her fingers and felt the hilt of the knife strapped to her wrist and, if she tilted her ankle, could feel the one hidden in her boot as well.

No one need protect Thérèse Marie Suzanne de Saint Omer. She could protect herself.

Miles surveyed the table in the captain's salon and nodded. The best linens. The very best china. Flowers—where had Piggy found flowers?—and the silver polished until it gleamed, the crystal with nary a fingerprint.

Miles didn't worry about the meal itself. Piggy was capable of turning out a feast even in the limited quarters of the *Nemesis*'s galley. How he did it Miles had never asked. He was merely thankful for the results!

One last look at the candle-lit room and Miles returned to the deck, where he leaned back against the rail, resting his elbows on it. He stared up at the stars, determined he'd not give the minx the satisfaction of thinking he watched for her.

Besides—he winked at one particularly twinkly star—he didn't need to, did he? He would hear the oars in the tholes, the splash of an oar catching an occasional crab. He needn't watch because he would hear—

"Ahoy!"

Miles swung around. "The devil," he muttered, wavering between falling into a temper and laughing at himself. He'd been gulled nicely, had he not? Very likely it was good for him to discover he could be approached without knowing it—but that didn't make it easier to accept it had happened!

"Ahoy, yourselves! *Bon soir* Captain Antoine-Clair, Armand Mouton! Welcome aboard the *Nemesis*."

Miles reached a hand to the woman ascending the ladder but she ignored it, climbing agilely over the side. Armand followed her, and hearing them, Toby crossed the deck. Commonplaces took the four of them into the salon, where Miles felt satisfaction that the woman's eyes widened before she caught herself and cast him a glance to see if he'd noticed. He grinned at her and found himself not at all displeased that a faint rosy color tinted her high cheekbones.

"Very nice," she said. "You do well by yourself." There was the faintest of puzzled notes in her clipped tones.

"You wonder how a mere captain may do so?"

Her lips firmed. "If you must have it, *yes. I do.* Perhaps it is not myself who is the smuggler, but *you*. Or perhaps you are *worse*. A pirate."

Miles threw back his head and roared. She glared and when that caught his eye he laughed still harder. But when she turned on her heel and headed for the door, Miles sobered. Instantly. As she passed him, he caught her around the shoulders and turned her back.

"I apologize, Madam Captain. Sincerely. A hundred times I apologize, but you've no notion how funny it is. You see, this *was* a pirate ship." Miles felt her stiffen. "Oh, no more. Not now. I won it from the pirate so it is mine now."

"The ship *and* his life," said Toby, a disapproving expression giving his features a stern look. "Captain Seward is not one to live his life sensibly and sanely but must be always playing with fire."

Miles and Thérèse Marie were at that moment exchanging a long look. Miles wondered at the speculation he read in hers, wondered what his own revealed and, not wanting to reveal anything at all, clapped his hands and turned away.

At the signal a sailor entered carrying a silver tray with a bottle and small glasses. The mood changed with the wine and again the conversation became general—but every so often Miles could see the questions in the Frenchwoman's eyes, could read her interest in getting the answers—and wondered why.

Did she experience thoughts similar to his? He certainly had questions that needed answers. And not all of them had to do with the smuggling!

Gradually, as the evening progressed, it became clear that they all understood each other no matter which language was used. Miles quit pretending he knew only a minimum of sailor French and Thérèse Marie allowed him to know she understood far more English than a simple maiden from a fishing village had reason to know.

When the meal ended, Thérèse Marie suggested they row ashore and walk off the gluttony that was making her feel excessively sluggish. Miles hesitated. He noticed Toby shaking his head and shrugged.

Standing, he stretched in a way he'd never have done in a drawing room with ladies present. "Why not?" he said. "It is a glorious night."

"Captain!" said Toby softly, but his tone carried a warning.

Miles spoke in a normal voice, his eyes not on the woman but on Armand. "I do not believe our new friends have set a trap for us. Why would they do so?" He was satisfied by the Frenchman's expression. It had not crossed their new acquaintance's mind to capture them.

"You would suggest we are underhanded and sly and would trick you?" interrupted Thérèse Marie. Her voice rose slightly. "You would impugn our honor?"

"You would call me out?" asked Miles. His eyes narrowed, but his lips spread very slightly in tightly controlled humor.

Thérèse Marie fumed. She glowered. "You know I cannot. But I would if I could."

"Just as well you do not. I am not a man one crosses without thought."

"Just so," said Armand, wishing to soothe his captain. *"Ma capitaine,* it was not such an impossible notion," he continued. "Mr. White is right to urge caution."

"As you would do if our positions were reversed?" asked Miles, the humor a trifle closer to the surface.

"Certainement," said Armand with dignity.

"And so you should," said Toby. The pair of first mates looked at each other and a bond was made. Each knew the other found it impossible to hold the least control over their particular captain and each sympathized mightily with the other!

"Do we walk?" asked Miles. His tone remained sober, but he felt very much as if he might not be able to contain his laughter much longer.

"I walk. I haven't a notion what the rest of you mean to do." Thérèse Marie stalked from the salon and crossed

the deck to where their dory was tied. She was releasing it when the others arrived.

"Allow me," said Miles.

Thérèse Marie was never quite certain how he arranged it so that she and he rowed into shore together, leaving Armand and Toby to come in the second dory, but she was not dissatisfied with the situation.

"Tell me," she asked, "how you come to own a pirate's ship. I would hear this tale."

Miles shrugged. "We were captured in the Levant and the captain held us rather than kill us. He thought to ransom us."

"Us?"

"Toby and myself."

Her eyes narrowed. "I would hear more. You are not to soften your tale because I am a woman and you think I should not hear the details."

Miles pulled the oars twice more. "As you have guessed, it is not a pretty tale. He was a brutal man who had his crew continuously in a state of near mutiny. He was also a gambling man." Miles recalled how difficult it had been to win only often enough so that the captain retained interest but not so much that the man would lose his temper. He gave the oars a harder pull. "That last night he and his men had made a particularly large haul from a ship they then sank. Celebrating, he drank more than usual and demanded I be brought to him and that we dice. Many of his men drew near to watch us play."

"So?"

"I tricked him. When I finally appeared to have lost everything, I wagered my life against his ship." The dory floated up to the narrow quai and Miles caught at an iron ring. "When he lost, his men, whom Toby and I had spent hours cultivating, stopped him from killing me anyway. We put the man ashore on an uninhabited island." Miles shrugged. "For all I know, he is there still."

"I cannot believe it was that easy," said Thérèse Marie.

Miles thought of the two beatings he'd endured that had left scars on his back, the bad food, the menial work he'd been forced to do, but mentioned none of that. "Ask Toby. He will tell you I thrive on danger."

Thérèse Marie nodded. "I too. There is something . . . I do not know, but one feels *alive* as never otherwise . . ."

Miles nodded. "Exactly. Few understand that."

"I admit I've no desire to die . . ." She cast him a speculative look.

"Nor I. And I have come close on more than one occasion. After the debacle of the pirate I feared my guardian angel had had to work overly hard to keep me safe and that perhaps he would run out of patience with me." In actual fact it had been just such a thought phrased far less poetically that had led Miles, a few years previously, to tire of his adventuring and return to England.

"Mine has been busy as well." nodded Thérèse, grinning. "From the time I climbed my first tree!"

"Did you too climb trees?" asked Miles as he helped her from the boat—and this time she allowed it, a fact not missed by Armand, who along with Toby, had reached shore some minutes earlier.

Miles and Thérèse strolled off, their mates following along behind. "He is a charming rogue," growled Armand.

"Yes, but do not fear. You may trust him with your ewe lamb," responded Toby.

Armand Mouton stopped, bristling. "I do not tolerate jests about my name," he said, very much on his dignity.

"Jests . . . ?" Toby frowned, and then his eyes widened. "Ah! Yes. I see. Ewe lamb. Sheep. Please believe I had not thought of your name, Monsieur Mouton, when I used that slang expression which is, perhaps, too English for you? The cant merely means that I called Captain Antoine-Clair a young female. I meant no insult either to you or to the young lady."

Armand relaxed. "I see. I am perhaps too sensitive, but it has long been the bane of my existence, that my name means a sheep." He sighed and then looked ahead . . . and then all around. He hurried forward, swearing volubly. *"Au diable,* where are they? Where has that misbegotten offspring of a monster secreted her? What is he . . ."

Toby grasped Armand's arm and pointed. "You see? I said he could be trusted."

Farther along the lane the two were seated on a fence, a good two feet of the stone from which it was constructed separating them.

"I believe they may be awaiting us?"

Armand thrust his fists into the air and growled. "I will take the brat and thrust her into a convent!"

Toby chuckled.

"You do not know! The terror she has put me through! She is my cross to bear. How can anyone keep such a one secure? And I have promised her father . . ."

"She has a father?" asked Toby, interrupting.

"Of course she has a—" Armand glanced at his still-too-new acquaintance. "Does not everyone?" he asked blandly, once again adopting that dignity behind which he hid when he was either upset or wished to be less than frank!

Four

"I don't like mysteries." Thérèse Marie clomped on down the lane, her pace keeping her somewhat ahead of Armand. "And I do not like it that he laughs at me!" If anything, her pace increased. "I do not like it, I tell you." She shook her fist at the moon riding high in the sky.

"You do not like the moon?" asked Armand, whimsically, the dinner wine followed by the brandy he'd drunk leading him to forget that when Thérèse Marie was in this particular mood she did not take well to teasing.

"Fool!" she said, turning just as he approached. She shook her fist right under his nose.

He stopped, looked at it cross-eyed, and then grinned.

"Idiot!" she shouted. "Mouton!"

Armand's eyes widened. "Thérèse Marie Suzanne Laurent, you promised," he said, with an alcohol-induced plaintiveness.

Instantly Thérèse Marie was contrite. "Armand! I am so sorry. You are correct that I promised and I have broken my word. I am the idiot. Everything bad you could say of me! Forgive me."

Armand tipped his head. "I don't know . . ."

"Please?"

"But you will do it again."

"I am an ass. A pig. I'm . . ."

"Moutonné?"

"Sheeplike?" It was Thérèse Marie's turn to show white around her eyes. *"Mais non! Moi?* Never."

"And me?"

"It is your name. You *are* Mouton, Armand, but not a sheep, *n'est-ce pas?"*

Armand sighed. "I loved my father, but I do wish he had been born with a different surname."

"Yes." Thérèse Marie sobered. "Sometimes I too have wished that very thing."

"You? But your father is the *comte."*

"Is he? A *comte* without an estate, is that a *comte?* He is but he is not." She sighed.

"To all here he is." It was obvious Armand spoke what he perceived the simple truth. "He has been a good man to his people."

Thérèse Marie stopped short. Her *father* had been good . . . ? *He* had . . .

She ran a few steps to catch up with Armand, who had slouched on ahead. "What do you mean he has been good to us?"

"He allowed you to use the yacht, did he not? He did not forbid you to cross to England even when it was dangerous to do so. He made it possible for all of us to live far better than most poor people in France."

"He has . . ."

Thérèse Marie shut her mouth. If the people on the estate thought him responsible, then it was best they continued to do so, but Thérèse Marie knew her father had allowed her smuggling for the simple reason he'd been unaware of it. Originally. When he did begin to suspect what she was up to, he turned away his eyes rather than confront her with his suspicions because, by her efforts, *his* life improved as well as that of the peasants.

She sighed.

But then she recalled her thoughts earlier that evening. He had not been raised to *do.* He was nearly fully grown when his parents were taken in the Terror. Up until then he had been waited on and petted and played with, his every order complied with. And he had perhaps been both too young and immature to take control and too old to change his ways. It was no wonder he became bitter and unhappy and seemed to her to be lethargic if not actually lazy.

Thérèse had never understood how he could spend day after day doing little or nothing. Reading a book he'd read a dozen times. Playing chess with the village priest one long hour after another. Strolling around the region, withdrawn from all around him, but even so treated like some sort of demigod by those he met.

It was *not* the life she wanted. Not one she could live if she had to. And then she recalled René's orders that she don her gowns and burn her trousers. Even though she knew she could not bear it, it was the life her father and his cousin would have her adopt!

She could not do it. She could not.

"Armand."

Once again the man had gotten several paces ahead, humming in the odd off-key fashion that meant he had drunk just enough that the world around him was perceived as rosy and good.

"Armand!"

"Hmm?" With the care needed by the slightly inebriated, he turned. "What is it?"

She joined him. "Armand, what am I to do?"

His eyes opened wide. "Do? What should you do? What you have always done, *non?*"

"René has decreed otherwise," wailed Thérèse. Not only did she hear her own tone, but saw Armand's shocked look. She ducked her head and bit her lip. "Ignore me. I have drunk too much," she said, lifting her chin and straightening her shoulders.

"What has Monsieur René decreed?" demanded Armand.

Thérèse sighed. "He says that the war is over."

"It is." A look of horror crossed Armand's face as he

suddenly wondered whether those particular rumors were true. "It *is*, is it not?"

"Yes. Of course it is."

"But that is good."

Thérèse nodded, sighed again, and strolled on. "For everyone but me," she muttered just softly enough so that Armand could not distinguish the words. "What the devil," she added more loudly, "am I to do with myself?"

"We will collect a boar on our next crossing. Old Gaston is demanding a boar."

"I know. I know." Thérèse's mouth formed a thin line and then relaxed. She nodded. "Yes of course we will get the old man his boar."

"That is good." Armand nodded and kept on nodding, unable to stop. He giggled. "I am quite drunk you know."

"I will see you safely home," said Thérèse.

Armand stopped and scratched his head.

"What is it?" she asked.

"That isn't right."

"What isn't right?"

"That last bit."

Exasperated, Thérèse asked, "*What* last bit?"

Armand's eyelids drooped. "I don't know."

Thérèse shook her head. "Come along, Armand." She took his arm and got him moving again. "And, in future, don't drink so much of Captain Seward's brandy!" The captain had pulled a couple of bottles from his pockets when the two first mates strolled up to where they sat on the chill stone awaiting them, and his mate had produced glasses as if by magic. They all sat in the moonlight talking and laughing and singing—she recalled one particularly lewd song the men taught her and felt her cheeks warm—and then finally the four separated, to wend their separate ways homeward.

Thérèse and Armand were very nearly to Armand's cottage in the middle of the fishing village when he stopped short. "I remember!"

"Now what?"

"I am supposed to see you home safely. *That* is what is wrong." With that he shook off her hand, took her arm, and marched her down the cobbled street to the end of the village.

The *comte's* village home had been constructed by knocking together a short row of cottages. From the outside it looked as it always had, a series of narrow but tall houses, each with a door opening directly onto the paving. Inside, however, there was far more room than needed by two people. Even so, Jean-Paul Laurent, Comte de Saint Omer, found the enlarged rooms totally inadequate. He often complained of feeling quite claustrophobic cooped up in them. Thérèse Marie, on the other hand, always felt guilty that the two of them lived in a space meant for five families!

Five

Long after returning to the *Nemesis*, Miles remained beside the railing. Toby, watching him stand there, silent, his eyes trained on the shore, grew perturbed. Finally he moved to the rail a few feet away. He remained silent, but occasionally turned a sly look toward Miles, hoping to find him less preoccupied.

"Go to bed, Toby."

"And you?"

"I will sleep . . . later."

"What is it?"

Miles turned, leaned against the railing, his elbows on it. He grinned, a sardonic self-deprecating smile. "But you know, *mon ami*. It is nothing out of the way. Merely that I do not like a mystery." And with that he went over the side, dropping into the dory. "Untie me, Toby. And don't worry if I'm gone all night. I mean to explore."

"To find where Mademoiselle lives?" asked Toby as he dropped the rope into the dory.

"Among other things." Miles used an oar to push away from the side of the *Nemesis*. "Don't wait up for me."

"Why would I be so foolish?" asked Toby, but Miles, already on his way into the cove, made no response. Toby watched until the dory disappeared into the dark and then, shaking his head, turned toward the cabin he and his son shared.

"Should I worry about him?" he wondered aloud. *Oh,*

not that he will run into danger from which he cannot extricate himself, not that. "What if he is . . . ill?"

Johnny, roused by his father's grumbling, chuckled sleepily. *"Lovesick,* perhaps. She is quite the woman, is she not?"

Toby straightened. It was not something a man his size could safely do inside shipboard quarters and the thump to his head very nearly felled him.

"Father!"

"Bah. It is nothing." But Toby explored his head with careful fingers. "Never again say anything so shocking."

"Shocking?"

"You would suggest Miles Seward has lost his ballast over a woman? Nonsense. No matter how much a woman *you* may think her!"

"It was you who wondered if our captain was lovesick."

"No, I wondered if he was ill. That is not the same thing."

"And in what way did he behave that you think him ill?"

Toby considered what it was that had upset him so badly that he'd actually awakened his son with his muttering. He recalled an oddly dreamy expression on Miles's face—an out-of-character expression. One he'd never before seen.

Could the boy be correct? "Bah! Nonsense," he blustered. "Captain Seward? *Never!*" Toby glared when his son chuckled. "You do not know him. You did not roam the world with him. You did not nearly die at his side."

"No," said Johnny, sobering instantly, "I was at home, growing up without you, watching my mother pine away for you."

Toby heard bitterness in his son's voice and sighed. "I know. It was wrong of me, but when I left her I didn't know about you. And we had made no promises to each other. She knew . . ."

"She knew and she understood, but she still pined."

"I returned in time to make her last year comfortable," said Toby a trifle defensively. "Thanks to joining up with Captain Seward."

Johnny sighed. "Yes. Thanks to him, you returned a wealthy man. I just wish you had done so sooner."

"I cannot change the past."

"No. Nor can anyone. I will not refer to the subject again."

"But you will blame me forever."

Johnny sighed.

By this time Toby had blown out the lamp, gotten into his bunk and pulled up the covers. He heard his son turn over. And soon he heard the deep even breathing of a sleeping man.

It was Toby's turn to sigh. That his son had not responded was answer enough.

Miles strolled along the lane in the direction of the fishing village. Was it only that afternoon they had sighted the *Ange Blanc* tacking toward the hidden cove just up the coast from the village? Somehow, it seemed far longer ago.

Uncharacteristically, Miles mused on the concept of time, on how it dragged on some occasions, how on others it seemed to flee from one on wings. But such philosophical thoughts were unsettling and, when the village came into view, he was glad of the distraction. He looked down on it and saw a village very like a hundred other such coastal towns he had visited on the French side of the Channel.

Or perhaps it was neater, not quite so drab as most? The few boats, lying on their sides along the narrow strand, looked, from a distance anyway, in excellent condition, and the short pier, from what he could tell in the bright moonlight, appeared very nearly new. The seawall extending into the water on the far side of the curve of the cove showed no sign of deterioration and the houses were all tightly roofed, which was not true in many villages where, thanks to twenty years of war, there was a shortage of men and supplies.

And, last but not least, all the houses appeared to be

occupied . . . also not true for other villages. Frowning, Miles turned inland, his mind turning to those walnut trees, the ram, and other oddities listed in the ledger.

The moon was dropping toward the western horizon when he finally turned back. It was too dark to see more and another hour or so before the dawn so there would be enough light he could confirm what he thought he'd seen.

But surely not. Surely it was merely the moon painting a romantic light over all and making things seem far better than could possibly be the case.

And, worst of all, he had a new and fantastic mystery to solve. The chateau. He had discovered its location and peered through several windows. The approach to the lovely old building had been very like what he would have expected of an abode deserted many years previously . . . but the inside! The moonlight streamed in, giving several of the rooms the appearance of being ready for immediate occupancy! He wondered who owned the place now, how often they returned to visit it . . . and why they did nothing to improve the exterior.

"I do *not*," he muttered as he pushed the dory away from the pier and into deeper water, "like mysteries."

Six

The next morning Thérèse Marie awoke with a feeling of anticipation. She lay there, feeling good about herself, her life, her future. . . .

All good feeling fleeing, she sat straight up in bed.

"My *future.*" She flopped back against her pillows. "Bah!"

Just then her door opened and the girl carried in hot water and a bucket of coals.

"Forget the fire," ordered Thérèse. "I'll not be here long enough that one is necessary."

"Mademoiselle. You are awake."

"As you see. Bring my chocolate and that will do."

"Fat Jeanne says you do not eat properly. She says you are to sit to your breakfast like a civilized person and—" The girl, seeing Thérèse Marie look about her for something to throw, backed from the room. "—I only say what you know she will tell you herself."

"If she sees me," muttered Thérèse. When the girl returned with her morning chocolate, Thérèse was nearly dressed. She took the cup, drank it down, grimaced at the bitter taste, and handed the cup back.

"The washerwomen come tomorrow. Fat Jeanne says you are to find your washing."

Thérèse sighed. "Very well. Now leave me alone."

"I only say what you know she will . . ."

Thérèse interrupted the chit. ". . . tell me herself."

The girl nodded. "It is so. Since you want nothing I will go and silently let myself in to your father's room and there I will build his fire. He will wish one."

Thérèse grimaced at the girl's accusatory tone. As if it were right and proper to waste coals when one would leave the fire behind in short order! She said nothing, however, merely waiting for the chit to disappear into her father's room before she went into the hall, opened the window set over a lean-to at the back of the house, and slipping out onto the roof, pulled the window shut behind her. The slates were slippery with morning dew and Thérèse took care. Reaching the corner where a rain barrel stood, she lowered herself onto it and then jumped to the ground.

Half an hour later she stood on the *Ange Blanc*'s deck and stared out toward where the *Nemesis* had been moored. It was gone. The anticipation with which she'd awakened dropped away for the second time. To replace it, an odd loneliness, a sense of loss, flooded in.

"No," she whispered, anxiety creasing her forehead. "Never. I would not be so foolish."

"You are never foolish," said Henri from behind her.

Thérèse turned on her heel. "I thought I was alone."

Henri nodded. "But you must not say you are foolish. It is not so."

"Everyone can be foolish on occasion, Henri, and I fear I have been foolish beyond permission."

She cast another glance toward where less than a dozen hours earlier she had spent the happiest evening of her life, where she had been treated as if she were no other than another sea-going creature with tales to tell and songs to sing. It had been wonderful to find a man who did not disapprove of her merely because she had interests a woman was not supposed to have and worse, from the point of view of every man she knew—even Armand's—a woman who acted on such desires.

But she had not fallen in love with Miles Seward. Thérèse Marie refused to accept that anything so ridiculous had happened. It was merely that she had enjoyed herself, the evening, him. . . . She pushed such thoughts aside. This was not the time or place to muse upon such things.

She joined Henri. "You have begun, I see. Good."

Henri went back to scraping the woodwork around the window to the main cabin. Thérèse Marie reached for another scraper and worked right along with him.

The constant effort necessary to keep the *Ange Blanc* shiningly white kept Thérèse Marie's body occupied, but not her mind, and she could not keep down the sudden unexpected memories. Miles, his head back, laughing, his tanned throat taut. Miles, neatly cutting his meat at dinner. Miles, his hand extended to her, strong, long-fingered, ungloved . . . Miles, that strong bare hand holding delicate crystal, touching it gently, treating the fragile glass with respect and consideration—a respect and consideration Thérèse believed would extend to any woman he touched.

Which led to thoughts of what it would be like to be touched by those long strong fingers . . .

. . . at which point she threw down her scraper, stomped into her cabin, and threw herself into her chair. She sat there glowering at the ledger lying open on her desk.

Open. The ledger was not in its drawer and it was open.

"That . . . that . . . He snooped in my desk, my papers!" she shouted.

When Armand opened the door to see what was wrong with her, she repeated herself. "But what did you expect? You told him to search."

"I thought he'd look for secret panels. I thought he'd look for a hold other than the one under the afterdeck. I thought . . ." She raised her fist and shook it, dropped it, and sighed. "I don't now what I thought."

"You didn't think."

Thérèse glanced at Armand. For half a moment she felt a need to blister him with her tongue, flay him with a vocabulary well suited to reaming him up one side and down another, although *not* suited to the mouth of a female! Unfortunately, what he said was true.

"Very true. I didn't."

"Are you all right?"

She shrugged. It was as near as she could come to admitting that, for reasons she only partially understood, she could not get Miles Seward out of her head. And since she had been alone forever, her mind her own, she was certain she disliked that, without permission, he'd taken up occupancy there!

Miles rode over thirty miles that day before returning to where he had left the *Nemesis* somewhat nearer Calais. He was tired from the unaccustomed exercise and feared he would be stiff on the morrow. Riding was not his favorite form of transportation, but had been necessary.

Because of it he was cross as a bear. Worse, instead of answering his questions, he had a dozen more!

Toby took one look at his captain and, without saying a word, led him into his salon, where he knelt to pull off Miles's boots and, still silent, poured a good tot of brandy. He handed it over without asking one of the questions he wanted answered. Instead, he took up a position near the window, leaned against the wall, and crossed his arms, waiting. . . .

Some ten minutes later Miles shifted position, suppressed a moan of pain, and looked up. "Thank you," he said.

"For the brandy?"

"For the silence. I hurt. That blasted horse had the gait of a half-broken mule and was quite as stubborn. And, as well, I am in a foul mood, Toby. A truly black mood."

"Want to talk?"

"Not just yet. I've got to think."

Toby watched his captain slouch down in his chair. The brooding look darkening Miles's features worried him. Toby wondered what had occurred to put his captain into this dour state so unlike his normal one. When Miles continued to merely sit there, that black scowl marring his brow, Toby compressed his lips and strode from the salon.

The mate looked in the door of the tiny galley where Piggy stood staring in a speculative way at the vegetables for which he'd rowed ashore earlier in the day. The two conferred and agreed that a special meal would improve Mile's mood.

It didn't. Nor did a good night's sleep.

"What is it?" demanded Toby when Miles retreated again to his salon and his chair. "What has you in such a stew?"

Miles looked up. "How often have you and I regretted the condition of a once-fine estate? Mourned vineyards that have become overgrown with dead or unpruned vines, or fields where the fences are down and scrawny cattle, if any exist, graze as they will. How often have we regretted the waste of good farmland? Of peasants living from hand to mouth, thin, ill, unhappy . . . ?"

The brief rant ended on a sigh and Toby frowned. "So?"

"So what would you say to an estate on which the peasants are rosy-cheeked, the children happy and healthy, the few men looking as if they were not anticipating the grave as a happy release and women who didn't drag themselves from one task to the next?"

"So?"

"Where the fences are down, yes—but, only where you can see them from a road. Where farm buildings look as if a good wind could blow them over, but if you explore you discover that, inside, they are tight and weatherproof? And where hidden dells contain small orchards or grazing sheep or a pigsty with sows and their young looking well fed? And what of neat gardens tucked behind untrimmed hedges that would shame even the laziest of English freeholders? What of a long whitewashed building with big windows complete with glass hidden away in a glade in the woods and in it, young women bending over their lace cushions, singing or gossiping, their fingers never still? What of others embroidering fine shifts, altar cloths, and other finery?"

"So? You have discovered an estate where the owner has managed to keep ahead of his government's depredations by hiding it all away. Why does that cause surprise? Not every aristo could have been loyal to Napoleon. Some must have had stronger ties to their people, their land."

"Ah! But there is no aristo! The estate is owned by a Paris-based consortium. On the other hand it will not surprise you to learn that none of the owners has visited. Ever."

"How do you know that?"

"Simple. I talked to the priest, a sad-eyed Frenchman wearing a patched *soutane* and scuffed and chipped *sabots* but excellent quality woolen socks. A man who sighed and complained and—" Miles's glower deepened. "—eyed me to see what I believed and what I did not."

"Hmm."

"And that ram had been put to a small flock of ewes not too far from where he was taken ashore."

"Well, one assumes that is why he was put ashore, after all!"

Miles grunted. "Yes, but according to the priest there isn't a *sou* to be had that isn't demanded by those in Paris. So whence came the *sous* which bought the ram?" His tone became less ranting when he added, "I don't know much about sheep, Toby, but that ram looked expensive."

"I think I begin to see."

"Yes, well see another thing. The *chateau,* when I found it, looks like the outbuildings and appears to be falling down around itself . . . except again one is deceived."

"You entered it?"

"Of course not. But I looked through windows and was very nearly caught by women coming to clean. Toby, I want answers!"

"So?"

"So I am damned well going to get them," said Miles,

pushing himself up from his chair. "Take us back to somewhere near that cove. This time they will not escape us!"

They didn't.

"Hold still," said Toby crossly. "I've got to see to this cut, dammit."

Miles lifted his arm higher to allow his first mate access to the shallow slash along his ribs. He scowled at his prisoner, who, her arms bound, leaned against the wall across the salon from him. She glowered right back.

Inside, however, where it did not show, Thérèse Marie was appalled. The cut was, very likely, not particularly dangerous, but it must hurt like the very devil . . . and yet, Captain Seward had not hurt her when he disarmed her and controlled her.

"What did you do with Armand and Henri?" she growled.

"They are in the brig," said Miles. "Where you will be once you've answered a few questions."

"My yacht."

"Bobbing along behind us like the good little ship it is."

"Bah."

"And the boar you *bought* in England is being cared for by my youngest crewman, who insists he knows a great deal about pigs. Not that he is happy about it. His uncle raised pigs and he ran away to sea to get away from them."

Thérèse repressed a quick grin. She could hear the lad grousing about his current occupation. "He better take damn good care of that boar."

"Why? Because you have yet to be paid for it?"

"Paid . . ." Her brows arched and fell into normal lines. "Oh. Yes. Of course."

She hasn't a notion of being paid! Still another mystery, thought Miles. "Ouch! Blast it, Toby, let be." He pushed his first mate away.

"I've got to wrap it."

"Leave it. It'll scab over soon enough. Especially after you've wasted all that good brandy on it!" He moved his arm this way and that, shrugged, and turned back to the enigma facing him. "The hog was the only reason you crossed the Channel? You didn't pick up any good woolens? You didn't want seed for spring planting, perhaps?"

"Spring planting was completed long ago. As you know. The hog was all we needed."

Thérèse Marie thought, with no little satisfaction, of the cigarillos she did *not* get for her father. This bastard would have loved to discover the tobacco hidden away in the cubby behind her desk. And the bastard had gone straight to it, had known where it was, and how to open it. She had not been pleased by that discovery. The carpenter who had installed her little hidey-hole had guaranteed that no one would find it, that it looked too much like the rest of the wall for anyone to guess of its existence!

"All you needed. All *who* needed?"

She sighed. "You snooped all over the estate. You know very well who *we* are."

"No I don't. I know a Parisian consortium holds the property. I know none of the consortium visits it and are most likely holding the land for future sale—

Thérèse Marie cast him a startled look, dropped her gaze instantly to the toe of her boot, at which she stared thoughtfully.

"—which thought appears to interest you," he said. "Think you might buy it?"

She shrugged. "With what?"

"With the profits from your smuggling, of course."

"What smuggling? You've seen proof I'm no smuggler."

"Hmm. You take your imports to Calais where you pay duty before returning to the cove, perhaps?"

"You know I do not." She pushed herself more erect. "But you are English. It cannot be of concern to you that I pay no French import duty!"

"Very true. What is of interest to me is where you pay the export duty on what you take out of England!"

Her glower, which had faded at the thought that she might find a way to purchase the estate, returned. "You'll just have to discover that for yourself."

"What I will discover is that you've paid no export duty. On anything."

"Bah. Believe what you will." *Which,* she thought, *since it is the truth, will be easy for you.*

"Thank you for the permission." He grinned at her, one of his more wolfish grins.

She bared her teeth in response.

He laughed. "You are the most amazing chit."

"Hardly a chit," she said, a faint sneer in her voice.

"Oh yes. Surely a hoyden and very likely spoiled rotten by doting parents." At the expression which crossed her face in an instant before disappearing, he modified that. "Or, more likely, loving but duped parents who haven't a notion what you are up to. What do you think you're doing?" he asked, sliding the question in at the end.

"I'm . . ." Her chin snapped up. "None of your business."

"But it is." A silky note caressed the words. "Oh yes. Very much my business. Did you not know? I am commissioned by the war office to catch smugglers, to bring them to justice. It is my duty to bring you in. To see you in court. To watch when you hang by the neck . . ." He stood quickly, jumping to her side and catching her. "Here now! None of that. You aren't such a weakling as to faint!" But she had. He held her against him, cradling her head in one hand and looking down into her face.

How, he wondered, *did I ever think her a man?*

He drew her up, his hand sliding around her side . . . and the soft pressure of her breast against his palm made him draw in a sharp breath. She moved, and reluctantly he pushed her against the wall, holding her up until her eyes fluttered open. They stared at each other.

Her voice was particularly husky when she said, "Put Armand and Henri ashore. Only take me."

"I knew you were not a coward."

"Will you put them ashore?"

Miles considered, his eyes narrowing. He liked that she thought first of her crew, that she did not beg for herself. In fact, he liked all too much about this woman he'd taken captive—and taken a wound from her knife in the process.

Perhaps a more serious wound than the slash currently throbbing at his side?

Perhaps a more permanent one . . . ?

Seven

"What will you do with them?"

Miles stared around the Renwick salon, clenched his fists, and ran a hand through his hair. Again. "Damned if I know."

Jason, Lord Renwick, laughed. "If you meant to turn them over to the authorities you'd have done so."

Miles raised his fists toward the ceiling of Jason's study, shook them, and growled.

At the sound, Jason's laughter was even heartier.

"It isn't funny in the least!"

"Tell me," coaxed Jason, his hand dropping to touch the nape of the huge white tiger, Sahib, lounging at his side.

Miles growled again, but more softly. Then he sighed. "I suppose I'd better since I definitely need help with this one. It started . . ."

Miles told how he'd chased the *Ange Blanc* on three different occasions and lost her, how he'd more recently trapped the yacht in the cove in which its captain usually moored her, how they'd met and dined, his search of the yacht and discovery of her records.

". . . So I went ashore and explored. Blast it, Jase, I hate mysteries!"

"No, you hate not knowing. It need not be a mystery. Merely that your curiosity gets roused and you will not rest until you've satisfied it. Only this time there is more, is there not?"

"If you mean that the captain is a young woman and one I find attractive, yes. That too is a problem."

"You cannot keep them in my storage room forever."

"I asked for her word and she would not give it."

Renwick hid a grin at the sour note in his friend's voice. "Why do we not ask my wife to speak to her, see if Eustacia cannot talk sense to your odd little smuggler."

"A better suggestion than I do what I am thinking."

"And that is?"

"Go in there and beat her within an inch of her life for being so foolish as to risk her pretty neck as she does!"

"Hmm."

Miles glared. "What does that mean?"

"You would scold her for doing what you've done all your life?" Miles frowned and Jason, getting no response, added, "Going adventuring?"

Miles chuckled. "I suppose I haven't the right, have I?" His smile faded, "I would still beat her for being foolish. For risking her neck."

"For something anyway." Before Miles could question that, he continued. "Thérèse Marie, you say. A pretty name. A feminine name. What is the rest of it?"

"She calls herself Captain Antoine-Clair. I very much doubt if it is her surname."

"Why?"

"Because the one person to whom I mentioned it, who was not part of her crew, quickly smothered a grin. The implication was clear."

"To you perhaps."

"She is well known in the region but *not* as Antoine-Clair. Jase, that estate is in better heart than Merwin's."

"Then it is in *far* better heart than mine?"

"I don't mean to insult you, Jase, and you've done miracles since you returned from India and—"

"Even though I'm blind?"

"—and perhaps I should not say the French estate is in such good heart as all that. What *do* I mean?" He thought for a second. "Well, it *is* when compared to other French estates, but the thing is, *someone* has taken great care to hide that it is prosperous."

"How?"

Miles described what one could see if one searched for it.

"It sounds to me as if someone has been bilking the owners of their profits for years."

"Undoubtedly."

"That doesn't worry you?"

"A consortium that took advantage of the Terror to acquire more land than they could ever care for? Land they are now beginning to sell for huge profits over and above what has been gleaned from them over the years?" Miles straightened. "Hmm."

"What?"

"I've just had a notion . . ."

"Will you tell me?"

"Let me think it out a bit."

"Very well. It is nearly time to dress for dinner. What will you do with your prisoners?"

"Perhaps my lady pirate will give me her word long enough so that she could dine with us. I would have you and Eustacia meet her."

"My valet told me she is dressed in male attire. He was rather shocked or I doubt he'd have mentioned it. I suggest you leave it to Eustacia. Have my wife speak with her. The word might come more easily if given to another woman."

"You do not say it, but you think she might feel easier if she knew she'd be chaperoned?" Miles laughed, thinking of the dinner she had shared on his *Nemesis* with him and three other men. "Jase, you may find more about my lady pirate!"

Miles went in search of Eustacia.

"You wish me to do what?" asked Lord Renwick's wife.

"Jase and I believe you will have better luck with the lady than I have had."

"Lady?"

Miles sobered and rubbed his chin with two fingers. "Eustacia, I cannot tell you exactly what it is that makes me believe there is much more to Thérèse Marie, *not* named Antoine-Clair despite her claim, than is immediately obvious."

"What is obvious?"

"Her courage," said Miles promptly. "Her intelligence. Her loyalty to those she cares for . . . I don't know."

"But what makes you think her well bred? That is what you meant, is it not?"

Miles frowned, thinking. "Table manners?" he suggested. "Her vocabulary, both French and English? Her accent when speaking English? English *not* learned in port taverns?"

"I see. Those things can be mimicked, but rarely totally successfully. I will take Sahib and speak with her."

"Sahib!"

"Yes. I have no desire to be overpowered by the lady and her crew, but I doubt very much she'd speak frankly if anyone else is there. Let me be certain I understand. You want her word that she'll not run away. If I cannot manage that, then her parole for the duration of our dinner at which she is to join us?"

"Yes."

"Very well. The children have heard you are here, Miles. They would very much like a visit to the nursery."

"I will go up and see them after I change."

Eustacia smiled. "That way you'll not be forced to stay long, is that it?"

Miles grimaced. "I never know what to say to them."

"Just tell them another story from your adventurous past," said Eustacia dryly, "and they will hang on your every word. You are their hero, you know."

His ears felt hot. "They are too young for such things."

"For listening to your tales?"

"For heroes!"

"One is never too young. Or too old. I'll see you at dinner—with your lady pirate in tow!"

"I sincerely hope so," muttered Miles, but Eustacia was already on her way to collect Sahib and get on about the business.

"I still don't understand," said Thérèse Marie politely. She had listened to Lady Renwick, asked a few questions, and shaken her head.

"It is very simple," said Eustacia, her hand on Sahib's head. The tiger had caused more than a little consternation among the prisoners when she'd first entered and Armand and Henri were still just as far away as the storage room allowed. "I ask, as did Miles, for your word. If you will not give a general one, then I ask it for the duration of dinner and the evening. Is it that I use English words with which you are unfamiliar?"

"No, no," said Thérèse Marie impatiently. "What I do not understand is why you wish it. I am a prisoner. I have been taken up for a smuggler. I am thought to be a criminal. You cannot wish a criminal seated at your table."

Eustacia thought of one particular politician, an acquaintance of their friend, Alex, Lord Merwin, who had come looking for Alex and had, perforce, to be invited for dinner and the night. That man was a villain if ever she'd seen one.

"One never knows who will sit there. On occasion I have wondered about perfectly respectable gentlemen, whether they are quite so upright as they wish to appear. On this particular occasion—" Eustacia's eyes twinkled and she could not hide a smile. "—I tend to wonder if the disreputable appearance is not the false one!"

Thérèse Marie tipped her head. "I assure you, I have behaved expediently at all times. I have disregarded the laws of two governments with no thought to the consequences, merely so that I could do what must be done. I am the criminal Captain Seward believes me to be."

"May I give you some advice?"

"Have I a choice?"

Eustacia smiled. "I believe you do not. I give it, willy-nilly. It is merely this. Do not make that admission to Miles—Captain Seward, I should say—until he has resolved the mystery surrounding you and your behavior."

"Mystery?"

"Oh yes, I think so. Do not you?"

Thérèse Marie smiled a tight little smile and a rather sardonic gleam could be noted in her eye. "You would say I have deliberately misled him?"

"Oh no. I would never be so impolite!"

Thérèse Marie laughed heartily. "I like you."

"I like you too. Will you give me your parole?"

The Frenchwoman bit her lip, suddenly sober. After a moment, she nodded. "But only for dinner and the evening," she warned.

"Very well. Starting now?"

Thérèse Marie shrugged. "I see no reason why not."

"Then come to my room with me. We are much of a size, I think, and although the fit will not be perfect, I will lend you one of my gowns."

"I would rather not borrow from you," said Thérèse Marie stiffly.

"I don't suppose you do, but—" Eustacia eyed the trousers the other woman wore. "—frankly, I do not care to have you prancing around my husband and the male servants dressed in that particularly intriguing fashion."

Eustacia did not inform Thérèse Marie that Jase was blind. He'd not see how his guest was dressed but it was definitely improper for a woman to appear in public in anything other than skirts—and servants gossiped. If things progressed as Eustacia suspected they might, she did not wish Miles's bride to have a reputation among the neighbors that would put her utterly beyond the pale!

"Well, Sahib?" she asked as she led Thérèse Marie to her room. "Have you made up your mind about our new acquaintance?"

"You speak to that animal as you would to a person?"

"You'd be surprised at the tales we could tell of this animal," responded Eustacia with a chuckle. "Well, Sahib?"

The big cat, pacing along beside her, looked up. He gave the odd sound that they had determined was the same as a cat's purr.

"You approve. Very well, then. You have work to do," said Eustacia.

The cat gave a sound one could only interpret as interrogatory.

"You'll know."

Thérèse Marie battled with her curiosity and lost. "What," she asked, "was that all about?"

"Hmm? Oh, you'll discover in time—or you will not, in which case I am wrong. Here we are. Just a moment while I ascertain that Jason has not yet arrived. Ah!" She spoke to Jason's valet. "You must dress Lord Renwick elsewhere. We require privacy."

The man bowed, collected the clothing he had laid out, and exited.

"You and your husband share a room?" asked Thérèse Marie. "Oh, excuse me. My curiosity has once again overcome my sense of propriety. Not that that is difficult. I fear my sense of propriety is not all that well developed!"

Eustacia laughed. "Oh, I do like you! You are aware, are you not, that curiosity is Miles's besetting sin? It has gotten him into more trouble than any man should have been in a lifetime, certainly too much for a man no older than he. From the tales to which I've listened it amazes me he is here to tell them!"

Thérèse didn't respond, but her mind worked furiously. Was it the captain's curiosity that had led to his hunting her down and capturing her? But what was there about her to make anyone curious? The thought slipped away and her eyes widened at sight of the gown Eustacia brought from her dressing room and held up for her approval.

"I could wear nothing so fine. Surely you've something less . . . less . . . less expensive."

"Why do I feel you'd have something other than expense in mind?" Eustacia studied the gown she'd laid on the bed. "Too ornate for your tastes, perhaps? But it is actually rather plain compared to what is worn in London these days. I've a local mantua-maker who follows London fashion closely but who charges far less than a fashionable mantua-maker would do. I can't think why I chose that particular shade, a walnut brown. It does nothing for me, but it will bring out the lights in your hair and your eyes are very nearly a match for it. It will suit you. You've the coloring for it. You need not feel beholden to me for borrowing it. In fact, I will give it to you."

"You are too generous."

"No. If you will not take it, I must give it to my maid. She is too young for such a dark color, of course, but will love peacocking around in it."

"I would not deprive her," said Thérèse Marie stiffly. "I will, if it makes you happy, wear it this evening, but that is all."

"You will return to your trousers?"

Thérèse's eyes suddenly twinkled with a rather devilish light. "Would you care to try them? I assure you they are far more comfortable than skirts. I would wear nothing else if I had any choice in the matter."

"Do you not?"

"My father berates me whenever he sees me in them. I take care to avoid him when dressed as a man! And his cousin is still worse. He has had gowns made for me to wear on those occasions I visit him."

"Then you do have relatives?"

Thérèse cast her hostess a wary look. "Does not everyone?" she asked, her tone suspiciously innocent.

Eustacia, not meaning to probe, realized she had, knew

it was what Miles hoped she would do, and decided it was something she didn't care to do. She *did* like this woman—trousers and all. And she didn't wish to make her angry.

"I apologize. The question was not a trick to find out about you, but honest interest. I do not mean to trap you into revealing anything you have no wish to reveal, so if, inadvertently, I again ask you something you wish to keep secret, all you need do is glare at me!"

"You are very good." But Thérèse Marie's eyes added true appreciation to the conventional phrase and the women smiled at each other.

The gown Thérèse slipped into fit her quite well. It was a trifle looser at the top than it would be on Eustacia, since Thérèse was less well endowed there, but it was by far the most stylish dress she'd ever worn. The material alone was of better quality and she could not help noticing how it felt sliding over her limbs.

"Let me take a few stitches here and here," said Eustacia's maid, tugging at the material. "And perhaps I should lower the hem a trifle?"

"It is not *too* revealing," said Eustacia. "I have seen skirts hemmed even higher—" She frowned. "—although I admit the girls wearing them are thought a trifle fast. Perhaps we should . . ."

"It is for one evening. We will ignore it," said Thérèse Marie shortly. She was unhappy with the fact that she actually liked how she looked in the borrowed finery. This was not for her. This was not the life she would, or for that matter, *could* live.

And then another thought entered her mind. What would Captain Seward think of the amount of silk-clad ankle she showed, a pair of her ladyship's sandals fitting quite well? Would he think she deliberately enticed him? The heat of a blush rose up the bare front of her gown, up her throat, and into her ears. Perhaps they should lower . . .

"Ready?" asked Eustacia, gathering up her reticule and

fan. "We are a trifle early, but I prefer that to being late. I have never been one for making grand entrances."

It was Jason, Miles, and Sahib who made the entrance. The two men dressed in formal evening clothes, the sleek tiger pacing between them, was a sight Thérèse knew she'd never forget. She was so struck she stopped speaking right in the middle of something she was saying to Prince Ravi, Lord Renwick's young Indian ward.

Ravi, who was used to having newcomers goggle at the sight of a wild beast given the freedom of the salon, chuckled softly. "He is magic, you know," he said softly.

"Magic?" Thérèse eyed Miles up and down. "There is certainly power there, but magic?"

"Oh yes. Sahib is a very rare beast and a magical one as well. You will see."

"Sahib? Oh! You mean the *tiger* is magical. I see."

Ravi frowned. He was unsure what exactly had been in the Renwicks guest's mind.

Miles came immediately to her side. "I feared you would refuse Eustacia's request for your word."

"It was expedient," she said shortly. "It is my guess I will eat far better than poor Armand and Henri, who are still locked up in that closet."

"A bit more than a closet!"

She shrugged. "As you say."

"Far better than the magistrate's cell to which I could have taken you all," said Miles, his irritation obvious.

"Why did you not?" she asked. The question had teased her mind very nearly since the three had been herded into the storage room and the door locked. At first she'd thought Lord Renwick was the magistrate, but a servant bringing food and water had said not.

"I don't know. There is a mystery. I dislike mysteries."

Her brows arched. "You, too? I have always needed to dig and probe and uncover any secrets I knew to exist. It is almost as if something in me forces me to do so."

Miles stilled, his eyes on hers. Neither blinked. *This*

woman, he thought, *understands as no one else has ever done!*

Sahib, followed by Lord Renwick, strolled up to them just then, distracting Miles. He blinked and then discovered he hadn't drawn breath for some time. He did so—and noticed that Thérèse Marie did the same.

"Have you been introduced to Sahib?" asked Jason, oblivious to what went on between the pair. His blind eyes stared somewhat to the side of Thérèse and she frowned. "It is something we do. Every guest must have a formal introduction so that Sahib knows they are acceptable."

She glanced at Miles, who pointed to his own eyes and shook his head. Hers widened. "I believe," she said, "that we already know each other although it was less than a formal introduction, is that not so, Sahib?" she asked, holding her hand out toward the cat.

Sahib politely sniffed it, looked up at her with his burning eyes, blinked once, and then flopped onto his side, turning up his tummy.

"What should I do?" she asked.

"It is my guess he wishes his stomach rubbed," said Miles slowly. "I have never seen him do that."

"Do what?" asked Jason, sharply. Whenever Sahib behaved in an unknown fashion he, unable to see it, worried. Such occasions were almost the only times Lord Renwick regretted his blindness.

While Miles explained to Jason, Thérèse, without thought for her gown, knelt and scratched Sahib. She looked up, her eyes glowing, and again Miles found his gaze locked with hers.

"He's wonderful," she breathed. Sahib chuffed softly.

"He likes you, Miss . . . Miss . . ."

"Antoine-Clair," she said, rising to her feet.

"But Miles insists that is not your name," said Jason, his voice as innocent as he could make it.

"If it is not, then Captain Seward must give me another. It is all to which I'll admit."

"Well, Miles?" Jason laughed. *"Will* you give her another?"

For reasons he didn't understand, Miles felt the heat of embarrassment in his ears. For the second time that day! "I will, of course, discover her true name," he said, his voice carrying a reserve unusual to him. "It is inevitable."

"How can you think it inevitable?" she asked. A combination of curiosity, fear that he might succeed, and, contradictorily, a belief that he could not possibly discover it, all mixed together to cause a morass of confusion. "Besides, I am who I say I am," she insisted.

"I think not."

"Nonsense."

"Let us not brangle," said Lady Renwick, coming up just then. "Tell me instead what it is like sailing your own ship? I have traveled on Miles's *Nemesis*, and liked it very well, but I cannot think how one knows where one is or plans how to get to wherever one wishes to go."

Once again the conversation became general. Miles and Thérèse enjoyed a discussion of the problems of navigation, a fast-paced repartee that grew far too technical for Eustacia, although Jason followed it fairly well. Tired of finding herself on the fringes of the discussion, Eustacia coaxed Miles into talking about his experience with Portuguese royalty, a tale that held Thérèse enthralled.

"Have you thought of going farther east?" she asked. "To India, perhaps?"

"It has crossed my mind."

"You, Captain Seward, will escort me home. You will take me and mine on the *Nemesis*," said Ravi with the arrogance of the born despot—which he was, of course.

"Ah. Prince Ravi, have you met our prisoner?"

Ravi bowed, said he was charmed to meet such a lovely prisoner, but then turned back to Miles. "When I leave here, *you* will be my captain. You will take me and my men home. And my tutor and his wife as well. But not—" There was a sudden sadness in the young man, which revealed his youth. "—I fear, Bahadur."

"Is the old man ill again?" asked Lord Renwick sharply.

"He is a very old man and frail," said the young prince with dignity. "I fear he could not survive the rigors of a long journey. I will leave him here, where you will make him comfortable for his last years."

"You will, will you? And what does Bahadur say to that?"

"Bahadur?" Thérèse softly asked Miles while the lad and Lord Renwick argued.

"He is an Indian hunter, a *shikari*. In fact he is the prince's father's royal hunter. The maharaja sent him to protect Ravi, but the old man suffered a severe illness after helping Jase save Lady Renwick from drowning and has never been the same since."

"Can he bear a long sea voyage?"

"I don't know. But I agree with Jase. He will wish to return with Prince Ravi to their principality in India. It is his homeland, and if possible, he will wish to die there."

"How sad."

"Sad?"

"That he is old and ill and far from home."

"Ah. I see." Miles eyed the young woman standing beside him listening to the prince explain why it would be better Bahadur remain in England. "I would suggest," said Miles, interrupting the prince, "a solution to this argument. Ask Bahadur what *he* wishes to do. And, if he wishes to return, then you should allow it even if you fear for the consequences. Your *shikari* is a man who faces life and does not blind himself to what is real. I think he will wish to attempt the journey even knowing he may not survive it."

"But . . ."

"But you would have him live a long life where he is a stranger? Where his beliefs are thought pagan and are, by most, scorned? Where he would be far from any who understood him?"

Prince Ravi's mouth formed a mulish line, his eyes narrowing. Then, suddenly, his shoulders drooped. "You would say I wish to preserve myself from pain rather than that I think of what is best for Bahadur."

"Yes."

The youth winced. "Yes. I see. Your harsh lesson, Captain Seward, is perhaps good for me, but I do not like it!"

He turned on his heel and walked away, not seeing the smiles the others quickly hid. Ravi, very much on his dignity, remained silent for the rest of the evening, only speaking when, finally, reluctantly, the group broke up. And then it was merely a polite good night to Thérèse Marie before she was led off by Lady Renwick to change back into her trousers before returning to her prison.

Except she was not returned to the store room but was taken to a bedroom at the top of the house. She expostulated, wanting to return to where Armand and Henri were imprisoned. Before she was locked in, she was informed, in Miles's most arrogant tones, that it was improper for her to share a room with the two men and that she could see them tomorrow and assure herself they were properly cared for.

"You would trick me. You will take them to a real prison."

"I promise you I will not."

"How can I trust you? I will not sleep for worrying!"

"I give you my word."

She stared at him, her eyes wide. She closed them, the lids fluttering from the tension. "This is what it means to captain one's own ship? That one must live with the consequences of one's actions?"

Suddenly feeling sorry for her, Miles nodded. "It was a lesson forced on me as well," he said. "Long ago. I was with a party of men who went into a situation from which not all of us escaped. I was arrogant and sure of myself—and very wrong. It is, as you say, a consequence with which I've had to live."

Miles did not wait for a response, but closed the door and turned the lock. As he returned to his room on the floor below, it occurred to him to wonder why he had admitted to this woman, this stranger, this captive, something he had told no one else. Not even Ian, his closest friend among the Six, knew of the nightmares he still suffered because of that particular error of judgment.

Eight

Twice more Thérèse Marie gave her parole. Twice more she dined with the Renwicks and Miles. And each time she returned to her small locked room with more to think about, more to absorb—more to regret.

"Why did I not meet him years ago? He would have loved the adventure I invented, would have aided and abetted me, and not have said it was wrong!"

But, retorted a small insistent voice in her head, *he tracked down smugglers for England. He sent them to real prisons, saw them hang!*

"But that was the war. It was the English guineas going to support Napoleon's war—that was what he stopped. He'd not have stopped me. Not if he'd known."

Am I so very certain of that?

The trouble was that she did *not* know. Not for certain. The next day she insisted she be returned to Armand and Henri, that she didn't like it that they were alone, that they didn't know how it was with her, that they worried about her as she worried about them.

"Ma captaine," said Armand when the door locked behind her. "You have suffered no . . . harm?"

"If you mean have I been ravished, then of course not. Even if Captain Seward were the sort to take advantage, Lady Renwick would not allow it!" She chuckled at the sight of Henri's reddened ears. "You are embarrassed that

I speak frankly. You know me well. How else would I speak?"

Henri shrugged. "Still, it is *not* something of which you *should* speak."

He sounded disapproving and Thérèse sighed. "Why," she asked, "is a woman forbidden certain topics when those subjects are most in her interest?"

"It is wrong," said Henri stubbornly. "I do not know why, but it is the way of the world that it is."

"Scolded by a wet-behind-the-ears scoundrel! Armand, you will have a long talk with Henri about his place in this world. He is not to scold me. Ever. But," she said, changing the subject before either man could respond, "how is it with you?"

"We are treated well," said Armand stiffly. "We are even allowed exercise in a walled kitchen garden. They have been planting a new asparagus bed," he said, his mood lightening. "You should see how they do it."

"Asparagus . . ."

Armand grinned. "We must acquire some. When we get the boar, perhaps."

All three instantly sobered. There was no guarantee there would be another trip. It was, in fact, unlikely. They were prisoners of a man who captured smugglers for whom he had no love. What their end would be Thérèse did not wish to know—and she feared for her crew. Feared for their lives—*their very lives*.

And it was her fault. Her fault!

René had warned her. He had insisted that she must stop crossing the Channel as a smuggler. In fact, it had been his contention that she must stop crossing the Channel as anything other than a passenger! She sighed. Should she apologize? No. It would only cause more worry in the men's minds than was there already.

Later that day she, too, was allowed to walk in the kitchen garden, where to her regret since it did not interest her as it did him, Armand insisted on explaining to her exactly how the Renwicks' head gardener had ordered the new asparagus bed dug.

". . . so you see, it will be well fed for many seasons with all that manure and verdure dug deep below the roots. They will grow down into it and will thrive. It is quite wonderful."

"And how does a French gardener differ in his method of planting?" asked Thérèse—and then didn't listen to his detailed response. On the other hand, it was impossible to be unaware of his enthusiasm.

If I ever get us out of this I will see that Armand has a small house and a field. He will retire from the sea and grow asparagus!

Henri was as bored as she. "I wonder if I could not scale that wall. They do not watch us closely. Surely I could do it and find your cousin and he would rescue you."

"René?" Thérèse chuckled. "You can see him creeping up to the house and breaking in? Rescuing us? *René* play the hero? He would be horrified at the very thought! And—" She sobered. "—you are to try nothing of the sort. Captain Seward would raise the countryside and you would be caught and this time you would not be put in a reasonably comfortable storage room, but taken before the magistrate and held over for the next assizes, where you would be condemned to hang."

"We are instead," asked the young man politely, "to wait patiently until Monsieur le Capitaine tires of playing with us and takes us before that same magistrate?"

Thérèse Marie turned away. "No, but we must plan and it must not be only you to escape but all of us. We will do it, Henri. I promise you."

". . . we must contrive a way whereby they may think they have escaped by themselves," mused Miles.

He and Jason were seated in the blue salon with Lady

Renwick, who neatly sewed a simple dress for a child in the poorhouse. "Why not simply let them go?" she asked.

"I cannot let them go. They are aware of the strength of my feelings about smuggling. To let them go when I believe them to have been smuggling—" He shrugged. "—they would wonder at it."

"As *I* wonder that you would allow them to escape!" said Jason.

Miles sighed. "There is a mystery. I must solve it. She will not speak of it and I can see no way of finding the answers unless I let them go."

"And solving the mystery is more important than your principles concerning smuggling?"

Miles frowned. "In this case . . . Eustacia, the items she smuggled were not the sort to make a person rich, which is, after all, the reason a crew turns to the trade. Instead, it appears to have made the peasants on the estate rich." He laughed. "Well, I do not mean rich as you are rich, but they are comfortable. Far more comfortable than in other parts of France. You would never believe how impoverished the French countryside has become. No farm animals with which to work. No men to do the work. In many places the populace is often hungry. But not there where Thérèse Marie has taken a hand!"

"Then her smuggling has been to benefit the estate?"

Miles was silent for a moment. "Yes. That sounds right. And if that is what she does, then *why*? And the only answer to that is that it was her family's." Miles suddenly seemed to relax. "Yes. Quite possible. Jase"— he spoke so sharply that Sahib started to rise and only lay back down when Renwick laid a hand on his head— "plan me a plan whereby my lady pirate may escape!" And then he threw back his head and laughed. "Oh, yes. She will escape and steal back her yacht and I will track her down still again!"

* * *

Two days later, after the Renwicks and Miles took Thérèse Marie to the river for a picnic and inadvertently-on-purpose allowed her to see a pasture in which several horses grazed, Eustacia walked purposefully down the hall to the storage room in which Miles's prisoners spent their days. She knocked and then turned the lock, opening the door and looking across the room to where the three played the only three-handed card game they knew.

Eustacia began the ritual request for Thérèse's parole. "Will you—"

A scream from the direction of the kitchen startled Eustacia even though she had expected it.

"—Oh dear!"

She turned and ran back the way she'd come, her skirts held up so she'd not trip. Behind her the three prisoners looked one to the other.

"We can only try," said Thérèse and headed for the door. She had become somewhat familiar with the house and, knowing there were exits to the gardens on all sides, turned away from the kitchen. "Ah. Now, gently," she told herself as she opened the door a fraction and peered out. Seeing no one, she opened it wider. "All clear," she whispered and the men followed her into a hedge-surrounded rose garden. "That way," she said, remembering where she'd seen the horses.

Riding bareback would not be easy, but was not impossible and would get them the farthest from the house in the least amount of time.

"I hate horses," said Armand, grimly eyeing the animals Thérèse and Henri brought toward him. "I cannot ride."

"You can walk then," said Thérèse, holding his gaze.

Armand sighed. "I will fall off."

"We'll not gallop. We'll not even trot with no saddles and only halters to hang on to. Now up with you."

"How?"

But Henri was showing Armand the way, and reluctantly

he climbed the fence and then eased himself onto the back of the gentle mare. "Now what?"

Thérèse had his horse by the halter. She used her knees to start her mare walking and the three headed toward the river.

"Well," said Armand some minutes later, "it looks as if we've escaped. Do you suppose the *Ange Blanc* is where they tied her up?"

"It makes no odds whether she is or is not. We'll not go near the *Ange*."

"We won't!"

"We head for René's. Our dear Captain Seward will not expect it and we are less likely to be found."

"I don't believe I can ride so far," said Armand after a moment. "I doubt I will be able to walk, either, if we travel long in this fashion!"

Thérèse, excited by their escape, laughed. "I too."

Later, when Armand was about to rebel in earnest, they passed a field pretty well surrounded by high hedges. "Here," said Thérèse. "We will leave the horses here."

"We haven't gone all that far," said Henri, glancing back the way they'd come. "We'll be tracked this far and then the hunt will be up for sure."

"It still appears as if we are heading for the cove where Captain Seward dropped anchor and tied up the *Ange*. They will believe us headed that way while we go *that* way." She pointed.

"Then let us do so *before* they catch up to us."

"I do not understand why they have not," grumbled Armand, sliding heavily from the back of his mare. He straightened—and moaned. *"Dieu!* I'll never walk properly again!"

"Yes you will and soon enough at that," said Thérèse crossly. She opened the gate, whacked her mount on the haunch, and watched the other two follow hers into the field. "I just hope no one comes checking this crop for a few days. We've left little in the way of tracks so perhaps they'll not follow even this far. Now come."

Thérèse Marie set off at a steady pace. She was not looking forward to what must be between twenty and thirty miles on foot!

"Well?" asked Lord Renwick when the three assembled for dinner.

"Very well," said Miles, complacently.

"So?"

"So what?"

"So where have they gone?"

Miles tipped his head. "Should I know?"

"I had thought," said Jason, slowly, "that it was because you cared that you plotted their means of escape."

"Nonsense." But Miles felt his ears burn. He glanced at Eustacia and discovered she was doing her best not to laugh. "There were mitigating circumstances," he added. "She did not profit by what she smuggled. Surely that makes a difference."

"She didn't so far as you know."

Miles's brows snapped together. If they'd been metal they'd have clanked. "What are you suggesting?"

"Perhaps the estate agent siphons off monies to give the family. Perhaps they receive more because of all she's done."

"Did she look as if she were a pampered chit living off the income of her family estate?"

"How would I know?" asked Jason, with no apology for the reference to his blindness.

"Her boots were excellent quality and, I believe, English-made," murmured Eustacia.

Miles's mouth turned down at the corners, emphasizing the frown marring his brow. "I have seen where she lives. In a fishing village! In a row house. She and her father live alone with one servant, perhaps two. And I believe they live pretty much on the charity of the people who belong on the estate. Perhaps her smuggling is payment for what is given them?" Miles heard a tone in his voice that sounded all too much like pleading. Shivers went up his spine.

What, he wondered, *is wrong with me?*

"Now that does seem a reasonable explanation," said Eustacia. She glanced at her husband, who she feared was about to say something more to upset Miles. "Payment for services rendered. A bartering sort of thing."

"Yes, but it doesn't explain why the profits are not sent to Paris as they should be," objected Miles, upsetting himself. He rose to his feet. "Jase, Eustacia, I believe I'll just take another little jaunt to France. Tomorrow," he added when Eustacia pointed out it was rather late to be setting off. He reseated himself and then, almost immediately, was forced back onto his feet when the Renwicks' butler announced that dinner was served.

Prince Ravi and his tutor joined them as they entered the dining room. "Captain Seward," said the prince, once all were served their first course, "I have been thinking about that thing I said."

"What thing, Prince?"

"That I sail home on your *Nemesis.* We must make plans."

"I am rather busy just at the moment, Prince, so if you mean to leave anytime soon then Jason will see that you've a proper ship for your travels."

The prince got a stubborn look. "I wish *your* ship, Captain. I know you and I know you will see me properly to my father's side. We need not leave immediately, but we must go soon. My father"—the young man looked exceedingly serious—"grows old. His advisors suggest I return before it is too late."

"Prince Ravi, I think yours is a plan we must discuss at some length—but not, perhaps, at the dinner table?" finished Lord Renwick, his tone a gentle reproof.

For a moment it appeared that the prince would argue

and then, suddenly, he sighed. "It is one of the most incomprehensible things about you English."

"What is, Prince?" asked Eustacia.

"This need you have to talk and talk and talk. I do not see the problem. It is time I go home. Captain Seward has a ship—" He shrugged. "—and so it is obvious. Captain Seward uses his ship to take me home!"

"And Captain Seward's life? He should interrupt his business, his plans, his needs, merely because you have said he should?"

"I am the future maharaja," said Ravi as if that settled the question.

And, for him, it did.

"Prince," said Miles after a moment's pause in which he controlled his irritation, "I am occupied at the moment with something which must be settled before I do anything else. There is also the problem that, if he is to go with you, Mr. McMurrey must discuss the wedding with his fiancée, must he not?"

Prince Ravi glanced toward his tutor, who blushed rosily. "I had forgotten. Mr. McMurrey, you will arrange your marriage instantly, please."

The *please* sounded odd, given that the tone was that of an order. Miles chuckled.

"What," asked the prince politely, "is humorous?"

"The notion," lied Miles, "that his bride will find it possible to arrange a wedding instantly. As you know, these things take time."

"I know nothing of the sort," said Ravi with more arrogance than he was used to displaying. "I have seen many weddings since I have lived at Tiger's Lair. Some have taken no more than a few days. I know this can be done."

"Yes, but it is not always done that way, and if Miss Browne's father is not to be more against this marriage than he is already," said Aaron McMurrey, "then we must do nothing to encourage his displeasure." He drew in a big breath. "My prince, if you must leave England precipittately, then I will be unable to come with you, even though it is the desire of my heart to do so."

Prince Ravi cast his tutor a look of mixed gratification and irritation. "I see. Since I wish it that you come, how soon can you be ready?"

The ensuing conversation bored Miles. His thoughts returned to his mystery and the solution that had occurred to him. As the meal ended, he told the others good-bye, that he'd be leaving very early in the morning . . .

". . . and," he finished, his eyes on Prince Ravi, "I will take no longer about my business than I must, since I have long had a desire to sail to the East where I may explore new regions and see a part of this incredible world I've not yet seen. Unfortunately," he finished, sounding sad, "I doubt I'll live long enough to see *every* corner of it."

While Miles made plans to return to France, Thérèse Marie and her crew sat on the back of a cart, swinging their legs. Thérèse bantered with the young cowman guiding the oxen pulling the wagon, making him blush and, without meaning to, the three adventurers become a part of his dreams for many years—especially the young woman dressed as a man.

The ride couldn't take them far, but it rested their tired legs . . . and every mile covered took her closer to her father's cousin. The moon set when they were still many miles from their goal. Armand found them an oast house, the door unlocked and a basket of apples stored in one corner.

"It will do," said Thérèse, shrugging off the unconventionality. But she wondered why she felt uncomfortable when never before had she been bothered finding herself alone with her crew. She had shared night watches on the *Ange Blanc* with the two men, sleeping between times, and never thought a thing about it . . .

Nine

Miles stood on the terrace before the Renwicks' home, talking to Eustacia. Her husband rounded the corner of the house, his cane tapping the path and Sahib following close behind. Miles watched idly and noticed that, as they drew nearer, Sahib seemed more interested in something in the garden than in staying at Jason's side—unusual behavior for the beast.

Miles's attention was caught by something Lady Renwick said and he looked down at her. "Paris? Yes, that's what I said. I mean to purchase that estate from the consortium." He said no more, turning his gaze back toward Sahib.

"Why?" asked Eustacia, the word dropping like a stone into the silence.

"Why?" Miles's lips firmed, giving him a grim look. Then he relaxed, but his eyes remained hard as stone. "Because," he said softly, "I do not like a mystery." He smiled, but it wasn't exactly a nice smile. "Why else? Once I am in my new *chateau* I will discover answers, will I not?" His tone deepened into a mild rant. "When, for instance, the agent takes me on a tour of the hectares I've bought and he must answer questions? When"—his voice grew still gruffer—"I see how our lady smuggler reacts to the discovery that *I* own her estate?"

"You would waste your fortune buying an estate you do

not want merely to satisfy your curiosity?" asked Jason, approaching in time to hear Miles's tirade.

Miles shrugged, his eyes on Sahib, who, stomach to the ground, crawled toward a particularly large clump of rose-bushes. "It sits in the bank doing nothing. The money, I mean. And I liked the looks of that area of France. It is likely the consortium is unaware of its true value. I will get it cheap. It will be a good investment, will it not? Why, therefore, should I not buy it?"

Sahib stopped and then inched forward, stopped, stretched his neck toward the bushes . . . and jerked back.

"Whatever is Sahib doing?" asked Eustacia, finally noticing the tiger's odd behavior.

"Stalking something?" suggested Miles.

"You do not mean he hunts?" asked Jason, alarmed. Sahib had never hunted for food in the whole of his life. He had been hand fed while a cub and, since, Jason supplied all his needs.

"He pokes his head toward those bushes and then pulls back. He's repeated the movement several times," said Eustacia, frowning. "I'll just go see what he's doing." She moved down the steps and across the grass toward Sahib.

"Go with her. Stop her if you can!" said Jason to Miles. "If Sahib *is* hunting, then he won't tolerate interference."

"I'll go, but even though I suggested it, I don't believe it is that. Sahib approached cautiously, but now acts more as if he were curious about what he's found than that he wished to harm it." Miles was already down the steps before he finished speaking.

"Sahib," he heard Eustacia say, "what is it?"

Sahib turned his great head, made the sound that meant he was pleased about something, and poked his nose back between two bushes—only to pull back instantly and wipe his tongue over his nostrils.

"Here, Sahib," said Miles, "why don't you let me see?"

Obediently, Sahib shifted back. Miles peered between the stems, holding one thorny branch aside with finger and thumb. He reached down with his other hand, and came back up with a spitting, squirming half-grown kitten.

"Is that all? One of the barn cats, I suppose," said Eustacia. "Now, Sahib, down!"

Sahib had risen on his haunches and touched his nose to the little creature—only to fall over in his need to get away from the sharp little claws striking out at him.

"A feisty little devil," said Miles, grinning. He held the cat up and looked it in the face. "You've taken on more than you can chew, *mon ami* David. You cannot fight a giant like Sahib!"

"David? The *cat?*" Eustacia cast him a horrified look. "Miles, you must *never* name a barn cat!"

"Why not?" He held the tiny creature farther aloft, looking up at it. Before Eustacia could respond, he added, "A boy cat. David it is."

Sahib touched Miles's thigh with his paw and Miles glanced down. Sahib opened his mouth in what could only be called a plaintive if nearly silent roar.

"You want him?"

Sahib seemed to nod and sat back on his haunches. He pawed—or perhaps *patted,* the ground in front of him.

"On your head be it, David," said Miles and set the kitten down before the tiger. The two felines stared at each other.

"Well I'll be . . ." said Miles softly.

"Whatever it is *you'll* be, I'll be too!" exclaimed Eustacia. She watched wide-eyed as the kitten wound between Sahib's legs and then, when Sahib lay down, crawled up his side to curl up on the tiger's shoulder. David purred. Sahib chortled his tiger purrs.

"I've a horrid feeling Sahib just adopted that cat." Eustacia sighed. "I told you not to name it!"

"Sahib adopted it before I gave it a name, but why, Eustacia, does one not name a cat?"

"If you name it, then it is no longer wild. It is yours." She brightened. "Aha!" She pointed a finger at him. "It is *yours* and I need not worry about it."

"Think again, Eustacia. Sahib isn't about to let me have that kitten!"

Sahib had looked over his shoulder, roared softly, and the kitten moved quickly to a position between Sahib's paws. The tiger sniffed it again and this time the kitten made no retaliation.

"What is going on?" asked Jason. With no Sahib to lead him, it had taken him longer than he liked to cross the flowerbed-strewn grass and reach his wife's side. "Tell me."

Eustacia described what had happened, giving Jason a vivid word picture of the behavior of the two creatures, and then accused Miles of being at fault. "He named the kitten before I could stop him. You know what that means."

"Named it?"

"David of all things. Miles, why David?"

"Rather Biblical, I thought." Miles grinned when she frowned. "Don't you see? That tiny kitten facing off with Sahib? What is more, it looks as if he won."

Eustacia still frowned, but Jason chuckled. "David fighting his Goliath, hmm?"

"Jase, it is not something about which you should laugh. We will have no choice but to keep it!"

Miles laughed. "Do you think you *ever* had a choice? Really? Can you see Sahib giving the kitten up—"

Sahib raised his head to stare at the humans surrounding him.

"—now he knows David?" Miles finished more gently.

"Fiddle!"

"Do you dislike cats?"

"Cats," said Eustacia firmly, "are all very well in their place, but that place is not inside the house!"

"Haven't you a kitchen cat?"

"A working cat. That is different."

"I believe David has a job of work to do."

"Job of work? For everyone else, you mean! He will be nothing but a nuisance, clawing the furniture and ripping up the upholstery and the drapery—and who will have the task of turning a barn cat into a properly trained house pet?"

Sahib roared. The kitten, which had been tracking a bug between the grasses, scurried back between the tiger's legs. It peered around one. Sahib put his nose down and the kitten batted at it—but there were no claws showing.

When the scene was described to him, Jason smiled. "You've no choice, Eustacia. Sahib has spoken."

"Now that is settled, I'll be on my way," said Miles, turning to where a light carriage awaited him.

The others strolled beside him and Eustacia asked what he'd meant, the kitten had a job to do.

"Entertaining Sahib, don't you think?"

Eustacia eyed the kitten riding on Sahib's back. She sighed. "It appears you are correct." They had reached the coach before she spoke again. She'd recalled something she wished to discuss with him before he left. "Miles, Prince Ravi was serious that you take him and his entourage to India. Jason and I discussed it and we too feel it is a good plan. *Could* you do it?"

"I could." Miles shrugged, "I *would*—if it were not for my own plans. And of course I *will*—if I return before the prince leaves."

"When will you be back?"

"I don't know." Miles frowned, then sighed. "Assuming you have made no other arrangements, we can discuss it then, and before you ask again, I haven't a notion when that will be."

"Then write us. I do not believe I can wait forever to know what you discover!"

Miles, half in and half out of the carriage, backed all the way out. "Write?" he asked, a bemused look in his eyes.

"You know." One could hear the laughter in Eustacia's voice. "You take a pen and ink and paper and put down words and then you pay the fees and send it to us!"

Miles grinned. "Perhaps I will. It never occurs to me anyone will be interested in what I do."

Sahib, the kitten still on his back, approached and stared up at Miles. He seemed to sigh and then, turning carefully so his burden didn't slip, he moved to Jason's side.

"Sahib?" asked Jason. The tiger leaned into Jason's leg. "A problem?"

The tiger growled very softly.

"Hmm. I see."

"What is it—" Miles was irritated for reasons he didn't understand—"that you think you understand?"

"Sahib is telling me it is time you learned to value yourself enough that you accept that others value you."

Miles turned disbelieving eyes toward Sahib and then lifted his gaze to Eustacia. "My dear," he said, his tone caustic, "have you thought about a room in which your dearly beloved husband can be placed for his own safety? It appears he is losing his mind!"

Before either Renwick could respond to that outrageous comment, Miles hopped into the carriage, tapping the ceiling as he did so, the signal the driver was to move out. Sahib stood between the Renwicks with the kitten on his shoulders, the tiny paws set between Sahib's ears. All of them, even Jason in his own fashion, stared until Miles disappeared.

"What did I say?" asked Jason.

"It wasn't so much *what* as that you attributed it to Sahib. Perhaps?"

"But when Sahib makes his thoughts clear should I not interpret it for those who do not understand?"

Sahib roared.

"You see?" Jason chuckled. "Sahib says I should."

Later that day, Eustacia, thinking about the scene, wondered if perhaps she had wrongly interpreted Miles's barbed comment. Perhaps Miles's retort was more that he recognized the truth of what Jason said and didn't like hearing it. Miles, it had always seemed to Eustacia, used activity as a means of avoiding thinking and disliked it a great deal when someone forced a home truth on him.

* * *

"René, stop scolding! I have heard it before and far too often at that! Besides, nothing happened."

"You have not come near to wearing holes clear through the soles of your boots? You are not footsore and tired and hungry? You insist nothing is wrong with this? Thérèse Marie Suzanne Laurent, you are the daughter of a *comte* and yet you consider it is *comme il faut* for such as you to traipse across the countryside like a Gypsy? *Enfin*, you look like a ragamuf—"

"Stop! No more!"

"—fin. And you must—"

Thérèse Marie turned on her heel and headed for the door.

"not . . . Where are you going?"

She stopped, her back to her cousin. "Away. Anywhere but where I must listen to you rant and rave and say over and over everything I've been saying to myself since before we escaped!"

"Ah! You feel guilty!" René's expression turned from anger to contrition. "My dear, I am so sorry, but you must understand what a shock it was to have you appear at my back door in such condition!"

"I am still in such condition," she said, her tone stern. "As are Armand and Henri!"

Dark splotches of color marred René's cheeks. "I am a bad host! Come. We will see what is in the kitchen so the three of you may eat. And we will heat water while you dine." He eyed her and closed his eyes as if in pain. "Lots of water. So you may bathe before you put on a gown. Enough for all of you," he added quickly when he saw her temper was again roused by the implication that her men could remain dirty. "I must also see what can be done about clean clothes for them but . . ." He looked puzzled at the problem.

"Henri is of a size he can wear something of yours—" she saw the notion a sailor would wear his clothes displeased René and frowned "—but I haven't a notion what can be done for Armand who is too big around the shoulders and too tall to fit into your things. Perhaps someone could wash and press what he is wearing?"

"I will send a message to old Sarah. She is an excellent washerwoman and will do far better than anyone else in making your Armand look respectable again! If only *you* had not arrived at the same time as they. It is not impossible that people may put two and one together and come up with four!"

"Those two and me? Making an equation to our disadvantage?" Thérèse shrugged. "I care not."

"And," said René complacently, "it makes no odds. You will cease this nonsense of wearing men's clothing and will stop your sailing to and fro and will become a proper lady. I will move from this poky little cottage and no one who matters will recall this little contretemps."

Thérèse Marie was too tired to wonder where René meant to move or to argue that there was no contretemps, as he called it. René took her silence for agreement and the subject was dropped.

For the time being.

Thérèse Marie was not about to become a proper young lady, sewing seams and practicing the pianoforte, and she and René would, more than once she feared, find themselves going over the same ground! Thérèse had a brief vision of herself running away to . . . to join the Gypsies in order to escape the fate René would design for her—and then laughed at herself for overdramatizing the situation.

But then another, even more quickly banished vision, entered her head: she saw herself running toward Miles Seward, demanding that he save her from a fate worse than death—in this case, the stultifying boredom of the life lived by a proper young lady, rather than the ravishment to which the phrase usually referred!

* * *

Miles and Toby, the latter dressed as a proper valet except for the beret he would not give up, rode slowly up the weed-choked drive. Off and on they glimpsed the chateau through the trees. Even such brief views showed it was in need of paint, that a number of windows were boarded over, and here and there a patch of tile from the roof appeared to be missing. Miles, thinking of the well-kept interior that he'd glimpsed through the windows, touched the papers hidden in an inside pocket and grinned a rather wolfish grin. Someone was about to get the shock of his life.

Or hers!

It had taken longer than he liked to buy the property. To his surprise there was another prospective purchaser. The other buyer had already put in a bid, but so low the consortium was dragging its collective feet, hoping to get more from him. After consulting with the original bidder, they accepted Miles's offer, which was considerably higher. They might have attempted to bargain with him, too, but he made it clear it was a take-it-or-leave-it-one-time-only bid.

Miles wondered who the other buyer might be and the grin faded, a frown appearing. There were those extra monies, the income that had not gone to the consortium, as it should have done. Had the estate agent held it back for the purpose of buying the estate himself? Had he decided he had enough to put in his bid? Miles's eyes narrowed.

"What is it?" asked Toby.

"It has just occurred to me to wonder who was bidding against me. What if it was the land agent? We more than suspect he was not honest with the consortium. Do you suppose he embezzled enough that he could make a not-contemptible offer?"

"Hmm. It has been years. If he saved carefully, it is possible."

"I must discover the truth. I cannot have an agent who is not honest."

"But we already have reason to doubt his honesty."

"We do not *know*. Perhaps it is merely that he didn't

collect from the peasants all he should have done, allowing them to live far more comfortably than most anywhere else in France! We know *that* is true, that Saint Omer is more prosperous than other estates we have seen."

Toby nodded and, reining in, said, "We have arrived."

They stared at the classical façade. "I like it," said Miles softly. "I like it very much."

"It is a mess," objected Toby. "If the inside is in the same condition as the outside, then there is work here for an army."

Miles's grin returned. "A regiment, merely. There is not half the work you'd think."

He dismounted and drew a long tether rope from his saddlebag. Toby took it from him and, winding the middle around a young tree, attached the ends to the horses' bridles.

Miles nodded. "We'll see to stabling after I've had a closer look at the interior."

"I thought you'd already looked inside."

"Only a quick peek through windows that told me some sort of skullduggery is going on. Come along now."

Miles unlocked the huge double front doors and shoved. The hinges groaned but were not so rusted from disuse that they wouldn't open. On the other hand, he didn't attempt to push them wider than was necessary to admit the two of them.

Inside, the two-story high entrance hall looked like any long abandoned building might be expected to look. "I thought you said it was kept up," said Toby. He sneezed from the dust roused by their entrance.

"It is. Or—" Miles wrinkled his nose at the dust and brushed away a cobweb "—part of it is. Come. We'll explore."

The rooms immediately off the entrance hall were in nearly as sorry a condition as the hall itself—until one looked more closely. Miles pulled the dustcover from a sofa and discovered new-looking upholstery. He went on to uncover a delicate escritoire and found it not only well polished but stocked with paper and ink. A bundle of uncut quills lay to one side.

The next room they explored told the same story and the next. Miles headed for the stairs. The set of rooms at the top was obviously the master suite. Here no pretense was made that the house was unready for occupancy. Everything looked as if the owner had just stepped out. Miles nodded to himself and strode to the armoire, which, much to his surprise, stood empty. He frowned. Was he wrong? Did no one live here after all?

Further exploration told the same story. The house, on the inside, was in very nearly the condition it had enjoyed before the *comte* and his wife were beheaded. Someone cared for it, kept it up, and cleaned it regularly—except for the rooms immediately off the entrance. But, so far as he could tell, no one lived here.

"I swear the mystery grows rather than wanes."

"And you, my friend, do not like mysteries!"

Miles grinned sardonically. "As you say, I very much dislike a mystery."

"So?"

Miles shrugged as he once again looked around the sitting room off the master bedroom. "You will await the wagon with our luggage and supplies. Move my things into this suite and do what you will with the rest. Piggy will oversee the kitchen, of course. I will find someone who can direct me to the agent, who will quickly find I am not to be bamboozled, as was the consortium! *I will have answers!*"

Now that she had time to think, Thérèse found she was more depressed than she liked that she had been guilty of allowing Armand and Henri to be captured. Thérèse Marie stalked the garden paths between René's neat vegetable beds. She walked first one way and then the other, her emotions roiling.

They might have been hanged!

Her skin felt tingly, a sure indication she had paled to an ashen color, and knowing her ridiculous and hated tendency to faint when her emotions ran too high, she moved to the bench at the end of the garden, where she sat down. Lowering her head, she waited for the feeling to pass. When it did, she opened her eyes and saw her cousin's well-polished shoes standing just before her. Her gaze drifted upward from his legs to his beautifully tied cravat—but climbed no farther.

"So!" he said, when certain she had recovered herself. "You understand, finally, why you must give up your adventuring."

"I doubt I can," she said sadly. "You have no notion what it is like, René, standing at the helm of your own ship, watching the waves roll under your bow, feeling the wind pushing you, knowing you are free as the birds flying overhead . . ." Her eyes developed a dreamy cast to them and a half smile hovered around her lips. "It is like nothing else in the world. I envy—" she stopped abruptly and glanced at René whose brows arched, indicating interest, perhaps suspicion "—*anyone* who sails the seas, coming and going as they please," she finished a trifle lamely.

"You did not use to lie to me, *chérie*," said René softly.

"I have not lied to you."

He eyed her. Then he sighed deeply. "No, you simply avoid telling the whole truth. Whom do you envy, *petite chatte?*"

Her mouth compressed into a hard line. "I am hardly little and I am not a cat. I'll thank you not to use that expression again."

He bowed. "I still wish to know whom it is you envy."

She glared. "Captain Seward, if you must have it! The man who took us prisoner and has my yacht tied up farther down the coast. Who will very likely sell it for what he can get! Who has made it impossible for me to continue my work!"

"Which you were to stop in any case." René frowned. "The loss of the yacht, however, is a more serious problem. We meant to use it during our infancy. Until the new company grows."

"We?" she asked dangerously.

"Your father and myself, of course," he said, meeting her gaze without wavering.

It was hers that dropped. "You will force me into a mold I do not fit. You will attempt to . . . what is that English expression? About pigs?"

"Make a silk purse from a sow's ear? *Chérie,* what nonsense. You are the daughter of a *comte*. You *are* silk."

Thérèse laughed but there was a sour note in it. "It is you who speaks nonsense, René."

"Come now, you cannot know until you try! You will find the Season a delightful experience and it will put from your mind all this nonsense of sailing and smuggling and all that. You will find a man you can love—"

A sudden unwanted vision of Miles Seward filled Thérèse's mind.

"—and you will wed and have children and your father and I will live—"

He paused, eyeing her sharply and she wondered what he might be thinking.

"—er, *earn* enough to support us in the style in which we wish to live. Think of it, *chérie!* Saint Omer will be bought back for the family to whom it should belong!"

"Bought—" Thérèse looked up, her eyes wide "—back?"

René nodded. "It is our plan."

"For the family?"

"Yes. For me, you see, as well as you and your father. I can return to France and live out my days in the rooms and halls that sheltered our ancestors. I've no heirs, *chérie,* and your father will not forbid it. In fact, he will welcome my company."

Thérèse rose to her feet, her hands fisted. "Have you any notion at all what will be asked for the estate? A fortune! Where will you get a fortune? From your honest business where you must pay duty here and duty there? When you've only one small ship? One not designed to carry cargo, designed to transport these goods you'll sell here and there? Have you . . ."

René covered her mouth with his hand, stopping the flow of words. "You are so convinced you alone can plan and do." He caught her chin, his expression sardonic. "My dear child, what do you think Jacques Rabaut has been about all these years?"

Thérèse went very still. "I . . . see. You and Father planned it from the beginning."

"Not the *very* beginning—" a chagrinned expression crossed his features "—but when *your* efforts bore fruit— literally, given fruit trees were your first effort to improve the estate—"

"For the peasants," she murmured.

"—then Jacques came to your father, talked to him. Your father came to me and we talked. And the plan was laid." René shrugged.

"Then, really, it was Jacques' plan?"

"His suggestion was the impetus but *his* offer was to give your father an allowance from the extra income which would not have existed if you had not played your games and which, rightly, belonged to my cousin in any case."

"My games." She suspected René did not care that her work had been done in order to benefit all living on the estate. "My *games?*"

"Were they not? A pleasant pastime? A means of occupying your empty hours? A diversion?"

"You have never understood, have you?"

"What is it that I have not understood?"

Thérèse felt her temper roused by his condescending tone and pushed the emotion down. She would not rant and rage at René. She *would* not.

"Well? What have I not understood?" he asked again, a certain complacency marring his good looks.

She glared but spoke reasonably calmly. "That I am not so self-centered, so immature, that I did not understand that we, the family, had and have an obligation to those on the estate. That we are responsible for them. That they look to us to keep them safe and healthy and that we must watch over their well-being."

The smirk Thérèse disliked faded from René's face, a cold look replacing it. "How very English of you, *chérie*."

The chill in his voice sent a *frisson* up Thérèse's spine. "Tell me where I am wrong."

His brows arched. "The peasants are there to see to *our* well-being, of course!"

Her eyes widened. "You believe that."

"We are the *élite*, Thérèse."

"Which means we've responsibilities for those beneath us."

"Which means we have a right to the good things of life!" he corrected sharply.

Thérèse eyed him. "You would induce the *sanscoulottes* to conclude they must do a proper job of it next time? Improve on what they and Madam Guillotine did the first time?" she asked politely.

René's skin paled. "You do not understand."

"I believe I do. Unfortunately." She cast a sad look his way. "If that is also my father's attitude, then I both pity you and fear for you." She turned on her heel and headed for the house.

"Where are you going?"

"To my room."

Which was true—so far as it went. But as soon as she could don her usual costume, she meant to collect Armand and Henri and begin the arduous journey back to the cove in which she'd last seen the *Ange Blanc*.

And once she'd found it—her mouth firmed into a grim line—she would, somehow, someway, steal it back and return to France. And once she arrived she would confront her father and see if he, too, felt as did René.

Surely not. Surely he felt some obligation to all the fine people who had hidden him from Madam Guillotine, who had fed him and clothed him and cared for him for decades even though, under the new laws, they'd no obligation to do so!

Dusk fell as she changed clothes and it grew dark as she and the two men walked away from René's cottage. They headed toward the coast, since it had occurred to Thérèse Marie as she pulled on her boots that her men knew the fishermen in the cove into which they usually sailed and, with luck, one of them would agree to drop three Frenchmen down the coast nearer to where the *Ange Blanc* was moored.

At least, where Thérèse hoped the *Ange* was still moored.

Ten

Miles strode around the estate at the side of an exceedingly grim Jacques Rabaut, forcing the man in directions he obviously did not wish to go. As they explored, he found himself more and more impressed at how cannily the people had hidden their efforts to improve their lot. The hills and dales were farmed in such a way that no one traveling nearby roads would see any of it. Grazing for sheep and milk cows was hidden away from prying eyes. Ragged-looking hedges were surprisingly tight, surprisingly dense. Copses hid what might have been a glimpse of neat gardens and small well-kept orchards. Geese and ducks were openly raised in a stream dammed to supply water to what looked a derelict mill—but which, if the noise meant anything, functioned very well. And an exceedingly noisome piggery covered the odor of a much more extensive and better cared-for operation hidden beyond it.

"You have done well, Monsieur Rabaut."

"We have done what we must."

"You mean to protect your crops from the tax men?" asked Miles, giving the land agent an excuse.

"For that and other reasons," said Jacques shortly.

"I find it surprising that everything is in such good order. Especially the chateau."

"Ah. Well, we had good masters here for generations. What was done to them was wrong."

"Madame Guillotine?"

"*Oui*. Many deserved their fate. Our *comte* did not."

"So you have done what you could to maintain things, but in such a way a casual observer would not notice?"

"*Oui*." The short answer was sullen in the extreme.

"But for what purpose?" asked Miles innocently. "Nothing you did could bring back the *comte*."

"Not that one."

"Ah!" That possibility had not occurred to Miles. "An heir exists."

Jacques' mouth pursed, his lips quivering with emotion. Then he nodded.

"You hoped the heir would find a means of returning to what should have been his estate?"

Again Jacques nodded.

"Hmm. There was another purchaser bidding when I put in my bid. Someone else would have bought it if I had not," said Miles. He spoke idly, but kept a sharp eye on Jacques and saw what he expected to see. First despair, then anger. "I will promise to be a good master," said Miles quietly. "I will not strip the peasants of the gains they have made, nor make it impossible for them to continue to prosper."

"You are not French."

Miles was surprised. He had often passed as French in far more difficult circumstances than this! "How did you guess?"

Jacques stopped and pointed. "First, your boots. They are English made. Your jacket. It is not French, but is also English." He spat. "When you speak your French is perfect, *oui*, but perhaps just a trifle too perfect?"

Silently Miles cursed. He thought he'd eradicated the tendency to speak with perfect grammar, thought he'd learned the idioms and where to elide and contract his words as would someone born to the language. But French was beautiful when spoken properly and it was difficult to force his tongue to obey him—unless he spoke truly gutter French learned in milieus it would be imprudent to reveal here and now! Miles sighed.

"You are correct. I am English. I have a fondness for things French and, now that it is possible, I would indulge myself." He spoke with just a touch of arrogance. It would not do for Jacques to think him a man who could be cheated or sidestepped. He had hoped to relieve some of the man's fears for the future by saying that he would not chouse the peasants of every *sou* they made, but it had not served.

The reason for Jacques's bitterness was very natural, assuming the other bidder was the heir! Just as those at Saint Omer tasted success, Miles's purchase of the estate was a disaster. And yet he was glad he had. It was a good property, lovely countryside and at the chateau he discovered new delights every time he turned around. Besides, he needed to know what part his little smuggler had in all this. And he wanted to know more history, more about the dead *comte* . . .

"I wish to hire servants for the chateau," said Miles, breaking a silence that was growing a trifle strained. "Both inside and out. The stables need repair and the gardens are a disgrace. If you wish to remain my land agent, as I assume you will, then please see to it at once."

"A cook?" Jacques did not admit to wishing to retain his place, but, tacitly his question admitted it for him. "That should, perhaps, be the first order of business?"

"I've a cook, but he will require help. I don't suppose the old head gardener survives?"

"He does. Whether he will work for an Englishman is another question."

"He cannot be a young man," mused Miles. "Tell him he has a free hand, as much help as he requires and then hire it for him. I will not argue expense and he need merely oversee the work."

Jacques nodded. He could not entirely hide that he was impressed. "I will promise nothing," he warned.

"You will do your best. You too wish to see the estate returned to its former glory."

Jacques sighed. "Yes. There is that, of course."

Miles cast a quick look at his guide. "It is unnecessary to tell you that I will not be in residence the year round. You know that you will have very nearly as free a hand as you've had all along."

Jacques stilled for an instant, just a hint of a hesitation in his stride before moving on.

"That does not mean that I will put up with the sort of accounting you did for the consortium. I repeat. I will not strip the peasants to the bone, but I *will* know how much income there is, what assets exist. You will *not* write fiction when you make your quarterly reports!"

Jacques grimaced. "What would you have had me do? They stole the property from the family. It was not theirs."

"You would say it is not mine although I paid a very good price for it."

Jacques shrugged. "It is Saint Omer."

"I can, to a degree, understand your feelings, but you must accept that times have changed, accept that *I* am the owner, and finally that I am *not* a tyrant who would cheat you of all your hard work!" Miles's eyes narrowed. "We did a great deal today once I convinced you I would not be satisfied to look at ragged hedges and broken down sheds. I will return to the chateau now. Does the heir live near here?' he asked, throwing the question into the conversation in the hopes of surprising information from the man.

"Monsieur le Comte is," said Jacques, and then hesitated slightly before finishing, "not here."

Miles hid a grimace. The man was sharp. The mild trick had not sufficed and he still did not know who the man was or where he could be found.

"Not here," repeated Miles.

Jacques merely nodded.

Miles refrained from pressing for more information, but his mind whirled. "Not here" could mean several things. Obviously, the man was not *here,* at their side, walking with them. But did he live *here* in the region, perhaps in a house on the estate that Miles had yet to find, a place that was smaller than the chateau but a not-contemptible dwelling for the rightful heir? In that case "not here" meant merely that he was away for the moment.

Alternatively, "not here" could be taken literally. Did he live in England, as did many refugees from the Terror? Or had he lived in England and returned to France with the king—to live in Paris, perhaps? More questions! It seemed that every time he turned around it was to discover still more questions!

And there is yet another one, is there not? he asked himself. *Why am I so interested?*

A vision of a slim young woman daringly dressed in male attire popped into his head—only to be pushed away. Instantly. Miles was never particularly introspective but he had a vaguely perceived intuition that to follow that thought to the end would lead to notions he didn't wish to contemplate! Was—he looked around as if someone could eavesdrop on his thoughts—afraid to contemplate!

Not long before dawn, Thérèse, Armand, and Henri were set ashore near the cove in which Miles had moored the *Ange Blanc*. They were, all three, relieved to see the yacht tied to a buoy only a little distance from the shore. The buoy suggested the *Ange* was not at anchor, which meant they would not be forced to raise it before sailing. The tide, which was still on the ebb, would be turning very soon now, so Thérèse hoped the yacht was merely tied.

"There is no time to lose," said Armand, his voice a mere thread of sound. A seaman all his life, he, too, knew the tide would not be with them for long.

"I know. But to move too quickly may also mean disaster. Henri, can you see anyone aboard her?"

"No one is where they can be seen, Mademoiselle Thérèse."

"Stop that!"

"Shush!" whispered Armand.

"I will not have it," she said, but more quietly.

"Let us discuss it later," said Armand, the barest hint of alarm in his voice. "Once we are properly at sea."

The three watched the yacht. "I think it is safe," whispered Henri.

"There is a cockleshell resting on the strand," whispered Armand, pointing to where the tiny craft was turned upside down.

"I saw it. What I do not see are oars," said Thérèse.

"Shoved underneath?" asked Henri.

"There are oars leaning against that cottage," said Thérèse, pointing.

"I'll get them," said Henri.

"You check the cockleshell. If oars are there, we need not chance waking someone in the cottage."

"Don't *you* get them," warned Henri. "They'll be awkward. Armand can manage much more easily." He moved swiftly, but as silently as possible down the strand, only the faintest clink of stone on stone coming to Thérèse's straining ears.

"Well done, Henri, but Armand clumps around like an ox," whispered Thérèse just loudly enough so that Armand could hear. He growled and she grinned.

"You are enjoying this," said Armand. Even whispered, the words sounded accusing.

"Yes. Ah! Henri is waving us forward. Watch your great huge feet!"

Armand reached the boat only a little after Thérèse. She had been teasing him, but it was true that he tended to tread heavily and did not always watch where he stepped. He and Henri lifted the frail craft and turned it. Thérèse picked up the oars hidden beneath it and followed the men to the water.

She glanced around. The hint of approaching day was a pink edge on the horizon to the east. Far too soon the tiny village would be astir and their chance lost. Armand stumbled, the clink of stone against stone sounding overly loud. Again she glanced around. Again she saw nothing.

"Hurry," she said, suddenly aware there were no fishing boats moored and wondering where the village fleet might be. "Night fishing will have ended. They'll catch the incoming tide."

The little boat was in the water and Armand reached for Thérèse, swinging her over the softly rolling ripples into the middle of it. He and Henri followed and Henri set the oars to the tholes. Then, softly, carefully, catching no crabs and swinging the sweeps low over the water so that no drips would alert awakening villagers, he moved the heavily loaded cockleshell toward the *Ange Blanc*.

They were within feet of the yacht when a door swung open in the farthest cottage. Thérèse's heart pounded. Was she so near success only to fail at the last moment?

"So go chase the cat, you foolish dog," they heard. The door slammed shut and the dog rushed toward the water. They could hear his snarls, growls—but no barking.

"Quickly," whispered Thérèse, her heart still beating like a wild thing in her chest. Her fingers felt like lumber as she worked at the rope holding the *Ange* to the buoy. Armand was already over the rail.

"Let me," whispered Henri, and Thérèse didn't argue but reached for Armand's hand. In an instant she was lifted over the rail and headed for the spar. She and Armand worked on the rolled sails. They were raising them when Henri joined them. Thérèse handed over her job and headed for the helm. Already the receding tide was gently bearing them away from land, which was good. Then a breeze ruffled the rising sail. Another gently bowed it. Still another and Thérèse felt the *Ange* come alive.

And then, from the shore, a feminine shriek followed by the angry quavering voice of an elderly person. Thérèse didn't turn to see which gender. Other voices joined those two, but it was obvious that unless the village's fishing boats returned that instant—and there was no sign of them—they had accomplished their escape!

Far enough from shore that Thérèse no longer feared recapture, exhaustion hit her, falling over her like a heavy rug and bearing her down. Unknowing, she fell asleep on her feet. Her gently bending knees touched the wheel and her head snapped up, her eyes blinking rapidly. She looked around. Henri was slumped down against the side of the cabin. Armand, his arms crossed over his chest, leaned near Henri, his eyes closed and his head nodding.

Thérèse forced herself to come awake, rubbing her eyes and slapping her cheeks. A wet finger tested the wind that she already knew was far too gentle to take them swiftly home. She forced her sluggish thoughts through the possibilities, and decided their best chance was to head *not* for France, but up the coast to the cove near René's, where they usually dropped anchor and where they could sleep off their exhaustion and—once they awoke, buy something to eat before sailing for France.

Thérèse grinned and, with care, turned the helm. It meant tacking their way up the coast, but was far better than the hours it would take to cross the Channel. They would be rested and fed. *And* they would find and buy that blasted hog she'd been foolish enough to promise the old pig man!

But she would not go back to René's.

Henri, cursing the stubbornness of pigs, herded the boar toward the piggery. Armand laughed and then laughed harder at the look the lad turned his way. But the boy's temper reminded him of Thérèse's, which had been razor-edged ever since she'd had one last confrontation with her cousin. The memory sobered him. René, hearing they were in the cove, came to see them and the scene between the cousins had not been one Armand wished repeated.

"Ma capitaine?"

"Don't say it, Armand."

"But what was I to do?"

"You needn't have promised."

"But he . . ."

"He is determined to make my life hell."

"He is not altogether wrong."

"He is. Armand, I will be forced to slit my throat if I must sit in a salon with needlework, smile politely at women I despise, pretend to listen to men woo me when I detest everything about the soft unprincipled fools. I cannot do it!"

"It will not be like that."

"Oh? You have visited London during the Season, perhaps?"

"There will be lovely gowns. And dancing," he added, inspired. "You love to dance."

"Yes I love to dance. Can you not see society matrons stare when I perform one of our country dances as I would in the village square?"

Armand choked back laughter. "Hmm. Yes, well, if you love dancing, then you love dancing. It need not be our hopping-about and kicking-up-our-heels sort of dancing."

Thérèse sighed. "You too. Traitor! I thought you my friend, Armand."

In that Armand heard a hint of the lonely child he had, when he was fifteen, taken under his wing and taught to sail. She had been a child, all arms and legs, her plaits flying in the wind, and had taken to the water like a mermaid, swimming in the cove with no fear, climbing the rigging in the yacht and clinging to the guylines as if born to them.

He sighed. "I am your friend. I will admit to you that I crossed my fingers when I made that promise and, in my heart, explained to *le bon Dieu,* so He will, I hope, understand that I meant not a word of it."

"Armand!" She swung around and threw herself at him, hugging him. "I should have known. I should have trusted you."

"Well, perhaps I should have told you once your cousin left us but there was that blasted hog . . ."

She had not lost her friend! Armand had not deserted her! Thérèse giggled. Relief filled her and she swung around and around until she was dizzy. "Ah! I should have known! I do not know what I would do without you!"

Twenty minutes later Thérèse burst into her father's house. There was no entry hall, the door opening directly into the large room that was their salon. She instantly stilled. "Father?"

He lifted his head from his chest, the glass dangling from his fingers dropping to the rug, the dregs of his wine running into the carpet, spotting it.

"Daughter," he muttered. "Ah. My loving daughter, who was here to soothe my wounded heart, to ease the pain, the disappointment. Who was here, looking like a *woman*—" he pointed at her trouser-clad legs "—instead of some fishing family's young and pampered son! You, *ma chérie,* are a disgrace to your name. You are—" he turned back to stare at the empty grate "—a disappointment from which I will never recover."

Thérèse Marie frowned in bewilderment. "But I escaped. And if I had not I would never have told them our real name! I would not have shamed you."

"Escaped . . ." His head rose and his eyes widened. Slowly, carefully, he rose to his feet. "You *escaped?*"

Her frown deepened. "If it was not our capture to which you refer, then what disappointment have you suffered? And what have *I* done?"

"Done?" He appeared to have forgotten that she'd been captured, his mind returning to his disappointment. "It is what you have *not* done. You have not grown to be the lovely woman your mother's daughter should be. You were not at my side to charm those—those—" he could think of no word bad enough and waved his hand "—those who have deprived me forever of what is *mine.*" Suddenly, huge tears rolled down Saint Omer's slightly fleshy face. His fea-

tures blurred, his body sagged. "It is over. There is no hope.
I must resign myself to forever existing in this—this—"
Again words failed him. "—excuse for a house. This *hovel.*"

"It is not a hovel," she murmured, but not so loudly as
to set him off in a tirade she'd heard far more often than
she liked.

"I doubt I can bear it now that there is no hope and how
I am to explain to René that all our plans, all our suffering,
was for nothing. Nothing. Nothing . . ." The tears rolled
faster and he knuckled his eyes, as would a small child.

Thérèse Marie moved to his side and led him toward the
stairs. With difficulty she got him up them and into the hall
that ran along the back of the several houses that, put together, partially gutted and reconstructed, comprised their
home. Half pushing, encouraging him vocally, she maneuvered him into his room. The bed was across what seemed
to her to be a great expanse of polished floorboards, but
evidently the sight of it gave her father new energy, because
suddenly he jerked from her support and staggered to it,
flopping across it—and almost instantly began to snore.

Thérèse stared at him. Disappointment, he'd said. Forever
lost. And he'd have to live . . . Her eyes widened. "You
tried to buy the estate!" Her frown reappeared as she continued to stare at the sleeping man. "So? You hadn't enough
to pay their price? So you must have more? So?"

She stared at him, her mind turning over and over the
bits and pieces he'd revealed, the slurred words giving her
only a few clues. She had wandered from the room and
into her own when a banging at the front door drew her
attention. One boot off and the other half off, she stilled,
listening. Footsteps. Fat Jeanne would answer the summons.
Thérèse finished pulling off her boot and dropped it to the
floor beside the other. They needed polishing. More, they
needed replacing. They had been damaged to the point she
wondered if it was possible for them to ever look reasonably
up to polite standards. One more thing about which she
must worry.

The woman who cared for the Laurents stuck her head, covered in the region's crisp white lace-edged coif, in the door. "That Armand. He says he must see you. At once." She looked disapproving. "This very moment—" her eyes narrowed "—but of course you've time to make yourself a lady!"

The disapproval in the woman's voice roused instant rebellion in Thérèse. "Before," she contradicted, already padding in her stocking-covered feet toward her door. "Out of my way, Jeanne."

For a moment the two women stared angrily at each other. Then the older sighed, stepped back, and gave an insulting version of a curtsy. Thérèse, not to be outdone, bowed in an equally insulting fashion and then, ignoring Jeanne's imprecations and malicious predictions as to Thérèse's probable future, she headed downstairs.

One look at Armand and she was glad she had. "What is it?"

"Someone has bought the estate. Someone owns it. All day, he was snooping into every corner of it."

"You cannot mean—?"

Armand nodded. "Someone," he repeated, "has just bought Saint Omer. He's moved into the chateau and he spent the day with Jacques who says he is nobody's fool."

"Who? Jacques?"

Armand gave her a puzzled look. "That is what I said. Jacques says the new owner is no one's fool and will not be put off. He led the way into places he'd no business knowing existed. And he seemed to know more than he should about *you, mon amie.*"

Thérèse whirled and looked upward in the direction of her father's bedroom on the floor above. "So that is what he meant."

"Who? Jacques?"

"Jacques! Jacques! Stop harping on Jacques!"

"But you said . . ."

"My *father,* of course. He said he must resign himself . . . But, when we have nothing, *where,*" she asked whirling around, "did he get the funds to make an offer on the estate?"

"But you know."

"I do?"

Armand looked astounded. "You do not?"

"Unless he managed to hide away Grandmother's jewels? Is that it?"

Armand's mouth formed a line indicating disgust and he stared at her. When she merely stared back, he said, "Jacques has been saving forever, holding back the profits. You know that. It was so that our *comte* could return to his proper place, could once again be the man he should be in the eyes of the world."

The man he should be! Thérèse gritted her teeth. *Oh, if only he were the man he should be!*

Thérèse wanted to rant and rave, wanted to tell Armand exactly what sort of a poor creature her father truly was, wanted to say that if the new owner were half so canny as Jacques thought, then very likely the estate was better off under him than it would be under her father's foot.

Her thoughts returned to her distressing conversation with René. Certainly their *people* would be better off with almost *anyone* rather than under René's heavy tread! And since René's will was stronger than her father's, very likely it would be René who managed everything to his satisfaction—and to the *disadvantage* of everyone else who lived on Saint Omer land!

But she couldn't. Couldn't say any of that. Armand and the others had remained loyal to a dream and she could not disillusion them. She would have to suffer her own disillusionment in silence.

And the suffering, as well.

She was, she realized, suffering. The estate had meant far more to her than she had known until this moment when she realized it was lost to her too.

Eleven

"So?"

Miles looked up at Toby's question. Otherwise, he didn't move. Nor did he answer immediately.

"What did you discover?" persisted the man, who was more friend than servant.

"It is as I thought. Only more so."

"Behind the scenes all is trim and prosperous?"

"Exactly."

"So why are you so glum?"

"I thought that buying the estate, coming here, that I would find answers."

"So?"

Miles's lips compressed into a brief expression of irritation before he asked. "So why do I merely find more questions?"

Toby coughed to cover a laugh but Miles heard and grimaced. "Did you discover the real name of your lady captain?" asked Tony when that was all Miles did.

"No."

"Did you ask?" asked Toby over politely.

Miles glanced up at him, back to the glass he held between the tips of his fingers, his elbows on the arms of his chair.

"So why did you *not* ask?"

Miles gritted his teeth.

"Perhaps because you fear the answer?" asked Toby, still far more politely than was normal between the two men.

"Fear it?" asked Miles, startled. "What nonsense. Why should I *fear* it?" Miles set the glass on the floor and heaved himself to his feet. "And don't ask why I don't *think* about it, *discover* for myself why. I don't *want* to think about her. The bloody mystery is keeping me awake nights!"

"Ah! That explains your edgy temper," said Toby, expressing satisfaction that one of his questions was answered.

"I am not in a temper!"

Toby's brows arched but he said nothing.

"I am *not*."

Miles said that quietly, tiredly, in such a manner that Toby felt instant apprehension. It was so unlike the man he knew, the tone of resignation, the defeated posture. "Captain . . ."

Miles shook his head. "I will find the answers I want. It is just that I don't know how to get beyond the bloody-minded secretive façade Rabaut wears like a suit of armor!"

Toby nodded. "I'll tell Piggy to become well acquainted with the woman Rabaut sent to help in the kitchen. Piggy will have her talking in less then no time and she won't even know she's telling secrets."

"Perhaps. I met the woman as I came through the kitchens from the stables. Rabaut chose her, I think, because she's as dour as a Scotsman and very likely as clamlike. But it's a better notion than any I've dreamed up, so do it."

"You'd never know it to look at him, Captain, but Piggy can charm the birds out of the trees when it's to his advantage to do so."

"Hmm. Make certain he knows it is to his advantage."

Toby chuckled. "Of course. I thought ten pounds?"

"Be generous. Make it guineas."

Toby's laugh was more relaxed. "Welcome back, Miles."

Miles met Toby's eyes and looked away. He grinned sheepishly. "Glad to be back," he muttered and then, more crisply, added, "I think I'll ride over to the fishing village in the morning. Now that I think about it, I suspect I was deliberately led away from it, which puts burrs under my curiosity. Rabaut does nothing without a reason."

The next morning, early, Miles allowed his gelding to amble toward the coast. He nodded to peasants walking along the lane toward their day's work, smiled at the children following—or hanging on to—their mother's skirts, and then wondered if there was a school for the youngsters. He made a mental note to talk to the priest about that, but it was of less importance than other things, and he put it halfway down the long list of problems he must look into when he had time. There was so much about which he must make decisions. Organizing the estate as he wished it organized would be neither easy nor instantly accomplished.

With any luck, he thought, *Rabaut will not prove a villain and will cooperate. The man did an excellent job here. I'd hate to find myself forced to let him go.*

Soon Miles could smell the sea. The nearness of water improved his mood and he urged the gelding to a canter, pulling up when he reached a high point of land giving him a view of the Channel.

His brows arched. He was above the protected cove where he'd first accosted the lady captain of the *Ange Blanc.* Where, at this very moment, the *Ange Blanc* rode at anchor.

Pleased, Miles's lips pulled into a tight grin. His lady captain, as Toby persisted in calling her, had escaped with her crew, the escape facilitated by the plot Jason had concocted. She also managed to steal back her yacht and that with no aid on anyone's part!

Miles recognized that what he felt was pride. Pride in her daring, her confidence, her loyalty to her men, her willingness to do what must be done to accomplish her goal . . . which in this particular case had not only been escape but retrieval of her craft.

He eyed the yacht. Beautiful lines. It was fast—as he knew from the times he'd attempted to capture her during the war—and lovely to look at. And well cared for. Any ship needed constant care. It soon became a hulk if such was not given it. The work was dirty and hard and continuous. Somehow he doubted she left it entirely to her crew and he liked that in her too.

In fact, he thought, frowning, *there is all too much about the wench I like!*

Miles's good mood faded. He was unused to the emotions the blasted woman roused in him. Tender feelings. A desire to help her even when he suspected she wanted no help. A need to be near her . . . *which explains why I am riding down toward the cove instead of toward the village?*

Miles pulled up. A *need* to be near her? What nonsense. "I don't need anyone," growled Miles and pulled on the reins a trifle more harshly than he'd have done if he were thinking straight. "I have never needed anyone." He pulled the gelding around and dug his heels into its side. "I will never need anyone . . ."

Miles's mind filled with a mental image of five young boys staring at him accusingly. He grimaced. "Very well. I *need* the Six. I need our tight friendship. But I need it for fun and companionship . . . not because I *need* it."

So why, he wondered, *has that image of five boys glaring at me changed to one of five boys rollicking with laughter and pointing fingers at me?*

As was his habit when he suffered an emotional prod, he put the thought from his mind and, again, kicked the gelding's flanks so that they trotted toward the fishing village, where he found a boy idling in front of a dusty looking shop.

"Two *sous* to care for my horse for an hour," said Miles.

The boy glanced in the shop window, breathed a trifle fast, and nodded, quickly—as if fearing that Miles might change his mind.

"Water him and take him where he can graze. Bring him back in an hour or so."

"The clock in the steeple will strike the hour," said the boy in a patois Miles had to strain to understand. "I'll not

Jeanne Savery

be late." One last glance toward the shop window and the boy led the gelding away.

Miles peered into the window as well and noticed a jar of hard candies. He grinned as he strolled down onto the strand and looked out over the water. A short quai extended out from one side of the cove, forming a breakwater, protection for the two fishing boats that bobbed on the gentle ripples. It took maybe five minutes to walk around the shore and reach the structure. The open-water side had a wall against which one could lean, and an old man rested his elbows there, a fishing pole leaning beside him and the line out.

"Catching anything?" asked Miles, approaching the oldster.

The man started, turned, looked Miles up and down, and grunted. He turned back to stare out at the swells rolling in with the tide.

Miles didn't push for conversation. He merely leaned nearby, his own elbows on the wall, and his hands clasped out over the water. He felt himself relaxing. Open water always had that effect on him.

If, he decided, *I don't have answers inside of a week, I'll leave. No one wants me here. I can hire an English agent to come periodically and check on Rabaut and for the rest— they can go on with their lives as they've always done . . .*

A week. He sighed. Would he see his lady captain again? He was ambivalent about that. Part of him wanted to see her. Wanted it very much indeed. Part of him, he admitted to himself, was scared to death of her.

Immediately, Miles shoved that thought to the very back of his mind. It didn't stay there. Why he should fear a slip of a girl—well, a firm-bodied and active woman—he hadn't a notion. It had nothing to do with the knife wound she'd given him when he'd captured her. That was merely something that happened when one engaged in a fight. So why would he *fear* her? He shrugged. He refused to worry about something so utterly ridiculous when there was so much else to think about . . . This time the thought stayed where it belonged, far from consciousness.

"Yes," he said in response when the oldster made a comment, "a truly remarkable day. One should not waste them."

"Especially at my age," was the dry response.

"At any age," said Miles firmly. "We all need memories of days like this for when we reach your age. Assuming we are lucky and live so long."

"Long life is good if one is healthy."

"As are you?"

"I've my aches and pains, but can't complain. You the new owner?" asked the man, his tone one of idle curiosity—although Miles suspected there was more to it than that.

"Yes. Miles Seward. English, before you ask, but very much an admirer of good French things."

The oldster cackled. "Our wines, perhaps?"

"Oh yes, and brandies and champagnes and . . ."

The chuckling beside him deepened—but then stopped abruptly and Miles turned to see why. There was a fish on the line. A good-sized fish if the man's struggles were an indication. He was old, but he was wiry, and Miles suspected would resent an offer of aid. Instead Miles watched and when, finally, the fish was pulled close to the wall, he picked up the fisherman's gaff and leaned over to catch the creature by its gill. He brought it up and over the wall and the old man immediately knelt to dispatch it and unhook it. He held it up.

"A goodly size," he said proudly.

"You will eat well today," said Miles, nodding.

"My woman will make an excellent soup. Very tasty."

"With her equally good bread it will be a feast for kings," said Miles.

The oldster hesitated and then cleared his throat. "Perhaps you would honor us by taking your midday meal with us?"

"Thank you. I would like that," said Miles and bowed slightly.

"We live in the cottage at that end. The free-standing one," said the old man. "Once, long ago, I was harbormaster. Back when there was a real harbor here. Before the war ended trade."

"With luck the harbor will need a new master. Perhaps you would teach a younger man what he must know to do the business properly?"

The old man's eyes widened. "Teach . . . ?"

"Or a woman if there is no man available."

Somehow the old man looked taller, younger. "I'll be glad to do it," he said. "And we will like sharing our meal with you. When the sun reaches there—" He pointed. "—then you come."

"Yes, I'll come."

The old man turned to return to shore, bobbed his head at an approaching man, and said, "Morning, monsieur. Lovely day, it is."

"Hmm. Take that fish to Fat Jeanne. I'll have it poached with my dinner today."

Miles's brows climbed his forehead. "And if he does as you say, then what does he have for *his* dinner today?"

"Hmm?" The newcomer seemed to notice Miles for the first time. "What he always has, I suppose. Get along with you, Dubois. Jeanne will be waiting."

The old man cast an apologetic look toward Miles. "I must . . ."

"Another time," interrupted Miles and smiled—but the smile faded when he glanced back at the newcomer. "That was not well done of you," he said softly.

"Not . . ." The man blinked. "The fish? But it is my fish."

"How can that be? Did you catch it?"

"Of course not," blustered the Frenchman. "Why would I catch my own fish?"

"Why would you not? If you wish fish?"

The Frenchman looked at Miles as if he were insane. "You do not understand."

"No. That is why I asked."

"I am not one to catch fish. They are caught for me."

"Ah. You mean to pay the old man for the fish?"

"Pay . . . !"

Miles nodded. "Dubois stood here under the hot sun patiently waiting for a fish to take his line. He looked forward to the soup his wife would make of the fish. He had invited me to partake of it with him."

"Ha! I see why you are perturbed. You wished a free meal. Well, then I suppose you must take your dinner with me instead."

"I think not."

"What?"

"The first invitation was freely offered. Yours is not. I go where I am wanted, not where I am not. Good day, monsieur." Miles nodded and passed the Frenchman, returning to shore with quick angry strides. He was halfway back to the small shop when he recalled that the boy would not return with his horse for another quarter hour or so. Miles looked around, wondering where the lad had taken the gelding, but saw no clue. He sighed and strolled toward the end of the cove where there were five tall houses built in a row. He was nearly there when a front door opened—

"—you!"

"Good day, mademoiselle."

Thérèse Marie sighed. "Well, it *was* a good day."

Miles chuckled. "I don't mean to recapture you and bear you off again," he said. "May I escort you wherever it is you are going?"

"If you are not here—" She eyed him suspiciously. "—to capture me, then why *are* you here?"

Miles's brows arched and he grinned a rather wolfish grin. "Can you not guess?"

For half a moment Thérèse felt hope rise in her breast, felt herself breathless and experiencing feelings that were disgustingly feminine. And then the world crashed down on her as the truth dawned. "You. You bought the estate."

He nodded and adopted an expression indicating he was exceptionally pleased with himself.

She frowned and stared out over the water. Speaking softly, she began to swear. "By the . . ."

Miles's eyes widened as the string of swear words fell from her lips and, gradually, a grin lightened his features. He waited for her to run down.

And then he waited for her to repeat herself. She didn't. Finally he touched her lips with his fingers. "Enough," he said.

Startled, Thérèse closed her mouth and stared at him.

"You live here?" asked Miles, as if he'd never heard her say a word out of the way.

"From the day I was born," she responded.

"Why did I expect to find you in a much larger house? With servants and perhaps a strict duenna."

She'd eyed him until that last bit. Then she laughed. "Me? You see me with a duenna?"

"Actually not, but I wanted to see you smile and you see? You did."

She sobered. "You are flirting with me. Do not."

"Why not?"

"I do not flirt. Instead—" She eyed him, wondering if she dared. "—I would rather we be friends. If that is possible when you are English and I am French."

"I see no reason why we cannot be friends," said Miles and repressed the glee he felt at her suggestion. He equally quickly repressed a question of *why* he felt so happy. "In fact I would like that."

"Then do not flirt with me," she repeated. "I do not like it."

There was however the faintest of questioning notes to that last, and both of them heard it. Thérèse felt heat in her throat just as he reached out and gently touched her cheek, which was, she assumed, also reddened.

"We will see," he said. "Ah! Dubois?" he asked when the old man came around the end of the house.

"I must see if I can catch another fish," muttered the old man, turning his head away.

"Another fish?" asked Thérèse sharply.

"That gentleman on the quai," explained Miles, gesturing, "requisitioned the first one."

"The *comte,* mademoiselle," said the old man at the same time, "wished Jeanne's good poached fish with his dinner."

"Dubois, wait." Thérèse, her mouth set in a hard line, entered the house and returned very shortly with over half the fish in a small basket. "There. That should make you and your wife enough for a meal."

"But the *comte* . . ."

"The *comte* has quite enough food for today's table. There have been times in the past, Dubois, when your contributions to his meals have been necessary. Today is not such a day."

"But he wishes . . ."

"There is sufficient. Fat Jeanne will contrive."

Dubois reddened, then smiled. He nodded and trotted off toward the other end of the village, casting a quick look toward the quai where the Frenchman smoked a cigarillo and stared out over the water toward England.

"The *comte?"* asked Miles.

"He rose to the title during the Terror when his mother and father met Madame Guillotine. He has nothing but his title, of course."

"Was the title not rescinded?"

Thérèse looked startled. "I do not know."

"Since he uses it, very likely it is his but if it was, then perhaps he could have it restored. It has been done for many."

"Perhaps for those who did something to deserve it— serving the king in exile, for instance."

"This particular *comte* has not?"

"He has visited England on one or two occasions, but

he did not like it that he hadn't the resources to make a proper bow to society." She shrugged, a particularly French movement.

"I see."

Miles wondered about the young woman's relationship to the man who played at being *comte* here on what should have been his estate. She was born in this house where that man lived? But why did *he* live *here*, in this small row house, when the chateau was kept up and he could have lived there?

More mystery!

But—his eyes narrowed as his gaze settled on the woman—*what is he to her?* Another question occurred to him, an even more disturbing question. *Why do I feel such a raging need for an answer to that particular question?*

The question was so upsetting and was another he was afraid to answer that he nearly turned away without proper good-byes and when he did recall his manners, she was already speaking. "I have work to do on the *Ange*, monsieur. Will you walk with me to the cove?"

Forgetting his unspoken decision to leave her until he'd sorted through his emotions—a process Miles always found more than a little difficult—he nodded, offered his arm, and strolled toward the lane leading up and along the higher ground above the Channel. Only when they were beyond the houses and he found the boy he'd hired leaning against a fence, watching the gelding munch the long grass of an abandoned enclosure, did he remember he'd ridden to the coast.

"Boy!"

The lad looked around and his features collapsed into one of alarm. "But the clock! It did not . . . surely it did not . . ."

Miles grinned. "No, you are not late. I am early. Your *sous,* lad." He dug into a small purse he drew from a pocket fitted under the waist of his trousers. The coins changed hands, the boy caught the gelding, and handed the reins to Miles, and then the lad took off at a run for the village.

"He will spend it on sweets," said Thérèse. "Sweets!"

"You disapprove?"

"His father died in the wars, leaving his mother with three children and no money. The boy should take the coins to her."

"The boy earned them himself."

"By being in the right place at the right time. Or some other would have done so."

"He *did* earn them."

"His mother *needs* them."

"You will note that the lad has slowed his pace, that he is no longer running, but is dragging his feet. Why?"

Thérèse relaxed. "He has stopped. See him sigh." She grinned. "He is taking them to his mother after all."

"As you would have done."

"I had no mother," she said shortly and turned to stalk along the path.

"I had neither mother nor father."

His voice stopped her and she turned.

"For their sins, a pair of fusty dusty trustees had the rearing of me. Which, to them, meant paying the fees to whomever, at that particular moment, had charge of me."

She stared at him and then continued on her way. "I wonder if you were truly worse off than I," she said. "No father at all would be better than one you cannot respect."

Miles stopped. It was as if lightning had struck. "You are the *comte's* daughter." Why had it taken him so long to see the truth?

She was several paces beyond him before she realized he was no longer at her side. She turned. "Surely you knew."

"How would I have known?"

"The yacht. How could I have had the yacht if I were not related to someone of a stature to own one?"

Miles studied her. He nodded. "Yes, a clue I did not take into account. Stupid of me."

Thérèse's eyes widened. "You admit you . . ."

He grinned. "That I occasionally make mistakes? That I do not always use the logic beaten into me at Eton? That I . . ."

"Enough." She sighed. "I have never known a man who was willing to admit he might have been wrong, that he might not have done something as well as it could be done. You continually surprise me, monsieur."

"What ridiculous men you must have known," he said blandly.

"Why do you say that?"

"My dear woman! If you ever meet someone so perfect he is never wrong, then I beg that you introduce me—and then run with me as quickly and as far as we can go! Such a person would be unbearable, would he not?"

Laughing, they proceeded on along the lane until they, as one, paused to look down into the cove at the *Ange Blanc*. "Beautiful," murmured Miles.

"Very," said Thérèse.

And then, shaking off the softer mood, which he attributed to the view rather than his company, Miles tied his gelding to a low bush near some grazing. He followed Thérèse down the hill and onto the pier, where she was already hallooing for Armand. The man, who was on the *Ange*, waved and went over the side and into the dory, where he picked up the oars and rowed ashore.

Twelve

"You are late," scolded Toby, who had begun to worry about Miles's long absence.

Miles grinned. He had torn off his cravat and untied his shirt before ever reaching his room. "Is that water still hot?"

"Tepid at best."

"Good enough." He finished stripping and stepped into the hip bath Toby had had waiting for him in his dressing room. "That yacht is really something. I wouldn't mind owning it myself."

"The *Ange Blanc*? You would buy it from the woman?"

"It isn't hers."

Toby frowned. "Then why does she sail it?"

"It belonged to her grandfather who lost his head in the Terror. Her father didn't exactly inherit it, but, on the other hand the consortium never made a proper inventory and hadn't a notion it existed. Everyone here has simply assumed it is her father's and never questioned her use of it."

"Then you don't have to buy it. You bought the estate lock, stock, and barrel, did you not?"

Miles's hand stilled, the soapy cloth held against one bicep. The tangy scent of sandalwood filling his head and the humor bubbling up inside made him feel ever so slightly dizzy. Chuckles turned to full-throated laughter.

But memory intruded on the irony and he sobered.

"Toby," he said, "I think you'll not mention that to anyone—" He glared. "—am I correct?"

Toby shrugged. "If you say so. But what game do you play now?"

Miles frowned. "Game?"

When he'd first captured his lady captain and her crew, he'd found it humorous, that he, by that act, owned her yacht—but her reaction, when he told her, was not at all amusing. She had been horrified, unhappy, beaten . . . it would never do to induce that reaction again! Especially since they'd agreed to be friends.

"Game?" repeated Miles softly.

Nor would it do for Toby to suspect he'd such a quixotic reason for keeping the information that he owned the yacht to himself. Toby would never cease teasing him!

"You know I always have an extra ace in any deck with which I play," he said, keeping his voice to a neutral tone.

Toby nodded. He poked his finger through a hole in one of Miles's stockings. Muttering that there was never a man who went through stockings as fast as Miles did, he found his darning kit. He seated himself, set his needles and yarn and scissors beside him, and dropped the darning egg into the heel.

Miles, eyeing Toby from under his lashes, was satisfied his first mate had no suspicions—and then wondered what it was he didn't want Toby speculating about. And then he wondered that he was wondering, and swearing silently, got himself out of the tub and dried off. Life had suddenly become overly complicated when he couldn't understand even the most basic of his own motives!

"I'd an invitation to dine in the village until the man was forced to retract it," said Miles, wanting distraction from whatever it was that kept him faintly preoccupied and more than a trifle unsettled. "I also met the heir to Saint Omer."

"Why do I have this notion you didn't like the man?"

"*He* was the cause of my missing my dinner."

"Oh?" Toby looked up from where he had just, for the

first time, woven his needle through the threads he'd laid down for the darn.

"Yes. My would-be host was harbor agent back before the Terror put an end to modest peacetime trading between the village and England." Miles described the ensuing scene where the *comte* demanded the fish be delivered to his cook.

"So?"

"So you'll be happy to know I restrained myself. I did *not* flatten the man."

"Why not?"

Miles laughed. "I never know when you'll disapprove of my behaving like Don Quixote and when you will not. In this case you appear to think I should have played that erratic knight's part."

"You had words instead?"

"Hmm. The idiotic man seemed to think he had a right to anything he wanted and that there could not possibly be the least objection to his taking it!"

"So the oldster was left without his dinner."

"No. But not due to the *comte!* Or to me. Our lady captain intervened. She kept back enough to serve the *comte* and gave the rest back to the harbormaster."

"And what did the *comte* say to that?"

"He didn't know. I suspect he'll never know. He'll have his poached fish and that is all he cares for."

"What, out of curiosity, does your lady captain have to do with the *comte*. But no. I recall you said she was his daughter!"

"For once in this business, I was *not* left with my curiosity clamoring! Yes, she is his daughter."

Toby stilled. "Oh."

Miles, nearly dressed, cast his friend a look. "What does that mean?"

Toby, startled, glanced toward Miles and then back at his darning. "Just 'oh.' Nothing in particular."

"Why don't I believe you?"

Toby's fingers caressed the new darn. "Do you want the truth?"

"Of course. When have I approved of lies?"

"There was the time . . ."

"Toby."

Toby suppressed a grin. "Oh well, then. If she'd been nobody in particular you could have taken her to your bed and gotten her out of your system. That she is the daughter of the *comte* rather changes things, does it not? You can't casually bed the daughter of an aristocrat!"

Miles felt his skin prickle and turned away to hide what he knew was suddenly pale skin. *Had* he been thinking of bedding the woman? Wanting to touch her and to teach her to want that touch? A mental picture of her, standing in the stern of the *Ange Blanc*, her back straight as an arrow, her hands, where she clutched the rail, strongly muscled under smooth sun-gilded skin, her complexion that curious golden color some women's became if they were not careful about the sun and the wind. . . .

But was that all that drew him to her? No. Actually those came a poor second to her bravery. Her loyalty to her crew. All the danger she'd faced, to keep the Saint Omer estate prosperous and in good order.

Yes, those things were far more important than that lithe body or the hair he'd thought cropped short. It was only short in front, the back tresses usually wound into a complicated knot against her head and covered by her hat, but today left hanging down her back in a long braid. He had a sudden urge to see that hair blowing in the wind when he sailed with her through foreign waters. . . .

Miles's thoughts came to a crashing halt and one utterly vicious word escaped him.

Toby swung around. "What?"

"Nothing. Nothing at all," said Miles and stalked from the room.

Toby was silent until the sound of Miles's footsteps disappeared down the stairs. "I'd give a great deal to know exactly what that particular *nothing* might be," he said, to himself, "and if that was *nothing,* then I'd like to know how you react to *something!*" He shook his head. "The man doesn't even know he's lost it," he said to the mended sock he held in his hand. "Lost what?" he asked as if the unresponsive sock had questioned him. "His heart, of course. I wonder how long it will take him to discover it is held captive in the competent hands of his lady captain!"

Every day the following week Miles kept Rabaut at his side as he poked into every niche and cranny around and about the estate. He checked roofs and outbuildings. He gave orders that hedges be trimmed. He sent the *Nemesis* back to England to return with necessary tools and supplies so that work could begin on the outside of the chateau and the grounds that the elderly gardener loved enough he would even condescend to work for the hated Englishman who had killed everyone's last hopes of seeing their *comte* where he belonged, the owner of Saint Omer.

Elsewhere on the estate fences were fixed, long-fallow ground prepared for late planting, and in the fishing village the nets were taken out and repaired. When Miles discovered there were not enough men left to man more than one of the fishing boats, he sent out agents to discover poor fisher families elsewhere who would be willing to come to a new village, where work would be available.

"And where do you think to house these strangers," asked Rabaut snidely when he learned of this latest folly on the part of the Englishman.

"There must be empty houses in the fishing village," replied Miles. "I have counted the population. There are more houses than families."

"Do you think so?"

"You would tell me I am wrong. Now you will tell my why."

Rabaut suddenly realized he'd revealed something that

had remained secret to that point. He stammered, attempting to think up a response that would not give it away.

Miles, his arms crossed, his toe tapping, and a frown on his forehead, waited. When Rabaut stuttered to a halt, he nodded. "I see. The *comte* does not live in *one* of the cottages at the end of the village, but in all of them. Who did he evict in order to have the whole of the row?"

Rabaut sputtered. "I did not say that."

"No, but I have wondered for some time how such a proud and foolish man could bear to live in one cottage in a row of cottages. I suppose the row was thrown together at some point and then furnished from the chateau?" When it appeared that Rabaut was unable to respond, Miles nodded again. "I see. Should I demand rent? How much rent? After all, the man is using five cottages, which should house five families. Five times the rent for one cottage? Would that be fair, do you think?"

Rabaut actually trembled from the emotions coursing through him. "You cannot. The estate is his. It is *not* yours. It was stolen. You cannot buy stolen property!"

"Finally. I wondered when someone would finally have the courage to suggest that. Nevertheless, I have bought it. In the eyes of the French government I own it. On the other hand, I don't see how I can, in any way, change the attitudes of your *comte,* who has behaved as he pleased for too many years and with no thought to how his actions affect those about him. He very likely does not care. I will not ask him to pay rent on the structure in which he resides, but I suggest, Rabaut, that you cease thinking of him as your master. If I cannot trust you to see to *my* interests, then I cannot retain you as my agent."

Rabaut's features fell into lines suggesting he was torn between loyalty to the *comte* and keeping his position. He sighed.

"You would like time to think about it?" suggested Miles softly.

"If you would be so kind. I have taken care of the *comte*

for many years now, have plotted with him and his cousin for the return of the estate to the family to which it rightfully belongs. Morally, *ethically,* if you will!" Rabaut looked faintly rebellious until a smile and a nod from Miles took the wind from his sails. "Well, it *is*," repeated Rabaut, "although I know you are correct that the king and government do not agree."

"Legally, I am owner," reiterated Miles.

Rabaut nodded and wandered off, his hands clasped behind his back and his whole bearing one of sad confusion.

"René!" Thérèse Marie blinked. "You? Here?"

"No thanks to you," said her cousin bitingly. "I expected you to come for me the instant I heard from your father what had happened. But you did not come. I had to travel to Dover and cross like anyone might do!"

"Why?"

"I have said. Because you did not come!"

"No, René, why did you *feel a need* to come?"

René's eyes widened. He seemed to become exceedingly still. "Why?" he asked softly? *"Why?"* he repeated. "Anyone of any sense would know why it is necessary that your father and I consult. Instantly. *And you did not come.*"

"Ah. Because my father was unable to offer enough to purchase the estate that was then bought by another, you have come to plot new plots? I see."

"There *was* enough. Your father, fool that he is, is greedy. Very likely he did not offer all."

"Even once he knew another offer had been made? I doubt that very much."

"We will see. Where is he?"

"Where is he ever at this hour?" Thérèse shrugged. "In bed, of course."

"You sneer. You who lower yourself to be up and doing with the peasants sneer at a true aristocrat who knows how to live life properly?"

Thérèse cast her cousin a look of sadness. "I pity you, René. You would bring back a past better forgotten and, although you know it is impossible, you continue to pretend you can do it. In your mind, you live in that age."

"Bah! You will never understand. It is our God-given right, Thérèse Marie. All have their place in the scheme of things," he finished with that arrogance he had used to hide from her. *"Ours* is at the top."

She eyed him. "You, René Laurent, are such a hypocrite." She turned on her heel and walked away.

Behind her, René frowned. For the life of him he could not discover the meaning behind her last comment. Finally, a trifle uneasily, he shrugged and continued on down the street toward his cousin's house. Once he arrived, René demanded breakfast of Fat Jeanne. He ate, savoring the good French cooking after so long a time away from it, and wondered why he had not visited his cousin more often . . .

"René?" asked Jean-Paul Laurent, coming into the breakfast room. He yawned. "Did you have to arrive with the dawn?"

Since the sun had been up some hours, René didn't bother to respond. "You should have sent the *Ange Blanc* for me the instant you returned from Paris!"

"Should I? Ah, excellent," he said, picking up a roll. "Just as I like them. But the *cherry* preserves . . . ?" he asked anxiously, holding the still-warm bread and looking around the table.

"Fat Jeanne said you would demand the cherry. She said to say you have eaten it all and you must do with peach."

Jean-Paul sighed. "Why is it too much to ask that I have cherry?"

"You can ask, but you have eaten it all and that is all there is to it."

"Punish her," said René when the maid left the room. "Make an example of her!"

Jean-Paul tipped his head and really looked at his cousin. "No. I like her. She—" A faintly lewd look accompanied the rest of his comment. "—keeps me happy. You will not interfere, René."

"Ah. But she presumes, Jean-Paul! There are others. Find one who knows her place."

"I have said you will not interfere!"

René's lips compressed. "Very well. But it is ever a mistake to allow such freedom to one's dependents. We will not discuss it," he added when it looked as if his cousin would argue. "Tell me instead why you did not buy the estate as we'd planned."

"The English scoundrel offered more than I could pay. They accepted his offer." Jean-Paul shrugged and looked at the bit of roll between his fingers, which he had not only thickly coated with good butter but also piled with peach preserves. He bit into it and half closed his eyes in contentment as he savored the combination of flavors and textures. *"Très bon!"*

"Jean-Paul, pay attention."

"Not when partaking of food, cousin," said the *comte*. He daintily wiped his fingers and then picked up his coffee, sniffing the warm aroma of good strong coffee.

René could get not one more word from his cousin until he had consumed what seemed a great deal of food. "You will get fat," said René.

Jean-Paul shrugged. "And if I do? No matter. I *like* good food."

He led the way to his private parlor, a room in which he had placed all his favorite furniture, a pair of exceptional portraits—one of his mother and the other of an ancestor—and in which a cheery fire burnt brightly in the small hearth. Jean-Paul settled himself before it and stretched his slipper-shod feet toward it.

"Now," he said and sighed. *"If* you must."

"How much, exactly, did you offer the consortium."

"Before I was finished, every last *sou*."

"Before you finished. In other words, after the other offer was made, you tried to top it and could not. I wonder—"

René looked very nearly angry enough to chew through nails. "—what might have happened if you had offered it all in the beginning."

"We will never know. Now, of course, something must be done to fix things. Rabaut says there is no wife. I have decided Thérèse Marie will wed the man."

René, about to open his mouth for another tirade, closed it. "Jean-Paul, I am surprised."

"Surprised?"

"I hadn't a notion you had it in you to come up with such a magnificent scheme! He will allow us to live in the chateau and, since he is English, he will return to England with his bride."

"That's what I thought." Jean-Paul, his smug look offending René no end, leaned back and went to sleep—or at least appeared to do so.

René, thinking that perhaps his cousin was getting old, left him to it, but would not have been particularly surprised if he had heard Jean-Paul's sigh of relief, nor that, his cousin gone, the *comte* reached for the book lying open and face-down on the table beside his favorite chair and that he then alternated between reading and staring out the window as he thought about what he'd read. Jean-Paul was something of a scholar, something that would have surprised René a great deal.

René meant to find Thérèse Marie and lay plans for her siege of the new owner of the estate. Unfortunately, from his point of view at least, he could not find her. She was not in the house, although she'd been dressed in a gown when he'd seen her and he knew she preferred trousers when she went out and about. It did not occur to him that she'd returned, changed, and escaped out the window over the shed at the back of the house and was off and away to the cove where she and Armand meant to finish up the latest round of scraping so that painting could begin while the weather held good.

When Thérèse Marie finally returned to the house long

after dinner was finished, he was very nearly in such a rage he could not contain it.

"You will have to wait," she told him when informed she was to come to the library, as her father called it, on the instant. "I must change."

"Yes you must, although I've no notion why that is so when you have been told to never wear those clothes ever again. But even so, you will first attend your father and myself. Now!" he said as she started up the stairs.

She turned, her hand on the railing, and looked down on him. "René, when will you understand that I do not take orders from you?"

"Then you will take them from your father!"

"Later." It occurred to her that René was in a mood to confiscate her male attire and destroy it, which would be a nuisance if she must replace it. It took her longer to change than might have been expected, since she felt a need to hide that part of her wardrobe of which her cousin would disapprove.

René, as she disappeared, gnashed his teeth in frustration. He stalked into his cousin's room and jerked the book from Jean-Paul's hands. "Why did you not put a bridle on your daughter long ago?

"If I had wed her to another, she'd not be available to wed the new owner."

"Bah! You will not evade me. I tell you, she is a hoyden and a ragamuffin and *impossible*."

"You should recall that it is because she is impossible that the estate flourished."

René shook his fists into the air. "Why does everyone pretend they do not understand me?"

Jean-Paul hid a grin. If anyone was impossible, it was René with his absurd demands. It was as if his disappointment that their plans had failed had turned him into another creature entirely!

Life, Jean-Paul knew, was no longer what it was when René left France nearly forty years earlier. And it would never be that way again. It could be good, but René, it appeared, had no intention of accepting merely *good*. He wanted the impossible.

"You cannot do it, you know," said Jean-Paul quietly, when René had stalked back and forth a dozen times. "And do not wear a path in my carpet. I haven't a notion when or how I could replace it if you ruin it."

"Do what?"

"Make life behave as you will it."

"Bah! You are the *comte*. Anything you will, that is as it will be."

"At one time, perhaps. As to being the *comte*—oh, of course I *am*, but without the trappings that is rather meaningless, is it not? It would, therefore, be best if we recovered the trappings. As things are, I merely *pretend* to be the *comte*."

Thérèse Marie, entering just then, stared at her father. "And does that satisfy you?" she asked. "Pretending to be what you are not?"

"Yes," he said complacently. "Come here, *chérie*." He gestured toward the stool placed at his feet. "We have a plan, you see."

Thirteen

Very early the next morning after a night filled with tossing and turning and worry, Thérèse Marie climbed out the window and walked rapidly toward the chateau. The morning dew wet the legs of her trousers and they flapped against her stockings, dampening them, making them chill against her calves. She didn't care. She had to find Captain Seward and warn him, tell him he must leave France, must instantly return to England.

The soft morning light soothed her agitation. Gradually her pace slowed. Despite the sense that his danger was imminent, there was really no reason to hurry. Her father and cousin would not rouse for another few hours, would not, even then, put in motion the plan devised the night before, when they'd talked long into the small hours—even after she had for the umpteenth time told them she would not cooperate, that she would not wed the new owner out of hand. Finally, her skirts swishing around her, she had stalked from the room and gone to bed.

But she hadn't slept. Not until she heard the men's murmurs in the hall and then the shutting of two doors and knew they, too, had gone to bed. Finally.

And even then she'd not slept properly. Dreams—nightmares, really—had awakened her again and again. When the early morning light made gray patches of her windows, she'd thanked *le bon Dieu* the night was ended, and crawled from her tangled bedding.

Besides, there was another reason she need not rush. At such an early hour, Captain Seward himself was unlikely to be out and around. On top of that she hadn't a notion what she'd say to him. Her mind went round and round, trying to find a solution to her problem. *Another* solution, because the only one she'd found so far was that the Englishman disappear so he could not be made a pawn in the Laurent men's plot.

But that cure was unbearable. He'd be gone. Her friend . . . *If only I could think of something else.*

If she could not, then she must go and get it over, must send him away, must watch him leave for England. He would be gone.

Gone far away where she'd never see him again.

Her friend.

Thérèse Marie's steps dragged, and finally she turned aside until she could lean against the thick bole of an ancient chestnut. Across the meadow a peasant child, carrying a stick longer then she was tall, herded geese toward a shallow pond. The geese, hungry, waddled along with little attention on the child's part. In fact—Thérèse grinned—the girl had laid aside the stick to go chasing after a butterfly that crossed her path.

Caught it too.

And stood quietly, the fragile creature cradled between her hands. She stared down at it for a very long moment, and then, smiling, tossed it into the air, watched it flutter along toward a clump of clover, and finally turned back to pick up her stick. The imp made an oddly adult sound of mixed disgust and distress and hurried after her flock, which had spread out slightly and needed encouraging before it would continue on toward the pond.

Something inside Thérèse expanded into an almost painful lump. That had been beautiful, the child, the butterfly. . . . She swallowed and discovered her hand covered her abdomen. Her head turned quickly this way and that, and relieved no one watched her shockingly revealing behavior, she took herself back to the path.

But a child? My own child?

The notion had never before occurred to her, that she might someday have children. Except, of course, it was ridiculous to think there was a man in existence that would take her for wife! So it was more than ridiculous that she yearn for a the child she'd never have. . . . Which, for some reason, reminded her that she must warn her friend. Must tell him that it was in his interest to leave France at once.

When he did, she would be lonelier than ever before and there had been times when she'd believed she would die of her isolation from others like herself.

"Not others like Father and René," she said aloud. "But like . . . oh, like my *friend* . . ." She shook her fist at the sky and turned on her heel, setting off once again to find Miles.

Miles moved around the bush behind which he'd hidden when Thérèse came into view. He hadn't decided what to do about her and, undecided, didn't wish to meet her.

When did I ever before behave so foolishly? he wondered.

And then he thought of the tender smile he'd observed on Thérèse's face when she'd watched the child with the butterfly. The hand she'd placed on her belly in that oddly protective movement . . .

Miles suffered from an odd combination of emotions and for once could put a name to them. There was anger that Thérèse thought of having a baby, that she wanted some man to give her one. Jealousy of whatever man she might choose, and a wave of protectiveness, a need, to see that that male, that stranger, who would certainly be happy to cooperate, did not hurt her.

And, worst of all, he was aroused by the picture in his head of Thérèse ready, waiting on his bed, her eyelids heavy with wanting . . . Miles's hand touched the front of his trousers and his next emotion was one of self-disgust. He *lusted* after a woman to whom he had offered friendship!

It was wrong. One was not aroused by one's friends. One hunted for a convenient lightskirt when one had needs of that sort!

Swearing softly, Miles strode off in the opposite direction of that taken by Thérèse Marie. Now he had a new reason for avoiding her! Until he had himself well in hand it behooved him to stay far away from her disturbing presence!

But getting himself "in hand" proved more difficult than he'd expected. It was midafternoon before he returned to the chateau, where Toby, who was watching for him, pounced on him. Toby drew him into the small side room in which those strangers, who were of a status above the sort sent to the rear of the building but not such that they could be offered a seat in the drawing room, were asked to wait.

Miles grinned. "What has tattered your sails?"

"Two things. You've company—No!" Toby stopped Miles from strolling from the room. "And I've a message from your lady captain. You'll want that before you see your guests!"

"Ah. Thérèse Marie was here?" It only then occurred to Miles to wonder why he'd not questioned the direction his friend had been headed. "What did she want?"

"I haven't a notion. She wouldn't tell me. And then she said she had to go, had to find you, so I suggested she write you a message—just in case the two of you didn't cross paths, as it were."

"We didn't." Miles frowned. "So?" Toby began patting his clothing here and there—and Miles's frown faded, his teeth showing as his lips spread into a grin. "I've *told* you you've had too many pockets sewn into your clothing!"

"Yes, well, give me a minute. Ah!" Toby pulled a folded and sealed missive from the smallest pocket in his vest. "Here you be."

Miles took it to the window, where he stood, the light coming over his shoulder. A tender smile grew as he read, but that was followed by a thoughtful expression, which ended with his lips compressed and a stern determined look. "I didn't like the man when I met him. I like him less and less the more I hear!"

"Who?"

"Her father."

"That's who came visiting and is fast doing away with a very good bottle of brandy! He and that cousin of his. If they *are* cousins."

"Cousin? Ah. René Laurent. Newly arrived from England. Thérèse Marie mentioned him in her note." Miles had rather skipped over that portion of Thérèse's communication and now unfolded the page to reread the passage. His teeth set off center, his lips slightly pursed, and his eyes narrowed.

"Don't like what you read?"

"If I'm reading between the lines with any accuracy, I think it may be this René who is the mastermind in all this."

"And what, if I may be so bold to ask, is *this?*"

"Hmm? Oh, they plan to trick me into marrying our lady captain, of course. She isn't pleased with the notion."

"She isn't? And what about you?"

"Hmm? Oh." Miles was certain his ears flamed red and wondered why. "Well, I've never thought of marriage. Bachelor material, that's me," he added with a quick glance toward Toby.

"A man's always bachelor material until he meets the right woman."

"If by some odd chance our lady captain were the right woman it wouldn't matter, would it? She insists I leave for England at once so the plan will come to naught!"

"I . . . see."

Miles cast Toby a glance pregnant with suspicion. "What do you think you see?"

"I'm . . . not certain."

Miles's brows arched. "Well, if you figure it out, I would appreciate it if you would explain it to me. In the meantime, I haven't come home and you haven't a notion when I will do so. In fact, you have just recalled I said something about riding into Calais in which case you believe I'll be very late arriving. Perhaps not until late tomorrow!"

"Now you are using the good sense I know you have. Where will you be when I get rid of them?"

"Be? Out looking for our lady captain, of course. We must put our heads together and come up with a counterplan to see that not only am I safe, but that she is as well."

"She?"

"If they mean to marry her off to me to regain the estate, then they will do worse to her if they fail. They will wed her to any man they believe they can manipulate into supporting them in the fashion in which they wish to see themselves supported!"

Toby sorted that long sentence into sensible bits. "Ah. Perhaps you could suggest she enter a convent."

Miles's shout of laughter was, very likely, heard through the chateau. He realized it and grinned. "Sorry, Toby, you'll have to lie if our guests are rude enough to ask about that laugh! But can you see any convent allowing my lady captain within the gate? I must go."

And he went.

Toby, shaking his head, crossed the broad entry hall and opened the door to the salon. He entered and waited until he was noticed.

René glanced at him, looked toward the door as if for someone else, and then, when no one appeared, back to Toby. "Well, man?"

"I made inquiries. I am told by a groom that Captain Seward rode into Calais. If he did that then he's unlikely to return until very late this evening. Perhaps not until tomorrow." Toby bowed, straightened, and waited.

The soft expletive escaping René's mouth was not a nice

one. In fact it was such that his cousin looked at him in surprise. Jean-Paul set aside his glass and carefully rose to his feet. "We will come another day," he said, catching and holding René's gaze.

"Yes," said René, who found his feet with far more ease than Jean-Paul had done, "we will come to pay our respects on another day."

Toby opened the salon door, followed the unwanted guests to the front door, and watched them stroll down the newly weeded, newly graveled, and well-raked drive.

"I'll just bet you will," he muttered and turned back into the house.

Miles had offered the excuse that he'd gone into Calais idly, but as he left the house, it occurred to him that not only was he not ready to see Thérèse Marie, but there were a few things he could see to if he did ride into the port. Besides, it would give him time to think up an alternative plan to Thérèse Marie's. He waited until his guests had disappeared before leaving the stables and riding off in an entirely different direction, one that meant a rather roundabout meandering ride so that he reached Calais just as the sun was setting.

Miles went immediately to his favorite hotel, asked for and got his usual room—although it meant moving a couple who, recently married, meant to travel though Europe for the next few months. When he discovered this, Miles felt mild chagrin at his unwitting interference, but did not feel so guilty as to hunt them down and apologize!

He ate an excellent meal and wandered out onto the streets, heading for the waterfront. The water. Miles sighed. *Why,* he wondered, *don't I forget this whole mess, return to the* Nemesis *and go organize a journey to India. It is what Prince Ravi wants. For that matter, taking the prince back to his homeland is what Jason wants me to do. And,* his thoughts continued, faint bewilderment coloring them, *it is just the sort of thing I'd have jumped at not so very long ago.*

He walked on a few more paces. *So,* he asked himself, *why am I here?*

A vision of Thérèse, her feet up on a chair, a mug of cider in her hand, and a song on her lips, filled his mind, which confused him even more. He'd never seen her in such a posture. Nor had he seen her drinking cider. So why did it seem so real? As if, unlike any other well-bred lady he had ever met, it was something she would do without a second thought?

Behind him, the door to a waterfront tavern opened and song and laughter burst out with a shaft of light. Miles realized he'd been hearing the voices but not really registering them. And he knew, from long experience, exactly what the inside of the tavern would look like. It was early in the evening and all was jollity and good will—unlike what it was likely to become in only an hour or two.

Had the barely heard voices translated, in his mind, into the picture of Thérèse in such a setting? How ridiculous. She was the daughter of a *comte!* She'd no business in a lowly tavern, lounging there, relaxed and singing bawdy songs. . . .

But then, she had no business dressing in men's clothing and swearing fluently. Or smuggling agricultural contraband from England to France—but she did. And she did it well. A surge of pride in her efforts filled Miles. When he realized what it was, it shocked him. And it wasn't the first time. But why pride?

In fact, why feel anything? But there was that friendship. It was acceptable to feel pride in a friend's doings. . . . Miles breathed a sigh of relief that he'd put his finger on the solution to that minor problem. He didn't, however, wonder why he felt relief. Instead, the thought of friendship reminded him that Eustacia had asked him to write and inform her what was happening.

Dutifully, he returned to his hotel, where he asked for

paper, pen, and ink and, although he found it difficult to begin, was surprised to discover he'd filled four pages back and front with his descriptions of what he'd done, what had happened, how he'd helped Thérèse finish the painting on the *Ange Blanc* . . . and the surprising news that her father was the *comte* and, if the Terror had not interceded, would have owned the property Miles bought while in Paris.

He reread what he'd written, wondered if he'd said too much about Thérèse—she seemed to crop up in nearly every paragraph—but shrugged and, folding it, sealed it. He found the proprietor, negotiated the rather excessive cost of sending the packet to England, and went up to bed.

The next day, as he strolled down the main shopping area, meaning to buy the one or two things he needed, he met Beau Brummell, which surprised him.

The Beau laughed. "You hadn't heard, then?"

Miles raised his brows at the faintly bitter edge he detected under Brummell's insouciant manner. "Heard?" he asked, allowing Brummell to grasp his arm and guide him into a nearby hostelry, where good smells from the kitchen make him realize it was past time he ate his first meal of the day.

Brummell made an excellent tale of his downfall and exile, but again Miles discerned an underlying chagrin. When the Beau managed to disappear just as the owner arrived with the bill, Miles felt a trifle chagrinned himself. He'd been nicely hoaxed, he thought, ruefully, but felt just enough pity for Brummell—despite the fact that the man had brought his disgrace on himself—that he cheerfully paid the tab and waited for Brummell to return from the necessary.

For his largess, he was well entertained by Brummell's famous style of banter as the two strolled from shop to shop. Miles's needs were soon met, but his brows arched at the sight of Brummell running up his accounts, buying trifles and bibelots. The man had in part gone into exile because of debt, had he not?

One would think, thought Miles, *that he would have learned his lesson!*

After an early tea, Miles made the excuse of a long ride home, and returned to the hostel where he'd left his horse. As he headed back to the chateau, it occurred to him that Brummell had never once asked why Miles was in France. The thought followed that it was just as well, or he'd have revealed that he owned property not far from Calais.

Brummell is the sort, thought Miles, *who would think nothing of dropping in for a visit and forget to go away!*

Thérèse was appalled. She stood under the open window and strained her ears to hear what else René might reveal.

"Of course he'll come. Why would he not?" asked René arrogantly when Jean-Paul asked.

"He is an enigma," said Jean-Paul softly. "He knows Rabaut has been cheating the consortium, but means to retain him as agent. Why would he do so?"

"Rabaut is an excellent agent. Very likely he thinks he can keep a close eye on things and, as a result, not be cheated."

"And he will, will he not?"

"Bah. Do you think Rabaut will not find means to continue supporting us? *You,* I mean."

"I very much fear you underestimate the man."

"He is English. What is there to underestimate?"

Thérèse had great difficulty controlling her temper. Keeping her equanimity in provocative situations had never been one of her strengths and hearing René insult Captain Seward had her seething. She wanted nothing more than to storm into her father's sitting room and give the two of them a piece of her mind.

Only because of her need to discover more of the plot about which she'd already overheard a distressing portion kept her silent and unmoving.

"He may refuse to wed her."

"He won't."

"How can you be so certain?"

"He is English!"

Thérèse blinked. *First, being English is an insult. Now it is a compliment?*

"The English are fools for their honor. He will feel honor-bound to wed her."

Ah! Not a compliment but another insult? René has very odd values, she thought, *if he thinks one should not find honor important! Why did I never see this side of him?*

"You are so certain," mused Jean-Paul. "I wish I were and then perhaps I'd not find the plan distasteful in the extreme."

"You are also a fool. How else do you think to live out your life at the chateau? Is that not what we have worked toward for years now? Will you let a scruple interfere with our goal?"

"Is it merely scruples that make me think it wrong to drug a guest and my own daughter in order to forward our plan?"

Thérèse Marie shivered. *That was it. That was the part I needed to hear. That explained how they thought to get the two of us into bed and compromise us into a farce of a marriage.*

She listened for a bit longer but heard nothing useful, merely René talking on and on, encouraging her father to accept the inevitable, to believe the plan was their only means to their end. Quietly she crept away. She had to think. Actually, she didn't have to think, but merely had to warn Miles of what her relatives planned.

As she once again set off for the chateau, she hoped he'd be easier to find than had been the case the preceding day!

Fourteen

"Not back?" Thérèse sighed. "And you've no word of when he'll appear?" she asked Toby, who, sympathetic, shook his head. "I must speak to him," fretted Thérèse, frowning. "Soon." She looked up and stared at Toby. "Before he receives an invitation to dine with my father and uncle."

Toby's brows rose. "That was why they came yesterday? And sat in the salon for so long?"

"They were here?"

"That they were *here*—" Toby grinned widely. "—explains why Miles is *not*. He suggested I tell them he'd gone into Calais and the next thing I knew, he *had*."

Thérèse smiled at the mild jest but the smile faded and her frown returned. She considered confiding in Captain Seward's first mate and friend, but was surprised to discover she could not bring herself to reveal her father's weakness in going along with René's evil plot. "Toby, I must speak with him before he accepts my father's invitation."

"You can wait here," said Toby.

Thérèse's frown deepened. "I planned to spend the day on the water, but I suppose I need not. On the other hand—" A quick flash of teeth gleamed before her grin disappeared. "—I am no good at all at twiddling my thumbs. What can I do?"

"Perhaps you need practice with the twiddling," said Toby, tongue in cheek.

"Nonsense. Today is Wednesday sooo——" She very obviously searched her memory, then snapped her fingers. "——it is silver-polishing day! I will help."

Toby held the door closed when she would have opened it. "Miles would not be pleased to find you doing such work for him."

"Then what would you suggest? What would be appropriately ladylike so I'll not bring *your* disfavor down upon my poor innocent head?"

Toby suppressed a smile and thought quickly. "Flowers," he said. "It would be a treat to have flowers, properly arranged, and placed where they should go. We've no one who can do flowers."

"And you believe I can? Merely because I am a woman I must know—simply *know*—how to arrange flowers?"

"Do you not?"

"I'm not very good at it."

"But you have done it. You will make a far better job of it than anyone else." Toby ignored the fact that Piggy had a way with flowers when he thought to put the talent to use.

He opened the door for her and led her to the back of the house to the room set aside for such work, although, likely, Thérèse knew the way far better than he himself! She went directly to the shelf near the door, where a flat basket and a pair of heavy scissors awaited her, snapped the scissors once or twice, shrugged, and went into the gardens.

A couple of hours later, she placed the last bouquet in the center of the dining room table and stepped back to look at it. Leaning forward, she gave it a quarter turn and checked again. She nodded, turned, and found herself with her nose very nearly pressed against a waistcoat made up of a gray satin material with a narrow darker gray stripe. The buttons, she noted, were silver. Well-polished silver.

Miles lifted his hands slowly. Slowly he placed them, flat and open, against her upper arms. She didn't move. She didn't even look up. For a long moment they stood like that, neither moving, neither speaking. Then Miles put his fingers under her chin and lifted it. They stared into each other's eyes.

Miles cleared his throat—and then wished he had not. As if it had been an order, Thérèse twitched, backed up a step, and turned away. "I apologize," he said.

"Why?"

"Why?" *Well, why did he feel the need to apologize?* "Because I startled you?"

"Very well."

When she said no more, Miles said, "Toby tells me you need to speak to me."

She turned and her eyes flew to the white missive he held between the fingers of one hand. "Is that from my father?"

"Yes."

"You haven't answered it, have you?"

Was there an urgency there? "The messenger waited. I sent back my acceptance." He eyed her shut eyes, the fact she obviously suffered some sort of distress. "Why, Thérèse? Why should I not have done so? Is it that you do not *wish* my presence in your home?"

Her eyes snapped open and she shook her head. "No, of course it is not that. But they've come up with a plot, a basely underhanded despicable plot!"

"Tell me."

She turned away, and when she spoke again, her voice was tight, slightly whispery from the tension. "They mean to drug the both of us and place us into bed together so that you'll feel honor-bound to wed me. Now that they have lost their opportunity to buy back the estate, it is the only means they can think up whereby they may legitimately return to live in the chateau."

"Thérèse, why has your father not lived here all these years? Why did he live in what he must consider inadequate housing in what is nothing more than a fishing village?"

She stared at him, shocked. Was he going to ignore the fact of René's plot?

"Thérèse?"

She sighed. "To begin with, he was afraid that someone would discover his existence, afraid of losing his own head. Once he was certain that would not happen, then he feared the consortium that owned the estate would turn him out." She shrugged. "My father is unwilling to give up what comfort he has for something that might become worse."

"I suppose that explains why he did not come forward in support of Napoleon, who would have confirmed him in his title as he did many others who willingly supported him."

"My father is not brave, but he could not bring himself to support the Corsican. And," she continued in a thoughtful manner, "if he had thought to do so, I suspect René would have done his best to dissuade him. I had not realized what a rabid Royalist René is until he came, hotfoot, to France when he learned Father failed to buy back the estate."

"Rabid?"

Thérèse repeated some of the things she'd heard René say about their status and rights and place in the world. ". . . so you see, he is not about to go gracefully back into the obscurity of his pleasant little cottage in England. He had believed his exile ended. He cannot accept the loss of the estate."

"Hmm."

"So you will also understand why you must not come to dinner. You *must* not."

Miles, who had had the sudden and unexpected thought that just perhaps he would not mind marriage to the minx, frowned. He eyed Thérèse and stifled a sigh. Perhaps he'd not mind their union, but obviously, she would.

"Thérèse, has it occurred to you that, if they fail to capture me, they might marry you off to just anyone with enough wealth to support them as they wish to be supported? Would you prefer to wed one of the newly wealthy?

For instance, someone who made a fortune producing war matérial for Napoleon?"

Thérèse paled. "I had not thought of that." She straightened, her chin firming. "No, of course I'd not want that, but it would not be the part of friendship to trick *you* into marriage. I'll not do it."

"I would prefer that to what might be the alternative for you," he said quietly.

She smiled and held out her hand, which he quickly grasped. "How like you! You would sacrifice yourself for my sake!" She shook her head. "No, it will not come to that. I will have a say in this and I will refuse to wed some upstart who would buy respectability. They cannot force me."

"They might have forced you to wed me, if we'd not been warned. Why do you think they'll not find a means of forcing you to their will in some other like situation?"

"You needn't be concerned. Now that I am aware of their tricks I can thwart them. What must be decided is what to do about you." She swallowed hard before saying what must be said. "I think you should receive an important message from England, one that forces you to return instantly and you regret it, but you cannot attend the dinner party. How would that do?"

He studied her. "Is it truly what you wish?"

"Hmm."

Rather noncommittal, thought Miles. *What, exactly is in her mind?* Unfortunately, her features were composed and told him nothing. "I wonder if it would not be better to go through with the dinner—but avoid the drug. It can be done, you know."

"If you know what it is in, then, yes, you can avoid it, but how will you know what to avoid?"

"I think we can safely say it will be in the brandy at the end of the meal."

"No, because I am not allowed brandy."

"They will serve you more wine, suggesting a last toast."

She frowned. "You seem so certain. How can you be?"

"Are you not willing to chance it? Thérèse," he added before she could respond, "it would give us time to think what to do."

"And if you are wrong? If they manage to put us to bed together? If they *insist* you wed me? Miles, I don't think I dare chance it."

"Why?" He regretted the harshness in his tone and instantly softened it by taking her hand in both of his.

"You are my friend." Her fingers squeezed his. "I don't wish to lose my friend."

Miles recalled thinking much the same thing. "I too have no wish to lose a friend. The dinner is not until Saturday. We have time in which to think about it."

"And I can continue listening at doors and at windows and see if I can discover exactly how they mean to accomplish their end. If we knew for certain . . . then perhaps we *could* avoid disaster." Her eyes rose to meet his. "This time."

"You dislike the notion."

She shrugged. "I prefer direct to indirect means. I do not like to act the spy. However that may be, in this case, it is necessary."

He eyed her. Then he nodded. It was her decision. He'd no right to try to dissuade her, even knowing she found her role distasteful. "We'll talk again tomorrow. I'll come to the cove, shall I? About noon?"

Saturday evening Thérèse still had no clue as to how the soporific was to be administered and she had not found Miles earlier in the afternoon to suggest, again, that he discover an emergency that forced him to cancel the invitation. She stared at herself in the mirror and grimaced. Compared to the gowns she'd borrowed from Lady Renwick, this one was not only old-fashioned but suited her less well. Then she shrugged. Why, suddenly, it seemed important to look attractive eluded her, when she'd never before concerned herself with such things.

Instead she checked the hall, heard her father and cousin talking behind her father's closed door, and crossed to the window. Hiking up her skirts, she crawled out, down the sloping roof and, with greater care than usual, down the water barrel route to the ground. Then she lifted her skirts and headed for the lane Miles would come down on his way to the village.

"Hello," he said, surprised to see her waiting for him.

"I have discovered nothing new. I am afraid."

"You?" His brows arched and he grinned. "Afraid? Nonsense."

"I am afraid for you." She stared him in the eye. "I don't want anything to happen that will make you unhappy."

Something inside Miles softened. He felt a smile tipping his lips and reached out a hand. Instantly she put hers into it and he gently closed his fingers around hers. "My dear!"

His expression made Thérèse feel shy and she dropped her gaze to where their clasped hands were held between them. "I would have nothing harm you. Ever."

"Nothing will harm me." He squeezed her fingers, drawing her eyes back to his. "If worse comes to worse and we find ourselves tricked into bed and you continue to feel the same about marriage to me, then I'll refuse to wed you and make certain the fact you've been compromised is bruited around the countryside. They will find no one else to wed you!"

She grinned. "A perfect plan," she said—although something inside her seemed to curl up and die. Even compromised, he didn't want to wed her!

And why, she wondered, *did you think he might? You have always known no man would marry such as you. Not willingly!*

"Will you walk on with me? I mean to leave my horse here in this small pasture rather than tie him up before your house all evening."

She nodded, fearing her voice might betray the ache that had settled into her heart. When he'd untacked his gelding and let him loose, he returned and offered his arm. It was only as they approached the front door that Thérèse recalled she'd sneaked out of the house earlier and that there might be questions if she returned by way of the main entrance.

There were. Her cousin reared back when he opened the door for their guest and discovered she was with him. "You . . ."

"Yes, René?" she asked sweetly.

"But . . ." He frowned.

"But?"

His frown became a scowl. "Never mind. Now. I'll speak to you later."

Miles looked from Thérèse to René and back. "He is angry. Why?"

"Because he must have been watching for me to leave my room and he didn't see me do so."

"Is that all? But why would that anger him?"

"He couldn't, you see."

"Couldn't?"

"I went out the back window."

Miles grinned. "Did you now? I wish *I'd* seen you."

"I am glad you did not," she said ruefully, her hand going to her skirts and pressing them down.

René actually gritted his teeth. Then he recalled his plan and shrugged. "She is a hoyden, through and through," he said on a sigh.

"She is a very lovely lady, brave and loyal and *capable de tout,*" said Miles, still smiling at Thérèse.

"Yes, well, I find it distressing that she forgets she is female," said René, a sour note to be heard. "However if *you* do not find it so, then that is all right, is it not?"

"I find her altogether delightful." Miles looked beyond René to the *comte,* who was frowning. "Good evening."

"Daughter, you will cease this banter and introduce us."

Thérèse, reminded that she was hostess for the evening, made the introductions.

Wine was offered—and refused.

It had occurred to Miles that his host and the cousin were more than a trifle jumpy and that they might have decided to do the deed instantly and have an end to it. When Jean-Paul looked glum, he decided he'd been correct and knew he must be on his toes. If he was tricked, then, of course, despite what he had said to Thérèse earlier, he would wed her, but, since she was obviously reluctant to see that happen, it was his responsibility to avoid it.

The meal was long and complex. Miles wondered that a village cook could produce such wonders and almost lost himself in experiencing new sauces and the various meats that went with them. The vegetables were cooked to perfection and the soup and fish could, neither, have been bettered.

"I congratulate you on your cook."

"I will tell Jeanne," said Thérèse. "She will be glad of the praise."

"Fat Jeanne was an apprentice at the chateau before the Terror ruined all," said the *comte*. "She learned well and has only improved over the years."

"She'd make her fortune in London," said Miles. "Although, that she is female would be held against her. It is thought that all great cooks must be male, you see, which is foolish in the extreme. Women are capable of a great deal. It is we men who would prefer they never discover just how much. It will change the world when they are allowed to develop their interests and abilities as men do."

"Nonsense. It will never happen. *Should* never happen, even if what you say could possibly be true," asserted René. "Women are the lesser sex. They are here to serve men."

"How odd," said Miles—and noted René's eyes narrow as he took a serving of the sweet just then offered. "I have always been of the opinion that men and women were to serve each other, each to the best of their particular ability, whatever that might be."

He reached for a pitcher of cream set on the table earlier and in the process caught his plate with his cuff. In the process of lifting the pitcher he also lifted the plate, the thick rum-flavored sauce and the fruit sliding onto the table.

"How awkward of me," said Miles, rising to his feet and daubing at the juices running toward the table's edge. He backed away to allow the maid to clean up the mess. When she had and offered more he shook his head. "I should not have taken the first. I have eaten far too much already. Tell me—" He spoke to the *comte*. "—how is it that you escaped the Terror?"

"My people were loyal. They hid me and lied to the men who came hunting me. Since everyone knew René was in England it was not difficult to convince them that I too had crossed the Channel."

"But you did not. How, Monsieur Laurent," he asked, turning to René, "did you support yourself in England? I have heard many tales of the hardships suffered by those who fled France."

René looked toward the *comte* and swallowed. "Oh, it was never so difficult for me. I did not choose to go to London, you see. It is far cheaper to live in the country."

Thérèse's brows clashed together and she cast a piercing look toward her cousin. "I have never thought to ask how you supported yourself, René. Do explain."

"It is no one's business but mine."

"Is it not? Did you, perhaps, keep records of the sales of lace and embroidery you organized for the estate women?"

René's lips compressed. "If you are asking did I take a commission," he said, his voice harsh, "then of course I did. Even you will admit it is the right of an agent to take a fee."

"How much?" she asked.

"This discussion is not suitable before strangers!"

"Hmm. René, do you know? I am fast concluding that *you* are the stranger, *not* Captain Seward!"

"Come, daughter, do not argue before our guest! I would propose a toast," continued the *comte* and turned to René. "Will you pour us our wine with which to make it?"

René's scowl lightened and he even smiled a tight little smile. "Of course. The special wine." He rose with alacrity and moved to the sideboard.

Thérèse caught Miles's eye and her own held a question. He nodded and she sighed. "Father, I will leave you to your wine. Good night."

As she rose to her feet so did the *comte*. "Not yet, please. As I said, I've a toast. You will wish to drink to the new owner of the estate, will you not?"

"The new owner?" Thérèse caught and held his gaze. "No, Father, I do not believe I do. Nor do *you* wish to do so! I will see you in the morning."

She left the room before he could object. Miles observed a quick glance between the other two men. The *comte's* eyes flicked toward the door his daughter had just passed through and back to René's. Very likely René meant to force the drink down her throat once he had succeeded in felling the guest.

Poor René, thought Miles. *He is destined for failure all around.*

The wine was served, the toast proposed, and when he had distracted his host and host's cousin Miles tipped his glass of the wine down his sleeve. Toby would scold him at the ruin of a good shirt, but that was just too bad.

Some hours later Miles thanked the *comte* for the excellent meal and an evening of good conversation. The last was a lie, since René had insisted on talking of France's past grandeur. By repeatedly bringing that discussion back to Saint Omer, however, he had learned something of the history of the estate, so it was not a total waste of time.

As Miles strolled down the street it occurred to him to wonder why the men had not tried a third time to drug him.

Perhaps they'd not had a large quantity of the drug and it was gone? He hoped so, although they would either acquire more or come up with another plan.

He sighed. It was far too lovely an evening to be thinking of plots and ways of countering them. He walked up the lane to the small pasture—and discovered more than his gelding.

"Thérèse Marie," he said, bowing.

She sighed and hopped off the top rail of the fence to the ground. "I began to worry. You are very late."

"Surely it cannot be more than one."

"Perhaps it is just that I'd no knowledge of what went on and feared that somehow they'd played off their tricks."

"They'd have forced a drug down your throat, I think, if they had managed to trick me, but they didn't try again."

"They didn't?"

"Very likely they'd too little opiate remaining to be sure of me and you too."

She nodded, turned, and leaned on the fence, lifting one booted foot to rest on the bottom rail. For a long moment Miles eyed her and then he joined her. "What are you thinking, friend?"

"That now you *must* go. I cannot guarantee that I'll have warning of their next plan. If you go, then they can do nothing and you will be safe."

"And you? I think you have forgotten my suggestion that they will turn their sights elsewhere if they fail with me. Your René is not about to live the rest of his life in an English village. Success was so close that he will have lost patience."

"He can live here with us and be satisfied with that."

"Do you think he will be satisfied, *mon amie?*"

"It is my problem. Not yours."

"But friends help each other when they've problems. When I was a schoolboy, there were six of us who banded together to aid and abet each other, help each other in any way that was needed. We are still friends, Thérèse."

"Lord Renwick?"

"He is one of the Six, as we called ourselves."

"I was shocked when I discovered he is blind."

"Not shocked by Sahib?"

Thérèse chuckled. "I like Sahib. He's wonderful."

"He thinks you pretty wonderful as well."

"Hmm. That is because I will scratch him as he likes to be scratched. Animals are well pleased by anyone who willingly indulges their whims."

Miles debated telling Thérèse stories of this particular animal's whims, which, mostly, dealt with arranging marriages for the Six! He decided not to.

"How was Lord Renwick blinded?"

"Jason was in India with the army when he went on a hunt for a man-eating tiger. Bahadur, of whom you know, was there as well. Jase and Bahadur shot at almost the exact same moment. Jason's bullet killed the tiger but it had already leapt at him and, while dying, clawed him badly. That would have been bad, but Bahadur's gun exploded, blinding Jason. He can see bright light from one eye and that is all."

"Tell me about your other friends."

Miles did, telling one story after another, most of which made her laugh.

"I envy you, you know," she said.

"Me? But . . ."

"To have so many friends," she interrupted. "I cannot imagine having so many."

"You have Armand and Henri."

She shrugged. "They are loyal to me, but not friends as I mean it. They, by choice, remain apart, you see. Keep to their place. They would never invite me to a meal in their homes, for instance, and would be appalled if I were to invite them to one at our house." She shrugged. "That is not friendship, I think."

"You have been lonely, have you not?" he asked after a moment.

"I did not know it," she said.

Miles noticed the verb form. Perhaps she had not, prior to meeting him, noticed it, but what of now? What of when he left as he would do? Eventually. He hated it that she would be alone again.

"Miles, please, will you not go?"

"No."

"But why?"

"We must solve your problem, *chérie,* before I can go."

"Have I a problem?"

"I cannot leave you alone to thwart their plots. I fear for you."

"I am perfectly capable . . ." She lifted a hand to pull his fingers away from her mouth. "You yourself said so!"

"You are capable of a great deal, but you cannot watch your back at all times."

"You have faced danger again and again! Real danger. Threats to your life."

He nodded. "True, but two points. First, more often than not, Toby was with me. I was not alone. And secondly, if I died, then it was over. If your cousin manages to marry you off to a monster, you will suffer day after day after day for the rest of your life."

She grimaced but was silenced.

"I am glad you see the difference. And that you accept you need someone at your back!"

"I will explain and Armand will watch over me!"

"That loyalty of which you spoke?"

She looked at him.

"Is it entirely to you? Or is it," he asked softly, "also to your father?"

Even in the odd light cast by a half moon, Miles could see her skin lose color.

Fifteen

"My dear!" Miles steadied her. "I did not mean to frighten you," he added softly. He didn't remove his hands from her upper arms even though she'd found her feet.

"How foolish of me," fumed Thérèse, wishing she didn't have this odd tendency toward fainting whenever strong emotion filled her.

"It is entirely possible that Armand will obey the *comte's* orders rather than yours?"

"I suppose it must be or I'd not have reacted in such a stupid fashion." Thérèse no longer felt faint. Embarrassment had replaced that weakness.

"Look at me."

She lifted her head slowly, huffed once—whether irritated with him or herself, Miles could not say—and met his eyes.

"I am here. I will not leave you alone to face this thing."

"You are too good to me!"

"We agreed, did we not, to friendship?" She nodded. "Then you must accept that there are consequences to that decision. One is that I not leave you in danger."

"But how, for the same reason, can *I* allow *you* to remain where *you* are endangered?"

He grinned and his hands tightened around her upper arms. "Thérèse Marie, I mean to help you whether you will or no. Accept it."

Her chin rose. "And I mean to protect *you*."

His gaze wandered over her face, liking more and more the strength he saw, the clean lines of strongly defined features. But the thoughts sliding in and around that liking were ones of which he was ashamed. One did not, he reminded himself, seduce one's friend. He firmly banished the notion.

"I have met your father now on two occasions," he said, once he'd done so. "Will you kindly explain how you grew to be the woman you are when he is the man he is?"

She chuckled softly, but there was a wry note to it. "I suppose because he had little to do with the rearing of me. The old priest took my education in hand once I grew beyond the care of Fat Jeanne—who was not so fat in those days. When I was very little I would sit on a high chair and watch her work and she would tell me tales of my grandfather and grandmother, of the old days and how things were." She frowned, the lines blackened by the shadow cast by the angle of the moonlight. "I wonder why my father did not learn, as I did, of the responsibilities of our position but only of the advantages."

"The only son? The only *child?* He was spoiled, perhaps?"

"I am an only child and I was not spoiled!"

"Very true." Miles's tongue was firmly in his cheek. "I wonder I did not think of that."

She laughed. "You would say I was spoiled in quite another fashion? That I will have my way, no matter what?"

"Yes, perhaps, but your way is a good way, so it is a benefit that you are stubborn, is it not?"

She wished his every compliment did not make her feel like a young girl just opening her eyes to the world. "You are far too kind." She feigned a yawn. "It is late. I am tired." She lifted her arms to his chest, meaning to push him away, but the temptation was too great. She rose on her toes, and placed a quick kiss on his chin. "I'm off to bed now. Tomorrow we will fight about whether you go or stay."

His hands tightened on her arms as he pulled her a fraction nearer—but that clear-eyed questioning look she gave him halted any possibility that he pull her still closer. Denied that he might kiss her as he wanted to do, very gently, he moved her back. Very carefully he opened his hands and, after a hint of a hesitation, dropped them to his sides.

"Yes," he said. "It is late. We will fight it out tomorrow."

"So you understand?" Thérèse asked Armand and Henri.

Armand frowned. "But it would be a good plan for you to wed Captain Seward!"

"Traitor!"

He grinned. "No. Think. You and he like each other a great deal. You have interests that match. You are both strong people and you both have strong morals which drive you and make you do what you do."

Thérèse glowered. She didn't like hearing someone else say things that she herself had already thought. Not when it was impossible that Miles would ever want to wed her. Truly want it.

"But," she argued, "you said it was that we were rash and impulsive and thoughtless that we got ourselves into difficulties!"

"That was when we'd been captured and I was thinking of Seward captured by pirates." He frowned. "But it is true, is it not? You are both of an adventurous nature. You would be good mates."

"We are friends," she said. *"Friends.* Do you understand?"

Armand sighed. "No, but very often I do not understand you. You make of something very simple something that is complicated. In any case, if you will not wed him then you are correct that we must find a way to see that you are not forced into a position where you must. But here he comes. I will take the dory in and fetch him out here."

Thérèse stood at the rail and watched. Her hand tightened

over the varnished wood. His smile. That glorious smile. It rammed a blade straight into her heart and Thérèse finally admitted the thing she'd been pushing from her mind for some time now.

Why, she wondered, *was I so very foolish as to fall in love with my friend? How did it happen? How could I have let it happen?*

"Ahoy!" called Miles, lifting a pair of bottles aloft. He held them in one hand, the necks between his fingers and they clinked softly against each other. "You'll not believe the wine Toby found in the cellars. We'll have it with our lunch, shall we?"

"Did you also bring lunch?" she asked, all innocence.

"Did not you?"

She grinned. "No." She backed up so that the two men could clamber over the side of the *Ange Blanc.*

Henri looked over his shoulder from where he was tying the dory to a cleat. "Do not be concerned, Captain. Armand's grandmother filled us a huge basket. She is very generous with her pick-nicks."

"Ah. Then I will not worry about my stomach." He eyed Thérèse. "Are we going to begin the day with our fighting?"

Armand looked from one to the other. "Fighting?"

"We are arguing about . . ."

Miles interrupted Thérèse. ". . . who is going to save whom from danger. She would send me away so that her cousin and father cannot trap me into wedding her. I fear that if she manages the trick, then she will be trapped into wedding someone, anyone, who has enough money to support the men as they wish to be supported."

Armand's eyes widened. "You did not mention that possibility!" he said, glaring at Thérèse. "But they *would* not . . ."

His voice died away as it occurred to him that perhaps they would. They were, he knew, decidedly old-fashioned, and it was not so very long ago that most weddings were arranged to the advantage of the whole family rather than for the individuals involved.

"Have you concluded they would not?" asked Miles softly when the silence had stretched out long enough.

Armand heaved a huge sigh. "Perhaps they would. *Oui,* it is not impossible that they would."

"So you see why I cannot desert her?"

"I see why you will not desert her."

Miles narrowed his eyes at the slight change in wording. "Friends," he said, "do not desert each other in time of need."

Armand eyed him for a moment and then nodded. *"Ma capitaine,"* he said, turning to Thérèse, "do we take the *Ange* out or do we not?"

"We do," she said.

The men, including Miles, readied the yacht for a day's sailing. Very soon they were beyond the rocks and out on the Channel. The bright sun glistened on the choppy water and a brisk breeze sent them toward England.

When they were well under way Miles took the wheel from Armand and stood there, his hands seemingly reading the tension of the sails and the movement of the keel from the vibrations of the wood beneath his hands.

"Shall we argue now?" he asked politely, not looking at Thérèse.

"It is too beautiful a day for arguments."

"It is too beautiful a day for your cousin and father to spend plotting, but would you deny that is what they do?"

She sighed. "I will not have you forced into something you would regret before the words were said."

"But you think I should allow it to happen to you?"

"It is a dilemma, is it not? Is there not a way we can both be happy, one for the other?"

Miles felt a muscle jump in his jaw. Was there a way? As he'd ridden slowly back to the chateau the preceding evening—the moon having set and the starlight insufficient for rapid travel—it had occurred to him that perhaps friend-ship was not all he wanted of Thérèse.

"You do not answer."

"Would marriage to me be so very bad?" he asked.

"You mean if we fail?"

He hesitated. "Yes, if you were forced to marry me, would you find it so very terrible?"

"I would not like to lose your friendship," she said.

"Perhaps we could manage to maintain our friendship."

She frowned. "Do you think it possible?"

Miles, who had never given marriage and what it entailed two thoughts together, let his mind wander over the marriages enjoyed by his friends. "My friends are all married. They and their wives are very happy together. I do not know if you would call what they have friendship, but they do not fight and they do not seem to tire of each other."

"Perhaps then it is possible? I have had no opportunity to observe friendship within marriage. Come to that, isolated as I've been, I've had little experience of marriages among our sort. Perhaps your friends, the Renwicks, are the only ones I ever knew. Oh, when I would visit René on my trips to England, the neighbor ladies would come to tea but—" Her eyes widened. "—it has just crossed my mind that I was never invited to their homes. Of course, I knew they came to visit René, not me, that I was merely playing propriety and making possible their visits . . ."

"René never took you to London? From something he said, I thought he went up for the Season each year."

"Only for a week or two. And no, he never invited me to join him." She drew in a deep breath and told Miles what René had insisted she should do.

"Give up your sailing? Attend tonnish entertainments? You?"

"You think I would be awkward and impossibly gauche?"

"Don't ruffle your feathers, little chick," he said, reaching out so that the tips of his fingers ruffled the hair escaping from the front of her hat. "It is not that you would embarrass yourself and others, but that you would hate it!"

Thérèse relaxed. "I told him that," she said, nodding. "He said I didn't know. That once I experienced it, I would love it—" Her lips compressed. "—and that I would find myself a husband."

They were silent for a long moment.

"Do you think," she asked, "that, even then, he had in mind that I would wed someone who would support him as he wished to be supported?"

Miles stared in astonishment. "Why would anyone support *him?* Your father, perhaps, but your father's cousin?"

"He would hang on Father's coattails, of course." She lifted her hat and pushed her hair back. "I wonder if Father might not have gone on as he has, neither happy nor unhappy, but—content, perhaps? If René did not push him, I mean."

"René is the villain, then?"

"Did I say that?"

"Since he is your cousin I should not have said it."

"He would have drugged you. And me. Would have tricked us."

"Yes."

"I would have to say that that is fairly villainous." She sighed. "Why must the world be so complicated?"

"That is why I prefer the sea. You have the deck under your feet, the sky over your head, and only the tides and the wind to rule you."

"I am always amazed when you put into words something I have long felt."

He grinned at her, one of his rather wolfish grins. "We do tend to think alike, do we not?"

"Yes. It is why we can be friends, I think?" she said quickly.

Miles, who was beginning to think it a reason they might be much more than friends, had forgotten that Thérèse did not feel the same. He very quickly turned aside from the direction his thoughts were taking him, and nodded agreement. "Yes," he said, unknowingly paraphrasing what Armand had said an hour or two earlier. "Common interests and common values, make for good friends."

They were silent then, enjoying the feel of the deck beneath their feet, the wind—which had risen slightly—in the sails, and the warmth of the sun shining down on them. Perhaps half an hour passed before Armand came to tell them he had laid their meal on the afterdeck and that he would take the helm while they ate.

Thérèse had lain awake long into the night going over every word she and Miles had ever said to each other. It was, as a result, very late when she finally awakened to voices in the hall.

Father and René, she thought as she rolled over to go back to sleep. Almost instantly she rolled back, out of bed, and onto her feet. She padded silently across the room and put her ear to the door.

". . . somewhere on the estate. He's always out and about. It will be easy."

"I'm not easy," said Thérèse's father. "Not in my mind. It is so very underhanded."

"Have you come up with a better plot?"

"I could offer him the child—and tell him the alternative if he does not agree."

Silences followed that and then a sigh. "You are so very naïve, Jean-Paul. So innocent of the ways of tonnish men. He would laugh in your face."

"He might not."

"And if he did not?"

Another sigh. This time Jean-Paul's. *"Then* we try your way?"

"You waste time. We do it my way from the beginning."

Thérèse wished one or the other would say something

to tell her what *that way* might be—other than the obvious, that it was underhanded!

"But who . . . ?"

"Rabaut will find help. He will not fail you."

Again silence stretched. Thérèse was about to give up and go back to bed when her father, rather hesitantly, asked, "Are you certain of that? Rabaut admires Captain Seward. He has not found him—even though an Englishman— someone to be despised."

"I have not heard him say any such thing!"

"He needn't say it in so many words when his other words imply it so clearly."

"Bah. He will do as he is told. He has been your man all your lives."

"We were friends before we grew up, but that was long ago."

"He has seen to it that you live a decent life."

"Yes. Everyone on the estate has been very kind for a great many years. I think it more due to Thérèse Marie, however, than to anything I have done."

"I do not understand you. Why do you and Thérèse have this ridiculous notion you must *do* something? You are the *comte!*"

"And my father before me was a very good *comte*. If he had been like some we knew, do you think our people would have helped me? In any way? Except, perhaps, to help me visit Madame Guillotine as did my parents?"

René was silent again. Then Thérèse heard, "Bah!" and footsteps going off down the hall. She waited. After a moment, her father returned to his room and the door closed. Only then did Thérèse turn, thoughtfully, toward her bed.

She stared at it. Then shook her head. If she had thought earlier to return to sleep, that was no longer a possibility. She was too completely awake, too worried.

"Armand," she said softly. "He will know what to do."

Twenty minutes later she was on her way to the cove

where it was most likely she would find her first mate doing one of the hundred and one things one must constantly keep after to keep a yacht in proper order. She was wrong and sat cross-legged on the pier, wondering where he might be. When Henri appeared, she asked.

"Very early a message came for him from Rabaut. A problem with which they must deal."

Thérèse jumped up. "How could René have gotten to Rabaut so quickly?"

"What has Monsieur Laurent to do with it? It is the old barn on Near Farm about which Rabaut worries."

Thérèse frowned. "What are you talking about?"

"The barn," repeated Henri patiently. "A beam cracked. Last winter in that last bad wind storm. The new owner wants it repaired and who better than Armand to do such carpentry?"

Thérèse relaxed. She shook her head at her single-minded inability to see beyond her own problems. "Yes, of course. I will find him there."

She stopped on her way back to land when Henri asked what he should do in her absence but, orders given, was off before he'd untied the painter on the dory. The old barn was a couple of miles inland but Thérèse no longer felt quite such pressure. It would take organizing to do whatever it was René had in mind. And Armand would discover from Rabaut what was in the wind so that they could counter it.

Armand already knew. Rabaut was still there and fuming after listening, horrified, to René Laurent's orders. René had just left for the village by a route other than that by which Thérèse arrived or she'd have met him.

"I cannot believe the *comte* would do such a thing," Rabaut was saying as Thérèse came up behind him. "And how am *I* to do such a thing? I cannot. It is not right!"

Thérèse caught Armand's eye and put her fingers to her lips. Armand smiled. "How is it wrong if the *comte* orders it?"

"But Captain Seward . . ."

"You like him," said Armand.

Rabaut nodded, unhappy. "I do. He is a good man. I did not believe it possible, English as he is, but he *is* good."

"Yes, I too like him. Did Monsieur Laurent say *why* he was to be hit over the head and brought to the village?"

"He is to wed our Mademoiselle Thérèse. Whether he will or no."

"And if our Mademoiselle will not?"

Thérèse grinned but it was not a happy smile.

"I don't see, from what Monsieur Laurent said, that she will have a choice."

"I wonder . . ."

"But it is a father's right to arrange his daughter's marriage. How can she do other than he decrees?"

Armand chuckled. "You know our Mademoiselle!"

The two men laughed together but sobered almost instantly. Rabaut sighed. "I do not like it."

"Nor," said Thérèse, behind him, "do I."

Rabaut swung around. "You!"

"Yes, 'tis I. Armand, what am I to do?"

"You would ask my advice?" asked Armand. His busy hands lifted, holding the plane he'd been running over the rough-cut timber which would become the new beam.

"Yes. Do not tease me. All I can think of is that Captain Seward must return to England where he will be safe. But he will not go."

"Hmm." Armand stared at his hands before looking up at Rabaut. "When are you to capture the captain?"

"Towards evening. They do not wish to keep him unconscious all day." Rabaut grinned. "I think they fear that otherwise he might manage to escape!"

"Yes, very well . . ." Armand returned to his planing.

"That is all?" asked Thérèse.

"You go to the *Ange Blanc*. You wait there."

"Wait for what?"

"Perhaps if Captain Seward will not go to England, then that is where *you* should go."

Thérèse frowned. "To England. But what will I do? Where will I go?"

"To Tiger's Lair, of course."

Thérèse's eyes widened. *"Mais oui! Très bien,* Armand! I will tell his friend that Captain Seward is in danger and *he* will know what to do!"

"And Lord Renwick's wife will keep you safe."

Thérèse hesitated a moment. "You would suggest," she asked, a frown forming, "that I *stay* there?"

Armand nodded. "Until your cousin gives up his notions and Captain Seward is safe."

"But you would have Rabaut hit him over the head and take him to René! I do not like that."

"No, no," said Armand quickly. "Rabaut and I will talk to Captain Seward. He will think it a fine joke on Monsieur Laurent and will cooperate and pretend he is hit on the head."

Thérèse Marie was less than certain that this would be the way of it, but her absence would put a spoke in René's wheel and that was all that mattered. "I will return home and steal away with what clothing I can manage before I board the *Ange.* How long before you come?"

"We will sail on the evening tide. About seven?" He waited until Thérèse had gone beyond hearing. "And we will have the captain with us!"

Rabaut, who had moved off to give Armand and the *comte's* daughter privacy, returned. "What!" he exclaimed at Armand's suggestion that he go home to his dinner and forget anything had been said about capturing Captain Seward.

"Rabaut, you do not wish to do this thing. So we will do an entirely different thing." His eyes narrowed. "But perhaps it is better you know nothing. I must finish this and then I will take care of the other and you may go home to your supper and have nothing to do with it."

"Then I am not to take the unconscious captain to the village later this evening?"

Armand grinned. "You do that." He winked. "If you can find him."

Sixteen

"You too worry about her?" Miles stared at Armand. The man was up to something, but what?

"Just come talk to her," said Thérèse's first mate.

"On the *Ange*? At this time of night?"

"She must not return to the village," insisted Armand. "She is in danger."

"Danger."

Armand glanced over his shoulder, all around. He lowered his voice. "I think her father's cousin is mad. You do not know . . ."

Miles interrupted. "That he wants me to wed her? Of course I know."

"But his latest plan . . ." Armand shook his head. "Come. Please. Talk to her."

"Is she frightened?" asked Miles, suddenly suspicious.

Armand silently begged his captain for forgiveness. "I did not wish to say that . . ."

"She would not like anyone to suspect she might be frightened. What has her cousin done?"

"It is only what he plans, Captain. He must not be allowed to succeed."

Miles compressed his lips into a hard line. "I will talk to the man."

"No!"

"No?" Miles's eyes narrowed. "Armand, you are hiding something."

Armand sighed. "Is it so much that I ask? That you come to the *Ange* and talk to her?"

Miles felt contrite at Armand's chiding. "No of course it is not. It is just that I am expected at the chateau very soon now."

"I can send Henri with a message," said Armand.

Miles nodded. "Yes, a good notion, that. I'll ride to the cove and send him to the chateau. You can follow as you will."

Armand sighed. "You leave me no choice, monsieur." He pointed toward something behind Miles and Miles turned. Armand dropped the cudgel he'd hidden up his sleeve and swung it. Miles dropped to the ground. "I am very sorry, *Monsieur le Capitaine,* but you are a very stubborn man and I will be late if we do not leave at once."

With a grunt, he heaved Miles onto the back of his gelding and led the horse by quiet ways to the cove. Lifting Miles into the dory was not easy, and also he discovered his prisoner was awakening. With another sigh, he tied Miles's hands and feet before taking up the oars and rowing out to the *Ange Blanc.*

"Armand," cried Thérèse, appalled. "What have you done!"

"Brought Captain Seward to the *Ange Blanc,* of course. Henri, come help."

"You have hurt him!"

Armand opened his eyes wide. "No!" he said. "Surely not."

Miles opened one eye. "If you did not," he said, his tone mild, "then I would not like to see what happens when you do hurt someone."

"Armand . . ."

"No. Haul sail, Henri. Let us get away before Laurent— or the *comte*—comes this way."

As soon as they were well away from shore, Armand untied Miles, who flexed his fists to get the blood back into them. "Did you have to pull them so tight?" he asked.

"I was nervous," explained Armand. He glanced to where Thérèse stood, a glum look on her face. "I knew she'd be mad."

"I see." Miles worked on the ropes on his ankles. "What happens now?"

"Now we go back to your friend's house where you will see that Thérèse Marie is kept safe."

Miles's brows rose. "Hmm."

"What," asked Armand, "did you think I had in mind?"

"That perhaps you were another wishing to see us wed."

"Eh? You'd be willing?"

"Thérèse Marie," said Miles, avoiding a straight answer, "has made it very clear she does not wish to honor me in such a way."

"You have asked her and she turned you down?" asked Armand, his eyes widening. "Blast her for a fool!"

Miles's brows arched. "I respect her wishes, Armand," he said softly. "Do not push her into something she does not want and would regret and, for which eventually, she would see me to blame. That would not make for a good marriage." He watched Armand's scowl deepen. "Promise me you will not mention this to her."

"But . . ."

"Promise me."

"Oh very well, but you are a pair of fools."

Armand stalked away and Miles turned toward where Thérèse watched from the stern of the boat. She beckoned and he moved to join her.

"You cannot be happy about this," she said.

"Perhaps Armand acted in a rough and ready way, but the notion is a good one. Eustacia will be glad of your company and your father and cousin cannot harass you into doing what you do not wish to do."

She bit her lip, staring out over the water. He saw that her hands were clenched tightly around the rail, and he touched one with a gentle finger.

She glanced at him. "Will you stay? I am . . . afraid to

stay alone. What will they think? No baggage worth mentioning. No forewarning. It is all so . . . so . . ."

"It is improper?"

"Yes. Exceedingly. Besides—" Her eyes widened and she turned a shocked expression up to him. "—when I was there before, I was your prisoner and I escaped. How dare you take me back there?" A further thought and her skin went still whiter and she wavered from side to side. "Or is that it? You return me to my prison?"

He slapped her. A very light sharp slap. "Thérèse Marie, make sense! It is you who kidnap me. Not me *you*. This was *not* my idea!" He watched her color return and, when he was certain she'd not faint on him, relaxed.

"I am a fool."

A bark of laughter escaped him when she repeated Armand's words. "Everyone is foolish now and again, Thérèse. You are not alone in that."

"My father will worry."

"So will Toby." A rueful look crossed his face. "I hope that particular fool doesn't go bursting into your father's house demanding my release!"

"Armand was supposed to have sent Henri with a letter but Henri is *here*." She turned and called to her first mate. Armand turned the helm back to Henri and approached a trifle warily. "Did you send the note to Mr. White?"

"Yes. Of course." He glanced over his shoulder. "Ah. You thought that because Henri is here, that I had not. You, *ma capitaine,* will write a letter to your father and it will ask that your clothes be packed up and I will bring them to you."

"I brought a bundle. It will do."

"Eustacia knows a very good seamstress in Lewes. Whatever you need, Thérèse Marie, can be made for you."

"But I must write him," she said, frowning. "I will, I think, merely write that I have gone away and will not return so long as they continue making plots which I dislike or disapprove."

"So how will they know to tell you that it is safe for you to come home?"

"Armand."

"Armand," said Miles slowly and, approaching the man, asked, "Will not the *comte* attempt to make you tell them where she is?"

Armand grinned. "But I will not know, will I?"

"And why will you not know?"

"Because I left her in Calais, of course."

"In Calais? By herself?"

"I have friends in Calais," said Thérèse. "Of a sort. They will think I have gone to them," said Thérèse Marie. "When I am not found there, they can hardly blame Armand. It is a good notion."

"But I too will be gone. How will they explain that?"

"You may send a message to your Toby to go away as well, and take your *Nemesis* away from port where you have it anchored."

"They will think I have kidnapped you."

"Why would you do that when *avoiding* marriage to me has been the problem?"

"But I am not supposed to know that, am I?"

"Perhaps they will think I told you. Perhaps I will say that in my letter, that you do not wish to marry and when I told you of their plots you said you'd leave rather than wed me."

"Hmm." He eyed her, his lids half concealing his thoughts.

"What does that mean?" she asked, suspicious.

"Hmm?"

"That."

"Oh. Nothing," he said. "Nothing at all." He turned the conversation away from personal things and the hours passed quickly.

In fact, the wind was so good and they arrived in excellent time and sailed into the cove south of Lewes, where Miles always cast anchor when visiting the Renwicks. Only his presence aboard kept the villagers from taking Thérèse and her crew captive. Once that was sorted out, Miles arranged for transport for himself and Thérèse, and before they had left the village, Henri and Armand were on their way back to France with letters to deliver.

Toby read his and swore softly. Then he sighed. He went to find Piggy and the two conferred, shook their heads over the idiocy of some people, and wondered, loudly, if they should pound sense into one of them! After that, they got to work, Toby seeing the house was put back under holland covers while Piggy had the kitchen put to rights. Very soon the two of them were off to Calais, where they boarded the *Nemesis* and sailed for England.

In the village things were no calmer than at the chateau. Armand faced René Laurent's tirade with a stoicism that baffled the Laurent cousin. Only when Jean-Paul forced René into a chair and stood before him so that he could look down into his cousin's eyes, did René finally run down and cease his ranting.

"I told you at the very beginning that Thérèse Marie would not take part in your plots."

"Nonsense. She is a woman."

"But an independent woman who knows her own mind."

"That is irrelevant! She is a woman. She will do as she is told!"

"If you can find her."

"You know, surely, the names and location of her friends in Calais!"

"Yes, but we will not find her there. I suspect we will not find Captain Seward at the chateau, either."

"But why?"

"Why? Because neither of them is stupid. Because you have not been particularly careful to keep secret your plans. Because Thérèse Marie has that streak of moralism in her which forced her to inform the captain of the plots she overheard."

"She did *what?*" René rose from his chair, forcing Jean-Paul back a step. "She did *what?*" he repeated even more loudly. "She was so disloyal as to reveal our secrets to a stranger?"

"You are screaming again," said Jean-Paul and sighed.

"And why should I not? How could she?"

"Very easily, I would guess. She does not wish to wed the man, so she would inform him of the plot so that he would go away and make it impossible for us to carry it out. Where is the difficulty in understanding that?" Jean-Paul was becoming more than a trifle riled himself, but irritating *him* was his cousin's behavior and not the fact that the plan had misfired.

"But she is your daughter. She should not betray you!"

"As we should not betray her?"

"*Her?* But—" René looked totally bewildered. "—she is only a woman!"

"She is also my daughter. I was against this plot from the beginning. I am glad she has run away."

René cast Jean-Paul a narrow-eyed look and set himself to convincing his cousin that the very best thing they could do for Thérèse Marie was to marry her off and as quickly as possible before she grew to an age where her idiosyncratic behavior became so ingrained she would become a laughingstock to all who knew her.

Armand, who had listened to the argument with interest, listened to only a little more of René's specious arguments before, thoroughly disgusted, he crept away, unnoticed by either man. He found Fat Jeanne in the kitchen and, after swearing her to secrecy, told her where Thérèse Marie had gone and that she was safe, and then—with one more admonition that René Laurent must not discover her—he went off home.

Armand was, he discovered, exceptionally tired. Skull-duggery was exhausting. He ruefully wished for the old days when all he need worry about was the British coast-guard on the lookout for smugglers. *Far* less of a problem, he decided, than René Laurent's desire to find a secure future and his willingness to use anyone in his path to reach that end.

Seventeen

Eustacia walked beside Thérèse Marie through the Renwick gardens, Sahib following along behind. Behind Sahib a nearly grown cat played, running to catch up whenever Sahib growled softly.

When she heard it again, Thérèse turned and watched the kitten jump at Sahib's waving tail. "He lets David play with his tail!"

"Hm. I wasn't happy when Sahib adopted the creature, but he takes good care of the kitten, teaching it and watching it, and cuddling it. You should see them sleep. It is quite a picture." Eustacia laughed. "Not long ago we couldn't find Sahib anywhere, which worried Jason no end. He cannot help fearing Sahib will revert to the wild you see."

"So where did you find him?" asked Thérèse, noting the smile flickering over Eustacia's lips.

"In the nursery. Sahib lay on his side with our youngest daughter curled up against him and the cat curled up next to her. Sahib watched the two of them with his great eyes blinking lazily and what I swear was a smile on his face!"

"He is a beautiful creature, but I don't know that I'd dare to allow him around my children."

"Nurse is afraid of him. When he strolled into the nursery, she ran out another door and locked it—leaving the children alone with him!"

"Why did she not go get help?"

"That door opens into a large closet. There was nowhere for her to go."

"Were you angry with her?"

"Jason was, but I pointed out that most people fear the tiger and that we are very lucky to have him. No one would dare hurt the children when Sahib is around!"

"I would think Sahib's behavior with the kitten would prove to Lord Renwick that he isn't about to become dangerous."

"Yes. Except Jase is blind and cannot see. If he could *see* Sahib's behavior, then, of course, he would be soothed, but he can only know what I tell him and I cannot seem to convince him Sahib is not about to become a normal sort of tiger."

"Yes, it is a problem is it not? You are a very brave lady to have married a man who is blind, I think."

"Nonsense. I married a wonderful man. That he is blind isn't at all relevant."

"Never?"

Eustacia was silent for a long moment. "Never has he failed me in any way. He even saved my life. And later, my inheritance. He is my husband, my confidant, my very reason for living."

"Your . . . confidant? I am not certain I know this word."

"Confidant. My friend. The person to whom I may say anything and know it will be understood . . . or if not understood, then accepted."

"But he is your husband so . . ."

"Does that mean he cannot also be my friend?" asked Eustacia when Thérèse stopped without finishing her sentence.

"I guess I thought it did," she said, her voice thoughtful. "Miles . . ."

"Is my friend," interrupted Thérèse. "I am thankful for that. He is not the sort of man who wants a wife cluttering up his life, and I do not wish to lose his friendship, so please, never suggest we might wed."

"But you are so well suited to each other."

Thérèse shook her head.

"And you are in love with each other—" Eustacia reached for Thérèse as her eyes rolled up but failed to hold her up and knelt beside her. "—and why should that thought cause you to faint?" she finished, a note of curiosity in her tone.

Sahib nosed Thérèse, looked at Eustacia and back to Thérèse. The kitten crawled up onto the fallen woman's chest and breathed into her face, mewed, and then squeaked when Sahib grasped him gently and lifted him off Thérèse. Sahib nosed the kitten under a nearby rosebush and turned back.

"Thank you, Sahib," said Eustacia a trifle distractedly. She chafed Thérèse's wrist. "Come on, my dear. Do wake up!"

Thérèse groaned. Her eyelids fluttered. "What . . . ?"

"You fainted."

"Again? What was it this time?"

"You make a practice of fainting?"

"Not because I *want* to."

Eustacia chuckled. "No, I don't suppose you do. Can you stand if I help you? Back, Sahib," she added.

Thérèse looked to the side and flinched. She had been this close to Sahib previously, but it had always been at her choice. Unexpectedly finding the tiger's huge head so close to her face was, she decided, a bit shocking.

"I can get up." She did so. "Now," she said, frowning, "what was it that sent me flat? What were we discussing?"

"I don't remember," lied Eustacia, wondering if it had truly been the notion she loved Miles that had sent her into a faint—or perhaps the notion he loved her?

"It must have been something. For some reason I faint when my emotions are running strongly. Usually, however,

I've enough warning that I can find a seat and put my head down."

"All strong emotion?"

Thérèse frowned. "No, I guess not." A quick flashing grin crossed her face. *"Anger* doesn't do it. I can be so angry I splutter and not feel at all like fainting. What other emotions are there?"

"Happiness?"

The frown deepened. "I don't know. I cannot ever recall being ecstatically happy."

"Fear?"

"I don't think so," said Thérèse slowly. "Fear for others, perhaps. When I realized that Armand and Henri might be hanged and it was my fault, then I very nearly fainted."

"Does it happen often?"

"Recently," said Thérèse, the grin once again flickering across her features, "it has happened several times, but recently my life has been chaos which is not usual!" She sobered, remembering that it was once again right royally messed up. "Did Captain Seward explain that I cannot go home immediately?"

"Yes. I should have reassured you immediately that you've a roof here for as long as you need it."

Forever? wondered Thérèse. She didn't voice that thought however, merely thanking her hostess. "Captain Seward said you would understand and be generous in offering hospitality."

"Somehow I don't think that sounds at all like Miles Seward. Did he really say such a thing?"

"Well . . . not in so many words, but it is what I understood him to mean. Was I wrong?"

"No. I merely meant that Miles never speaks in such formal phrases, so I could not believe it was what he'd actually said." Eustacia put her arm through Thérèse's. "I will like having you here. I almost never travel because I do not like to leave Jason and it is difficult for him to go elsewhere, so I am always happy when we have company."

"Perhaps . . . no!"

"No? What do you mean?"

"It crossed my mind that I must find a position somewhere. I just wondered if perhaps . . . but no."

"You wondered if perhaps I needed a hired companion? Now why did I never think of that!" She eyed Thérèse. "You would find it burdensome to merely be our guest?"

"Yes. I could not bear knowing I was a charity case."

"Even if I reminded you from time to time that you are my friend?"

"Are you?" asked Thérèse, startled.

"Oh, I think so. At least, I *hope* so."

"I have had so few friends," said Thérèse a trifle shyly, "that I am not certain I know how to be someone's friend."

"Oh, I think you do." Eustacia chuckled. "It is merely that you need practice, perhaps. We will discuss the hired companion thing again if we must, but I hope you will merely be friend and companion."

Sahib pushed past them and loped down to where a gate had been set into a hedge. Up and over and gone. The kitten mewed, and suddenly Sahib had his feet on the gate and looked back at them. He roared softly and the kitten bounded toward the gate as well . . . but could go no farther.

Lord Renwick and Captain Seward appeared behind Sahib and Miles peered around the big cat. "Ah! We have found them, Jase. They have been strolling in the enclosed rose garden. Get down, Sahib, and I will open the gate."

"Does that animal understand when people talk to him?" asked Thérèse, her eyes widening. Sahib had, obediently and instantly, removed his paws from the gate and backed away.

"We think he must understand most everything said to him. It is the only way to explain some things that have happened," said Eustacia. "Were you looking for us?" she asked the men.

"We were. We have decided it is a fine day for a picknick and have ordered one made us for us. The old barouche will be at the front of the house in half an hour."

"We go to the river?"

"I thought you might enjoy it?"

"You know I will."

Thérèse watched the two. Their words were common everyday words, but the intimacy of tone, the love revealed with every inflection, set her heart beating harder and an odd emotion rose up within her.

Envy, she thought. *I am envious of their closeness!*

She glanced at Miles and found him looking at her. She cocked her head slightly, wishing she could read the expression in his eyes. His face revealed nothing, but those eyes burned into her and said. . . .

Said what? "What is it?" she asked.

He blinked. "I . . . don't know." Miles could not bring himself to admit the odd feelings filling him. Admitting to himself that he was jealous of the bond between his friend and his wife and that he had felt a sudden deep desire to experience that same sort of thing was in and of itself more than he could bear. That he wanted that bond with Thérèse—well, he didn't dare put that thought into words.

Friendship, he reminded himself. *She wants your friendship.*

Miles, always diffident when it came to believing that anyone could wish to know him, to become close to him, was exceedingly grateful that she offered so much.

Prince Ravi stalked upriver from where everyone tumbled from the barouche. He had, once again, been put off when he wished to discuss the notion of Miles taking him and his entourage home. He couldn't be aware of just how tempting Miles found the project, how much he wished to run away from the emotions plaguing him, away from Thérèse. . . .

But he couldn't. He stared at her back. She stood within

the gazebo Jason's grandfather had had built near the river, her hands on the rail and her feet slightly spread. A tender smile tipped his lips.

She would, he thought, *stand just so at the rail of the* Ange Blanc. *Or the* Nemesis. . . .

He quickly banished that last traitorous thought. He even banished the question that followed, that of *why* it occurred to him to think of her on the *Nemesis*. Still, he could enjoy the warmth filling him, the satisfaction that watching her gave him. That hurt no one. Except perhaps, himself.

Thérèse turned, leaned back against the rail, and met his eyes. She smiled a quick warm smile when a blush rushed up into his ears. "Miles?"

He strolled toward her. "I was just thinking you'd stand just so at the rail of your yacht."

It was her turn to feel heat in her neck and cheeks. "René would say it was unladylike to stand that way."

"René has exceedingly conventional ideas about women."

"What do you mean?"

"I mean he thinks of them as all one sort of person. Or perhaps two? Those one might marry and . . ."

"The others?" she suggested when he realized that what he was about to say would not do.

"Yes. Two sorts. I, on the other hand, have observed women and long ago concluded that, just as there are many sorts of men, there are also many sorts of women. Each is an individual. One cannot say you are unlike a lady merely because of the way you stand. A lady is a lady because of what is inside, what she believes, how she behaves toward others—and believe me, Thérèse Marie, you are a lady to your very core!"

The blush, which had faded, rose again to plague her but she smiled. "Thank you. That is the first compliment I have ever received that I value."

"The first—" His brows snapped together. "—that you value? But how can that be?"

She screwed up her mouth into a *moue* and relaxed it. "Men tend to be very commonplace when giving compliments. They say the same thing to every woman. So I know, when one tells me how lovely I look or how beautiful my eyes, that he says merely what he would say to any woman."

"But your eyes are beautiful. And you have a wonderful face. Why do you think they lie?"

She frowned. "Nonsense. I have a mirror, Miles Seward, and I know I am nothing special!"

"Perhaps it is that when you look in the mirror it presents you with only the very sober face one dons when looking in a mirror. It never sees you when your eyes sparkle or when your expression says so much more than your words or . . ."

She held up a hand stopping him. "Nonsense, I say! You embarrass me. Please stop throwing the hammer . . . have I that right?"

He laughed. "It is an English cant expression that says one is giving false coin, yes."

"False coin? Counterfeit?"

"Counterfeit compliments. But you are wrong if you believe that is what I do, Thérèse. I like your face. It is a good, strong, honest face that will wear well as you age, unlike far too many tonnish maidens with rosy cheeks and innocent sweetness. *Treacle* sweet with a touch of *sulfur* when you dig down inside them!"

"A good tonic, you would say?"

"No! Merely the bitter coated with the sweet!"

Thérèse chuckled. "Yes. I see that same thing in village maidens who are desperate to wed. They seem so very innocent and yet I know they are not. And I know they would say the things they do to very nearly any man. Merely to flatter one into asking for her hand." Thérèse grimaced. "I have always thought young men must be particularly stupid to be bemused by it."

Again Miles laughed. "But, my dear, you don't think they are *thinking*, do you?"

"Miles Seward! You watch your tongue," said Eustacia from behind him. "That is outside of enough, saying such a thing to a young lady!"

"But this isn't just a young lady, Eustacia," he said, holding Thérèse's gaze with his own. "This is my friend."

"I do not wish for him to watch his words, considering whether what he says is suitable," said Thérèse. "I like it that he feels free to say what he pleases to me and that he allows me an equal freedom to say what I wish and that I will know he does not look down on me if it is something not exactly suitable for a woman's tongue."

Eustacia laughed. "You two. When will you realize you are a pair?"

Both Thérèse and Miles felt the heat of embarrassment and both, instantly, looked away from the other, flicked a glance back, found the other had as well, and again looked away.

Miles cleared his throat. "I believe I will go . . . see if the prince has caught a fish!" His long ground-eating strides soon had him beyond hearing.

"You must not say such things," said Thérèse softly to Eustacia, whose mouth was compressed into an angry line. "He does not wish to wed. He must not be pushed to do something he does not wish. To shackle that free soul? It would kill him."

"You are wrong, Thérèse. It is that he cannot believe there is a woman alive who would have him without wishing to change him out of recognition. You fear any man you wed would attempt to turn you into that sweet innocent you and Miles were discussing so freely so you too fear to wed. But don't you see? You and Miles like each other just the way you are!"

"We are *friends*."

"But," said Eustacia softly, "you have thought, occasionally, that you would like to be much much more, have you not?"

"I will do nothing to harm our friendship!"

"Ah! By not admitting it, you have admitted you have wished for more. And Miles, I believe, has wished for more as well. But both of you are so lacking in self-confidence when it comes to relationships that you both fear upsetting the applecart by changing what you have!"

Thérèse swallowed hard. "Perhaps what you say is true, but it is irrelevant, is it not? We like what we have and what we have is friendship. I will rock no carts of apples!"

"And neither will he." Eustacia sighed. "I wonder if Sahib thought Jase and I so silly when we each felt we were unmarriageable."

"You! But you are perfect! I can see where Lord Renwick, blind as he is, might feel a trifle reluctant to burden a woman with that, but why ever did *you* feel inadequate?"

Eustacia's fingers rose to cover the birthmark marring one jaw. "This. I had been told since I was very young that no man could tolerate looking at such a blemish, that I would never find a husband, and that I must resign myself to spinsterhood. So I did." She smiled. "But then a really nasty man began courting me and I could not bear him, and I was very lucky to be taken into this house by Jason's aunt who found he liked my voice. Jason is sensitive to voices, you see. And he needed a secretary who could help him with his writing." She actually grinned widely. "And then we fell in love!"

"And lived happily ever after."

"Well, no. Not right away. There was that idiotic feeling of inadequacy. Both of us suffered from it."

"So how did you get beyond it?"

"I doubt very much that we'd ever have got beyond it if Sahib hadn't put a paw into the situation." She giggled, thinking of the night Jason had suffered from a nightmare and Sahib brought her to him and then, literally, pushed her into Jason's bed. "His paw is impossible to resist, you see, when he puts it into a situation!"

"No, I don't see, except that you believe Sahib played a role in your wedding Lord Renwick."

"He has played a part in getting each of the Six happily married and—" Eustacia cast Thérèse and impish look. "—I suspect he will find a way to convince you and Miles that you must wed. I have seen him eyeing the two of you when you have been occupied with each other."

Thérèse felt a *frisson* rush up her back. Contradictory feelings filled her and she turned, once again gripping the railing and staring out over the water.

"Ah," said Eustacia, an apology in her tone. "I have said too much. I do not mean to upset you, so I'll say only one thing more. Sahib is never wrong. He *knows*."

Before Thérèse could respond, Eustacia walked off to where her husband stood talking to the elderly Indian who had been introduced as Bahadur, one of Prince Ravi's entourage. Thérèse saw her clasp Lord Renwick's arm and lean her head into his shoulder. Only for an instant, however, and then she straightened and joined the conversation.

Farther up the river Miles turned away from watching the two women and lifted the landing net, waiting silently while Prince Ravi worked a large fish into shore.

What, he wondered, as he waited, *did Eustacia say to Thérèse to upset her so?*

He found out a few hours later when Eustacia cornered him and, her hand firmly around his wrist, walked him into the conservatory. She turned to face him. "Why do you not marry her?"

Miles's defenses immediately stood to attention. "When what we have is perfect, why change it?"

"But Sahib is convinced it could be far *more* perfect."

Miles felt his ears heat. "Nonsense. If this is what you said to Thérèse Marie when we were by the river, then it is no wonder she was so irritable."

"When was she irritable?"

His lips smiled but his eyes did not. "You have not noticed? Ever since you had that little talk with her it has been obvious. I should not have left the two of you alone."

"If she is irritable, then it is because you are blind."

Miles felt those prickles one feels when one's skin turns a pasty white. "And in what way am I blind?"

She eyed him. "You are angry. Is it because you are afraid?"

"Yes."

Eustacia's mouth dropped open. She closed it, and laughed a soft wry chuckle. "Well. I guess that admission ends *this* discussion. I see you haven't the—" she paused, wondering if she had the nerve to use the word, decided she did, and nodded once, firmly "—the *guts* to reach for happiness beyond anything you have dreamed exists!"

Eustacia turned on her heel and left Miles standing there staring at a bloom. He lifted one finger and gently caressed the petal of a large golden pink flower to which he could not put a name. But the petal reminded him of Thérèse's golden cheek when it was infused with blood, which, whenever she suffered from embarrassment, made him want to touch her. Just as he did the petal.

He couldn't caress her, but the petal was there and no one would know the feelings boiling inside him. The desires. The dreams . . .

Eighteen

The next afternoon Thérèse walked in the garden with the tall young man dressed in the bright silks and satins he loved. "That is a particularly fine coat," she said.

He touched the sleeve. "Yes. I liked the material the instant I saw it. I knew I had to have a coat made from it. After today I will not wear it until I dress to greet my father."

"It is for ceremonial occasions when you go home, is it?"

"Yes."

Thérèse watched him mouth the phrase "ceremonial occasion" as if committing it to memory. She had already learned that Prince Ravi loved words but this was the first occasion she felt she had added to his vocabulary. "Will you be glad to leave England or will you miss it?"

Prince Ravi frowned. He put his hands behind his back and paced several steps deep in thought. "Will I miss England," he repeated softly. He turned his head to glance at her. "I had not thought of it, but do you know? I fear I may. Or more exactly, I will miss people I have come to know well."

"You may write them letters and they will respond. You need not lose touch entirely."

"Yes. I will do that." But the frown did not fade. "Why is it that life will not arrange itself just as one wishes it arranged?"

"How would you arrange it, Prince?"

"When I go home, which I must do, then I would take all my friends with me. They would live with me, advise me, and continue to help me understand this very difficult world."

"I believe your tutor is to go with you, is he not?"

"Yes. He and his wife." Ravi scowled. "If ever she *is* his wife!"

"What do you mean?"

"They knew long ago that they would wed. But they do not wed. And I wish to go. I would already be well on my way—" Again he glanced down at her. "—if it were not for *you.*"

"How is it my fault that you have not gone?"

"Captain Seward is to take me in his *Nemesis*. He will not sail until he is certain you are safe."

Thérèse felt her heart slam into her throat. "Surely . . ."

"Surely?" he asked when she did not continue. He saw that she wavered on her feet and he reached for her arm, helping her to a bench in a nearby gazebo. "Are you all right? Should I find Lady Renwick?"

"I am fine," she said after a moment. "Surely it is not because of me that Captain Seward remains in England?"

"But it is. He discussed it with Lord Renwick only last evening as we played billiards—" He broke off, snapping his fingers. "—which reminds me. I have not ordered a billiards table shipped to my home. I must not forget to do that. If I do it soon, then perhaps it will have arrived before I do and I need not forego my games!"

Thérèse wished to think about Miles, about this new information, the notion that he remained in England for her sake. "You better go see to that now, while you are thinking of it. I will remain here," she added as she saw he expected to escort her back into the house. "It is lovely out and the weather will not remain so beautiful for much longer."

Ravi bowed and hurried off but Thérèse had little time for thinking. Miles peered in and, when she did not look up from studying her feet, cleared his throat. That caught her attention. "Captain!"

"Miles. You call me Miles."

"Hmm." She eyed him. "The prince tells me you stay in England only because you are worried about me. Why? Lady Renwick has said I may stay here for as long as is necessary. Forever if need be."

"I do not trust your cousin. From all you've said, I believe your father would not harm you. Not intentionally, anyway. But René Laurent is another kettle of fish entirely."

"Another . . . !" Thérèse sputtered into laughter.

"It is not funny, Thérèse Marie!"

"Oh, but it is. I can see, in my mind, this very odd picture of Fat Jeanne's soup kettle, whole fish bobbing around in it and there is René, just another fish! Can you not see it?"

Miles's mouth spread into a quick grin, his teeth flashing white against his tanned skin. "Oh yes. Perhaps I will draw it for you. A cartoon."

"Yes. With his mouth open, like a fish gaping!"

Miles chuckled but soon sobered. "Yes, but however much you make me laugh, *chérie,* it is still true that he is a danger to you. If he did not lead your father about by the nose, then I would not be so concerned, but he can and does and it is not good."

Thérèse, who had hoped to divert him, sobered. She nodded. "Yes." She sighed. "I never knew him. I didn't understand."

"What do you mean?"

"All those years when I went back and forth across the Channel. All that lace and embroidery he sold for us. I have seen similar things in your Lewes shops and the price is far higher than what he claimed to have received for the work. Did he, all those years, lie to me? Or is it that a shopkeeper sells it for so much more than he buys it?"

"What funds had he to live on here in England all those years?"

"I do not know, do I?"

"Don't be sad, Thérèse. It is not your fault if he used your work to support himself."

"But he cheated those who *did* the work. It is not fair. It is wrong."

"You assume that is what he did."

"Yes."

He waited, expecting more. "Just a simple yes? Why?"

"Because one of the first things he did when he returned to France was to demand to see the women who did the work. There were complaints afterwards that he said they must double their output, but if they did that, then who would work in the gardens and care for the animals and the cooking and cleaning and everything else that must be done? The two women who came to me were unhappy. They did not see how they could disobey René's orders, but they saw no way of doing what he asked and all else as well."

"What did you do?"

"I talked to my father who instantly saw the problem and *he* talked to the women. I wonder what he will do when René discovers his original orders were countered, and that Father asked only that the women do what they could to increase their output."

"René is a greedy man."

"Then why did he not wed an heiress and be done with it?"

"He participates in the Season?"

"A few short weeks each year."

"Perhaps he tried, but there are many French gallants living in London. He would be one destitute Frenchman among many, without so much as a title to make him palatable to a wealthy father."

"He once said he still loved my mother. I think he lied."

"Very likely." When she didn't respond he asked, "Does it make you so very unhappy?"

"At one time I thought of him as the man my father should have been. How could I have misjudged the two of them so badly?"

"Your father's nature made it easy, did it not?"

She sighed again. "We have gone far from the discussion I meant to have with you. You should begin planning for your journey east with the prince and his people. The lad needs to go and it is the time of year for beginning such a journey, is it not?"

"The weather along the south of Africa will get better as it worsens here in England, yes. But we've time yet."

"Time to see me safe."

"Yes."

"Perhaps one of your friends would know of someone who would hire me as a companion."

"You would die of boredom."

"Dying of boredom is better than dying each time a husband I cannot love demands his rights of me."

A muscle jumped in Miles's jaw. "I will marry you myself before I allow that to happen to you!"

"But you do not wish to wed."

"And you, *chérie?* Would you find it distasteful to be wed to me?"

"You are a wonderful man, Miles Seward. How could I possibly find it distasteful?"

"Then we should wed."

"No."

"Why not?" he asked, surprised anger in his tone.

"Because," she said patiently, "we are agreed that we will do nothing that will interfere with our friendship, are we not?"

Miles was silent. Then he sighed and nodded. He had had to work himself up to making that proposal, knew he'd done it badly, and knew he reaped the reward for his cowardliness.

How, he wondered, *do I convince her we would not lose from our marriage, but would gain from it? How? And when,* his thoughts continued, *did I begin to believe they would improve? Or is it merely that I wish to have her in*

*my arms, and with me always, and I would hoodwink myself
into believing?*

"What is it?" she asked.

"Hmm? Oh, I was just feeling the fool for panicking
that way. We will come about without such drastic measures
as weddings we do not wish."

Thérèse turned away, swallowing hard. *Did I really think
he would try to convince me?*

The two remained silent for a long time. Then, coming
toward them, they saw Lord Renwick and Sahib. Miles rose
to his feet. "Shall we go meet them?" he asked, needing
activity to counteract the unwanted thoughts and emotions
rampaging through his very soul.

Sahib looked from one to the other as they approached.

"If he were human," said Miles softly, "I would swear
that was a sigh."

"But why would he sigh even if he were human?"

"I fear he's taken the notion into his head we are a pair,
Thérèse, and very likely Sahib thinks us very slow at rec-
ognizing it. But he is wrong, is he not?"

Something of a hesitation in Miles's questioning tone
caused Thérèse to cast him a quick look, but they had
reached Lord Renwick by then and Miles was already asked
why his lordship was doing his best to suppress chuckles.

"Have you room aboard the *Nemesis* for a billiards table,
Miles?"

"A . . ." Miles's eyes widened and a shout of laughter
burst from him. "Perhaps we should set it up on the fore-
deck. Can you not see us playing in a high sea?"

The thought of balls rolling up and down the table all
by themselves had all three laughing. When they sobered
to the point they could talk, Miles said, "Of course we can
take the lad's table. I will send Toby in the *Nemesis* up to
London and have it packed into the hold in such a way we
need not worry about balancing the weight around it. Has
the prince made the order yet?"

"No. I told him I would discuss it with you and I have.

You may do the honors with Prince Ravi. Now that is settled, just when do you think you can sail East?"

When Miles hesitated, Thérèse spoke, forcing herself to say the words. "He can leave as soon as the *Nemesis* is ready. I would say not more than a couple of weeks. Three at the most."

"You assume there are no repairs," said Miles, his voice a trifle harsh, "that the keel needs no scraping, that the hundred and one things have been ordered that we may need on such a journey?"

"I know very well the *Nemesis* needs no repairs, doubt it needs the bottom scraped, and suspect you've everything you need stored in a warehouse somewhere, long ago ordered to meet such a need. Two weeks at the outside."

"You know him very well, do you not?" asked a bemused Lord Renwick.

"How could I not? Is he not like me? I would never allow repairs to remain undone. A ship becomes sluggish, hard to maneuver, and loses speed when the keel needs scraping, so I know Miles Seward would see that done as often as necessary, and since he is the sort who is impatient to begin a venture once it crosses his mind, then he has prepared for any such eventuality long ago! What is so difficult about that?"

"She has you there, Jase," said Miles, smiling a fond, very nearly besotted smile.

"No. She has *you* there."

They all laughed, but Miles and Thérèse eyed each other in a speculative fashion that was not lost on Sahib. The big cat growled softly and the kitten crawled down off his perch on Sahib's back. The two felines touched noses.

Just as the trio of humans set off toward the house, the small cat ran between Thérèse's feet in such a way she was tripped . . . and was, of course, caught by Miles, who reacted instantly. The feel of her in his arms was very nearly more than he could bear.

She is my friend, he reminded himself. *She is not some-one I may seduce into my bed!*

"What has happened?" asked Lord Renwick, a questing, questioning expression appearing on his countenance.

Miles, brought to attention by the question, set Thérèse onto her feet, but he could not tear his gaze from hers. "Happened? That blasted kitten tripped Mademoiselle and I caught her. No damage done."

Except, thought Thérèse, *to my heart.*

Much later that evening, Thérèse paced her room, wondering why she'd been such a fool as to fall deeply in love with Miles Seward, of all people. Why with a man who would never marry, who was married to adventure and travel and would never wish to give that up for a wife and family. She sighed.

"It isn't fair," she muttered. "Not when I too crave adventure and travel!"

That thought teased her mind for some time. In the middle of the night she awoke and discovered she'd been dreaming about it. And when she woke in the morning she realized that somehow a decision had been made.

She *would* travel. She *would* have adventure. And, one way or another, she'd do it at Miles Seward's side even if she weren't his wife!

Prince Ravi sat near where Lord Renwick and Miles discussed Miles's new French estate. "I'll need a manager there, as I have in Portugal, but finding anyone like that retired officer, someone who loves Portugal and the Portuguese, but someone I can trust to see to my interests . . . well, it isn't easy, finding someone like that, is it?"

"You could ask Ian. He'll know."

Miles chuckled. "How does Ian always know someone who will fill the need whenever any of us have a problem like this one?"

"He likes people. He gets to know them. Everyone from

the boot boy to Lord Clarence! And he remembers. Write him, Miles."

"He'll need to work with my French agent. Rabaut knows the estate and the people. If it weren't for Mademoiselle Thérèse Marie's cousin, I would trust *him* to see to things, but René Laurent is not to be trusted." Miles sighed. "I wish I could see my way clear to helping that gentleman on his way to the far south."

"The far south?"

"The very far south. Botany Bay comes to mind!"

Renwick chuckled. "Yes, I see, but that is an English prison colony. I doubt the French government would approve of a French citizen finding his way there. Shall I write Ian for you? I've a letter to him begun and we can add that bit to it if you'd like."

"Very well."

"Another reason to put off leaving for India," said Prince Ravi, his tone a trifle sour. He brightened. "One problem *has* been settled. My tutor and I go to London in only a few days now for his wedding. He and his wife will also shop before the ceremony for their stay with me in India."

"Miles, will the *Nemesis* carry as many people as we mean to send with you?"

"Not with as much comfort as you and I would like, but Prince Ravi's men are used to crowded conditions and mine will double up."

"Will there not be personality clashes with so many in such small space?"

Miles's mouth firmed into a stern harsh line. "Aboard ship, I am king. My law rules. Our route lies close to land nearly the whole of the way and I can set ashore anyone who becomes a troublemaker." The stern look faded and he chuckled. "It is also true that we may go ashore at most anytime, having a break from each other."

"It isn't dangerous?"

Miles shrugged although he knew his friend could not

see him. "Along some stretches of coast, yes. One must take care, of course."

"Will we never leave?" asked Prince Ravi.

"If I could only be certain Mademoiselle would not be in danger . . ."

It was the prince's turn to shrug. "Take her with us."

Miles stilled, his face losing all expression. Then he shook himself. "No. Impossible."

"She would be chaperoned by the new Mrs. McMurrey," said Jason softly. "There could be no objection."

Miles swallowed down the sudden joy roused by the notion. He shook his head. "There would be talk."

Jason chuckled. "From all I've been told about your Mademoiselle Thérèse, there will always be talk. She is not one to fit the mold any more than you are, Miles."

Miles frowned. "I would be the cause of the talk, however. Eccentricity is one thing. Scandal is quite different."

"Miles," said Jason, his hand dropping to Sahib's head, "why will you not consider wedding her?"

"We are friends. I would not lose that."

"But why should you? The best sort of marriage *includes* friendship. There should be more, of course, but friendship is as important, and perhaps more lasting."

"You would say there is friendship between you and Eustacia? Nonsense. You love one another!"

"Two kinds of love, Miles," Jason scolded gently. "Or perhaps three. The love between a man and woman's bodies. The warm love of spouse for spouse. And the comfortable love between friends. Did you think one could only have the one or another?"

"It isn't love," said Miles dryly, "what I have had with the bodies of certain women."

"No of course not. But what one has in bed with a loved companion is something quite different."

Miles was silent. The he sighed. "She is not interested in marriage. I find it hard to admit, Jase, but I asked and was turned down."

Sahib lifted his head, his brow ridged in frown lines that Jason rubbed gently. Sahib turned his great head to look up at Lord Renwick, then turned back to stare at Miles.

"What is it, Sahib?" asked Lord Renwick.

Sahib rose to his feet, carefully balancing the cat sleeping on his back, and paced closer to Miles. Again he stared.

"He is looking at me as if he would read my soul," said Miles, whimsically. Inside he wasn't feeling whimsical. In fact, he felt as if what he'd just said was true.

Suddenly Sahib opened his mouth and roared. The cat woke with a start, jumped from the tiger's back, and hid behind Lord Renwick's chair. Sahib roared again.

"Nonsense," said Miles, his gaze held by the tiger's hot look.

"What is it?" asked Lord Renwick. "What is nonsense?"

Confusion filled Miles. "I . . . I don't know." He drew in a deep breath. "Yes I do. There for a moment it was as if I understood Sahib."

"What did you understand?"

"I . . . don't know."

Sahib sighed, turned around, and returned to Lord Renwick's side. He settled in his usual place and, after a long moment, the cat reappeared and curled up between the tiger's paws.

"*I* know," said Prince Ravi. "Sahib told you to wed the woman. He knows it is the right thing to do."

"Sahib is a tiger, Prince," said Miles, "and I will not have my life organized by a tiger!"

"A magical tiger," said Prince Ravi firmly. "Are you not, Sahib?"

Sahib roared softly, caught the kitten between his paws when the young cat would have scrambled away, and very gently put it back down. He purred a tiger's chuffing purr. The kitten batted at Sahib's muzzle, then turned in a circle, and settled back down.

"You see?" said Prince Ravi as if it were settled. He rose to his feet and stalked to the door, where he turned and pointed at Miles. "Marry her," he ordered, "and let us be gone!"

The door closed behind the young man with a decided snap.

"He has made up his mind to go and cannot bear the wait," said Lord Renwick. "I thought I had trained him to patience."

"Only when it is not something he wants!" said Miles, glad to discuss anything but Thérèse Marie. And then he rose to his feet as the door opened to admit Ian McMurrey, elder brother to Prince Ravi's tutor. "Ian!"

"We were," said Renwick, also rising, "discussing you only a few minutes earlier. Now I need not finish my letter to you and you and Miles can discuss his problem face-to-face. Is Serena with you?"

"And the children. We will stay until my brother goes to London and then we will accompany him and be there for his wedding." Ian sobered. "Miles, I came down to Tiger's Lair because there is a Frenchman in London looking for you. He's also looking for a young Frenchwoman he says you abducted. Someone knew we were friends and sent him to me."

"And what did you tell him?"

"That you would abduct anyone was nonsense, and from what I had heard of the young lady, it was far more likely she abducted you."

Miles crowed with laughter. "But you are correct! She did!"

"Not exactly," said Thérèse Marie, entering with the other women in time to hear the exchange. "My first mate abducted him and it was done before I knew what he planned. Perhaps he abducted the both of us, now I think of it. Neither of us was safe from my cousin's machinations. Is my father also in London?"

"That would be the Comte de Saint Omer?"

"Hmm."

"Yes. I did not meet him, but I heard he was in London."

Miles turned from where he greeted Lady Serena, Ian's wife. "They are both in London?" His eyes narrowed. "I wonder . . ."

"Wonder what?" asked Thérèse, going to him and laying a hand on his arm.

"Ian, you were not followed were you?"

"No. It occurred to me Monsieur Laurent might think I would lead him to you, so I made certain I did not."

"I wish you were going to Scotland rather than back to London."

"Why?"

"I would send Mademoiselle Thérèse Marie with you."

"We could, I suppose, send her to my father."

Miles blinked. "Your father! That old curmudgeon? I'd not wish that fate on my worst enemy!"

Ian laughed. "You did not know him before my mother died. He is like that again. Tony's wife returned him to us when you all came up for that first christening. He'd begun changing before you left, but we feared it would not last. It has though."

Ian smiled over his friend's head to where his wife stood. It was a special smile, one of love, understanding, and contentment, and one Miles discovered he envied with all his heart.

"In that case," he began . . .

"Stop!"

He turned a surprised look on Thérèse.

"Tiens! Am I a package to be shipped here and shipped there!"

Miles started to laugh but changed it to a cough when Thérèse glared at him. "You are a very nice package, *chérie,* but no, not one to be shipped here and then there. Would you not, for me, go to Scotland, where I believe you would be safe?"

He caught and held her gaze. She bit her lip. He tipped his head.

"Please," he said.

"I . . . will think about it."

Thérèse Marie turned and almost ran from the room. *He wants to be rid of me,* she thought and managed to contain the tears until she reached her room.

Miles looked from one to another of his friends. "What was that about?" he asked. His male friends looked as confused as he felt, but both Eustacia and Serena looked disapproving and were shaking their heads. "What did I do?"

"Why," asked Serena of Eustacia, "are men such fools?"

"When you understand it, explain it to me," responded Eustacia tartly. "Will you see to Thérèse or shall I?"

"You go to Thérèse, who knows you best, and I will take Miles by the ear and lecture him on the sensibilities of young women."

Miles, looking from one to the other, backed off. "Now wait a minute!"

"No," said Lady Serena, moving toward him just as quickly as he backed away. She shook her finger. "You, Miles Seward, will come with me. Now." And as she had threatened, she took him by the ear and pulled him toward the door.

"Save me," called Miles to his friends, half laughing and half serious.

Ian's rumbling laugh followed him through the door. Renwick's chuckles made a counterpoint sound and, suddenly, covering both, Sahib roared.

"Oh, oh," said Miles. He removed Serena's fingers from his ear and, quickly, before Sahib could follow, he shut the door. He turned to the servant posted in the hall.

The footman, trying very hard to retain the sober expressionless countenance of the well-trained servant, instantly straightened.

Miles rolled his eyes. "I am a laughingstock, but," he said, his eyes narrowing, "on your life, do not let Sahib out that door!" Then he turned to Serena and meekly suggested they go to the conservatory for her lecture. "The verdure will ease my soul which you will sear."

"Very poetic," she said, speaking judiciously. "Why do you not use that romantic streak with Thérèse?" She didn't wait for a response, not expecting one, but turned on her heel and led the way toward the lush growth of the Renwicks' conservatory.

"Am I allowed to defend myself?" asked Miles when they reached their goal.

"No. You will, instead, listen."

Miles groaned. "You mean to lecture me."

"Yes I do. Miles, you have no notion at all how you hurt her, do you?"

"Not the most diddly bit of a notion," he replied promptly.

"Do not make a joke of it." A certain bleakness Serena had never seen before could be seen in his eyes. "What is it, Miles?"

"I *must* make a joke of it. If I do not it hurts too much."

Serena leaned back against the potting table and crossed her arms. "It. What is it?"

"What we are discussing!"

"And what are we discussing?"

He eyed her. "You are a sly cat, Lady Serena McMurrey!" She didn't smile and he turned away. "You will make me say it, will you not?"

"Yes."

"It. My feelings. My idiotic inadequacies." He twirled back on his heel. "Well? Is that enough?"

"We'll begin with this nonsense of your inadequacies. In what way are you inadequate?"

"Among many, an inability to stay in one place for more than a moment."

"Why is that an inadequacy—no," she added before he could speak, "continue. I am listening."

He shrugged. "I am nothing. No one. I have done nothing with my life to compensate for it. A vagabond. An adventurer if you will."

"I will it *not!* There is something nasty about an adventurer, Miles Standish, something unsavory. And that is not you. No, I will not have it that you are an adventurer. Vagabond? I find that one difficult as well. You were not exactly a pauper when you went off on your adventures—which is different from being an adventurer—and, from what I hear, made for yourself a fortune Golden Ball would not find contemptible! How is that inadequate?"

When he would have responded, she held up a hand and he closed his mouth.

"You have on a variety of occasions, found yourself in tight corners," she continued. "Very tight corners. And often you have had friends and acquaintances with you for whom you felt responsible. Did you ever shrug your shoulders and leave them to rescue themselves—or not, as the case might have been? No," she responded, even though he held up one finger. "On every occasion you have put yourself in deeper danger in order to see everyone safe. And yes, I know of that one occasion for which you would say you were responsible for the deaths of several. Did they follow your orders? Or did they insist on attempting their own escape?"

Miles blinked. "But I should have *made* them . . ."

"No. You were not only very young, you were not in command, and, even so, you saved most of that ridiculous group of explorers."

Miles turned aside. He fiddled with a leaf. "There must have been a way . . ."

"It must be nearly a decade since that badly conceived exploration into the African desert. You did your best to talk them out of it. When they insisted on going, you joined them, which you need not have done. When it fell apart, you lead a fair number of them back to civilization. How can you demand more of yourself than that?"

"But . . ."

"Miles," she interrupted, *"dub your mummer."* When his brows arched and his mouth closed on suppressed laughter at her use of the cant phrase, she nodded. "You did *more* than could reasonably be asked of any man. Cease beating yourself."

"Yes ma'am." He pulled at a nonexistent forelock.

She sighed. "Another jest. Miles, why else do you feel you are not worthy of Mademoiselle's affections?"

He drew in a sharp breath. "You don't mind kicking a man when he's down, do you?"

"Not if he is in need of it. Now tell me. Why?"

The bleak look returned with a vengeance. "It is not so much that I am not worthy of them as that I am unlovable."

Serena reached out and slapped him. Hard.

His hand flew to cover the sharp hot mark on his cheek. "Why did you do that?"

"You have five friends. Is their love worth nothing to you? And what of we, their wives? Is our love of no worth? You? Unlovable? I haven't a notion how you concluded such a thing, but of all the idiotic things you've said to me that is the most ridiculous of all!"

"But . . ."

"But? *Can* you say you are not loved?"

"No." He swung away. "No, there is Jason and Ian, Tony and Alex. And Jack, of course. They are my friends. Have been my friends forever it seems." He turned from her. "And yet . . ."

"Yet?" she asked softly when he paused.

"And yet I have always felt it a mistake, that one day they will see through me to the empty core and will shun me, forget me . . ."

"Damn those old men who had the raising of you!"

"Hmm?"

"They were fools and idiots and . . . and . . . evil!"

"They saw I had very good care," said Miles gently.

"No. They saw you were fed and clothed. That you had good schooling. But did they *care* for you? Did anyone *care* for you?" When he didn't respond she went on softly. "Children need the knowledge they are loved. If they do not get it, they ever after believe there is something wrong with them. And that is you, Miles. You believe it when it is so *wrong*. It was not *you* at fault but your guardians!"

Miles stared up into the foliage above her head. The warm moist scent of green growing things filled his head and, just barely discerned, a sweeter odor teased his senses. The faintest of scents. He wondered what it was and then berated himself. Serena was trying to help him. That she was spouting nonsense did not make it right for him to ignore her.

"You do not believe a word I say, do you?" she asked.

"Well"—he grinned a quick flashing grin—"no. But I am willing to listen all the night if it will make you happy."

A very odd noise came from deep in Serena's throat.

His eyes widened, and when he laughed, it was a real laugh. "Ah! You've been taking lessons from Sahib!"

She stamped her foot. "Blast it, Miles Seward, do you think I would bother with you if you were not worth it?"

He tipped his head, thinking over what he knew of Lady Serena. "Now *there* you have an argument that makes me stop and think. You do *not* suffer fools lightly. Very well, Serena, I will mull over what you say. I do not promise to change. I doubt I can at my age, but I will try."

"Then I have not utterly failed." She turned on her heel and went quickly back into the house. It took her a few casts, but she found Ian and, when she did, caught his gaze, held it, and walked straight into his arms. "I love you," she murmured into his cravat. "I wonder you had the patience to teach me to love you. I am so glad you did."

Ian, cuddling Serena close, stared over her head at Thérèse Marie, who had been talked into rejoining the group by Lady Renwick. Her eyes opened wide and she blinked twice. He made a "you-see-how-it-is" face at her and she grimaced in return, a "maybe-for-you" sort of face. And then she rose to her feet and strolled to the window, where she fiddled with the cord that tied back the drapery while she stared thoughtfully out the window.

Perhaps she would not cancel her plans for the future after all. She would chance it . . .

Nineteen

Two days later they all entered carriages—including Sahib, who rode on the special bench built into the Renwick carriage, where the forward seat had used to be. Five hours later they entered the McMurrey town house. Everyone would attend Ian's brother's wedding. Even Thérèse Marie, although she insisted that, since she had not been invited, she could not go. But Aaron McMurrey, once her predicament was pointed out to him by Ian, immediately proffered an invitation, so that problem was solved.

"Miles," she said softly. Dinner was done and everyone relaxed in the McMurrey library. She had drawn him away. "I have never met the bride. Surely she will not want a total stranger at her wedding."

"I would lay odds that there will be many strangers at her wedding. Half her own relatives, for a start."

His comment drew a smile, but Thérèse Marie shook her head. "No, she will feel she must be polite to me and on such a very special day I would feel an intruder. Please do not force me to go. I will explore London while you are all gone."

Miles shook his head. "No. You forget."

She frowned.

"Your cousin is in town. What if he saw you?"

Her frown deepened.

"You'll come to the wedding where I can keep an eye on you!"

She bristled at his suggestion that he must watch over her and in her irritation forgot her concerns about the bride. "I can take care of myself."

"Will you not allow me to worry about you?" When she didn't immediately respond, he added, "It is a role of friends, you know."

She sighed. "I have had little practice at friendship. It is like when I worried about you before we left France?"

"Very like. Except I'll not knock you on the head and carry you off!"

She chuckled. "I apologize again for Armand's behavior. But I am glad you are no longer where René may lay plots and bring you to disaster."

"Such a terrible fate he had in mind for me!"

She laughed, but there was a bit of strain in it.

"Aha! It is not that you worried about me married to you, but that you worried about you married to me!"

She sobered instantly. "No. Never think it. You are a wonderful man and any woman would be lucky to have you as her spouse."

This time Miles sobered. "No. That isn't true. I'd make a terrible husband, Thérèse. You know I cannot be still, that I must be up and doing. A wife would want a home, a place to call her own where she could raise her children, could invite her friends, could do all those things women do."

"The things women do . . ."

"What is it, Thérèse?"

"I think such things would drive me insane, Miles. I guess I would make an even poorer wife than you think you would be husband."

He watched her walk away. When she joined Serena and Eustacia, accepting a cup of tea from Lady Serena, he quietly left the room and, a few minutes later, left the house. Once outside he dithered . . . and then turned toward the park. He had strolled for perhaps twenty minutes when he saw Aaron sitting on a bench and staring out over the Serpentine. For a moment he thought of turning away and leaving the solitary figure alone. And then he thought of how he would feel the night before his wedding and decided that perhaps the younger man would like someone with whom to talk.

The wry thought followed, that he was, perhaps, not the best person to listen, since he was not and would never be married, but he would do his best.

"Should I go away?" he asked, approaching the bench.

Aaron looked up, smiled. "Mr. Seward. No, please, join me. I have been thinking of Beth, and feeling . . . inadequate."

"Inadequate?" Miles passed him a quick look. "But in what way would *you* be inadequate?"

"She is so very wonderful," said Aaron. "I would be a better man for her, wish only the very best for her—and, of course, will do my best to see she has her heart's desire in all things—but I cannot hope to meet her expectations. Not immediately. Her father is a very wealthy man. She will feel deprivation, perhaps even need, during the years I do not have the wealth to give her all she wants."

"She knows you, who you are, and what you have and have not."

"Yes. But does she *know?*"

"Ah. I see. Tony's Libby was her best friend, was she not? For years? And Libby had very little."

"Yes . . ."

"It is hard to accept that a woman chooses with her eyes open, is it not?"

Aaron laughed. "We would think of them as big children who must be cared for and cosseted and kept from all harm! And yet she is excited about traveling to India, living there. She has read everything she could find about the land and the people—especially Lord Renwick's book. She knows of the dirt and poverty and the dangers. And still she wants to go!"

"You seem amazed."

"She is a woman. Yet she craves adventure. Is that not something about which one should be amazed?"

Miles frowned. "A woman. Who craves adventure . . . ?"

"You see? You too find it a startling concept. And yet I wonder if it is as uncommon as we would assume. Think of the women who have followed their men into the savage land across the Atlantic. They have braved dangers, met them, and faced them down, dangers that we cannot even conceive." Aaron turned a quick glance on Miles and smiled. "Well, perhaps *you* can, but I cannot."

"It is a wild and beautiful country," murmured Miles. His thoughts were no longer on the conversation, but on the very odd thought that a woman might *prefer* adventure to a home and safety.

"Yes. As is India in a different way. I hope we do not contract any of the diseases about which I've been told. That is my biggest worry, that one or both of us fall fatally ill."

"There are many illnesses of which our doctors know little or nothing. After we sail I will pack a kit for the two of you and teach you the uses of the different medicines. Things I picked up in my travels and which I have, with my own eyes, seen to be efficacious."

"You are very kind. I will feel much better knowing we've such a thing with us."

Miles nodded, but he could not concentrate, his thoughts drifting again and again to the picture in his mind of Thérèsa, slim and straight and proud in her male attire, asking him to release Armand and Henri and take only herself prisoner. The courage she had shown, the loyalty to her crew . . . and the terror, barely hidden, that she herself would hang by the neck until dead.

He shook his head. *No, I cannot ask it of her. However much she would enjoy the good things, she might die and I'd be damned for taking her into such danger.* He heard Aaron speaking and said, "Excuse me, I was thinking. Please begin again?"

"I merely said that I thought it rather late and that I am ready to return to Ian's. Will you come or do you mean to stay out longer?"

Miles debated staying, thinking longer about Thérèse and how wonderful it would be to have her at his side as he sailed around the globe. But he had decided, had he not? It would not do.

"It is late. I too will return." He looked sideways. "Will you sleep?"

Aaron chuckled. "Oh yes. And dream. And my dreams will be very good, I think!"

Miles smiled. "You have chosen a lovely young woman. You are a very lucky man."

"Luck? Yes, that she was Libby's friend and that Lady Renwick invited her to Tiger's Lair, *that* was luck. And that she loves me as I love her? Is that luck or is that fate? Or something else . . ."

Aaron's hands were clasped behind his back and he strolled more slowly than Miles liked, but Aaron was a man on the verge of a great change in his life and Miles, sighing softly, moderated his stride to match Ian's brother's and strolled through the park without speaking, allowing Aaron his thoughts. . . .

Which are pleasant, thought Miles, *judging by that smile flickering over his countenance.* And added the rueful thought, *Would that mine were.*

The wedding was large and, if the bride was unhappy that her father had gone overboard to show the nobs that his daughter was as good as anyone, she never once let on. She maintained her poise until she and her new husband entered their carriage and it was no longer needed. Then she turned her thoughts to the few days they'd spend at the same seaside residence that had, a few years previously, been lent to Ian McMurrey and his new bride, Lady Serena.

"But you," teased Aaron, "will not hold a knife against me when I come to you this night."

"Then it is true that Lady Serena defended her virtue against her new husband?"

Aaron laughed. "She certainly had a knife and I believe she would have used it if she had found it necessary, but Ian only went to her to suggest they learn to know each other better before they came together as man and wife. They had never met before that day, you see, both appearing at the altar at the behest of their fathers."

"Iniquitous!"

"It might have been, but they fell in love. My father preens himself on his good judgment in insisting that Lady Serena be brought into our family. Ah, but, Beth, my dearest love, I do not wish to discuss Ian and the problems he and Serena had. I wish only to speak to you . . . and *of* you . . ."

And as he did just that, making love to her with his words, Miles and Thérèse Marie sat silent, in a carriage returning to Tiger's Lair. Neither could think of a thing to say. Nothing they felt *able* to say. In less than a week the *Nemesis* would be laden with all that was needed for the long voyage to India. Miles would leave.

We will, he thought, *be separated by half the world.*

It was a situation he didn't wish to face. Although he wanted to, he could not open a discussion that might, in the end, mean they'd *not* find it necessary to part. He feared to discover there was no hope and that they must! Thérèse, hugging her plan not to be left behind, feared giving a hint of it. Both remained silent, except for commonplaces, the whole five hours of the journey!

They saw little of each other over the next few days. Miles had to oversee the stowing of all Prince Ravi had purchased once it occurred to the young man he might never again see England. Much to his surprise, he had discovered he *would* miss it. The prince also prepared a list of items he ordered Lady Renwick to purchase for him every six months or so and send out to him.

Eustacia, reading down it, repressed a smile. "My prince, I will send some of this, but do you really think Cook's fairy cakes would survive the journey? Instead, why do you not ask her to teach your cook the way of them and, if there is some ingredient he cannot find in India, then I will send that."

So, along with everything else, Prince Ravi's private cook took lessons from the Renwick cook who, in return, was finally taught the way of several Indian dishes that the Renwicks had learned to like.

Thérèse stayed out of the way, watched all the activity with burning jealousy, and once they returned from their few days alone, had hours in which she got acquainted with Aaron's wife. Beth McMurrey was not so preoccupied with her new husband that she did not perceive Thérèse's carefully hidden angst.

"Come with us," she urged one day.

"I cannot." Thérèse did not add that, if she could figure out how to do it, she meant to do just that, however much Miles did not want her to do so.

"But you would escape your cousin's machinations. He would never find you if you were aboard ship and on the high seas!"

Thérèse shivered. She recalled the day in London when she'd strolled along Piccadilly with Lady Serena and Lady Renwick, who searched for the perfect gifts for a lady going far away from London for several years. The usual sorts of gifts would not do at all. They had been staring at the window of a shop selling linens when Thérèse caught her father's reflection. Coming along behind was her cousin. With all the casualness of a lady who has made up her mind, Thérèse immediately slipped into the shop.

"What is it?" Eustacia had asked when she saw how white Thérèse had become.

"I saw them. They are here. Looking for me," whispered Thérèse.

"They didn't see you, did they?"

"I think not. No, there they go . . ."

"That is your infamous cousin?" asked Lady Serena, staring after them. "I believe I met him once at a *soirée.* Is that possible?"

Thérèse explained about René's coming to London each spring.

"Ah. I do not blame you for avoiding him. I did not like him at all. An insinuating sort of mushroom, I thought, and wondered at Chartley for having him as his guest."

"Chartley?"

"An elderly gentleman who keeps much to himself except for a couple of weeks in the spring when he is seen in the company of your cousin."

"A recluse, much older than René, but he comes to London with my cousin." Thérèse shivered. "I find more and more about René that is despicable."

"What is it?"

"If Chartley is a recluse, why does he go to parties he must dislike very much?"

Eustacia tipped her head. "You would suggest your cousin knows something that Chartley would not want known?" She frowned. "But how can he? He is so much younger . . ."

"His parents lived with the court in Paris. Perhaps his mother or father left journals . . . ?"

"Pardon?" she asked when she realized that Beth had said something, which, lost in her memories, she had not heard.

"You love him, do you not?"

Thérèse was glad she was sitting, because she felt the blood leaving her head. "Very much," she said in a soft voice. "Too much to make him unhappy."

"But he is unhappy," said Beth, frowning. "Why?"

"He is my friend. He does not wish to leave me when he knows nothing is resolved."

Beth frowned. "But . . ."

Thérèse put a hand on the young woman's wrist. "Believe me. We have spoken about it."

Beth bit her lip. "You are certain you did not mistake each other? That each of you has thought you understood the other but each of you has come to wrong conclusions?"

"It is moot in any case. I would make a terrible wife for any man."

"Perhaps for just *any* man," retorted Beth instantly, "but for Miles Seward?"

Thérèse felt her heart beat harder. *Does Miles need the sort of wife I would make him?* she wondered. *Is it possible? Am I right to make the plans I do?*

"Think about it," said Beth. "Before it is too late." She rose to her feet. "I must go. Aaron fears I have brought too many trunks and suggests I sort through them and see if there are any I can leave behind."

"Ask Miles. He will know if you've too many."

Beth thanked her for the suggestion, and with only one last glance toward where Thérèse stared blankly out over the rose garden, she hurried off to the house.

Lord Renwick and Sahib found Thérèse still sitting there sometime later. Or rather, Sahib discovered her and led Jason to her. "Good afternoon," said Lord Renwick, not absolutely certain there was anyone there to whom he was speaking.

"Oh! Oh, Lord Renwick!" Thérèse forced her dark thoughts to the back of her mind. "Won't you join me?"

"You are thinking of Miles, are you not?" asked Lord Renwick when he'd settled himself beside his guest.

"I will miss him a great deal. He is my friend, you see."

"We are your friends."

"I know. And I am more than grateful that you have taken me in. But Miles was my *first* friend."

Sahib growled softly.

"And," suggested Jason gently, "perhaps more than a friend?" When she didn't immediately reply, he hurried on. "No, forgive me. That was something I should not have asked. Miles will miss you too, you know. And he will worry about you."

"He mustn't." *And he won't, if I can only keep my nerve,* she thought. "I can take care of myself," she finished.

"And you have friends now who will see you are safe."

"Yes. That is good."

"But you will miss him."

"Very much." *But only if I cannot bring myself to . . .* Sahib growled again—a trifle less softly this time.

"Sahib says you should go with him," said Jason, a touch of humor in his voice.

"Sahib says? Or you say?"

"The both of us." Jason frowned. "Are you aware that Miles persists, despite our best efforts, in thinking himself . . . not quite good enough? Or something?"

"He is a wonderful man."

"Yes, but *he* doesn't believe it." Jason chuckled. "It is quite unbelievable, is it not? Serena says it is because he was not loved as a child, that he was cared for and taught and all his needs seen to—except that most important one."

"How terrible. Even when my father was most deeply lost in a sort of sadness that left him lethargic and unable to do anything much, even then I knew he loved me."

"Yes. And I think there may have been servants who loved Miles. Once or twice, he spoke of a maid who spent her free time playing with him and mentioned an undercook who encouraged him to stay with her in the kitchen and talk to her. But they would never say they loved him, would they?"

Thérèse thought of Fat Jeanne and remembered all the times the woman had hugged her and smacked loud kisses on her cheeks and called her little cabbage. "Perhaps . . ."

"In any case, he grew up thinking he was not deserving of love and finds it strange that we all love him—and fears that someday we will discover what he really is and will stop."

"Which is one reason he goes running off on his adventures? He cannot be caught out if he is not here for the catching?"

"I had not thought of it in exactly that way." Jason chuckled. "Yes, something of the sort may send him running! You would be very good for him. If you loved him." She said nothing. "You *do* love him, do you not?"

"Yes," she said softly. "Yes, I love him. Very much indeed."

"Have you told him so?"

"I cannot burden him with words he does not wish to hear."

"Or words he fears to hear? Or fears he'll *not* hear?"

Again Thérèse was silent. This time Jason did not probe. He feared he had gone too far as it was. He felt Sahib stirring at his feet, felt him move, and knew he laid his great head in Thérèse's lap. Jason's sensitive ears heard Thérèse's fingers digging into the skin, probably around Sahib's neck and under his ears the way the big cat liked.

Perhaps, thought Jason, *Sahib can do what we cannot seem to do and put some courage into one or the other so that they do not lose each other!*

Thérèse, staring down into the glowing golden tiger eyes, sat there with her fingers digging into his fur, and wished she had the courage to ask Miles if there was any possibility, ever, that he might learn to love her.

Twenty

The day arrived when the *Nemesis* would sail on the evening tide. Everything was done. Prince Ravi's entourage was aboard and getting as comfortable as they could in the space provided for them. Bahadur had overseen the removal of the temple from the room in which it had been installed at Tiger's Lair. He, too, was aboard ship and, with reverence, establishing a shrine in a place where it would not be in the way of the sailors.

The rest of the company were still at Tiger's Lair, where Sahib watched first Thérèse and then Miles and, when possible, the both of them together.

"Jason, what is wrong with Sahib? It seems as if I trip over him every time I turn around," said Miles, when, for the third time, he had nearly done so.

Jason was talking to Prince Ravi and didn't respond, and not more than five minutes later, Miles was just in time to catch Thérèse when she did trip and fall. They stared at each other for a very long moment. Then, breathless, Thérèse breathed her thanks.

"It was nothing. I am just glad I was there to save you from a bad bump." But he didn't release the grip he had on her upper arms. "I will miss you," he said so softly she barely heard it.

"I wonder if I can bear it," she responded, resolving that she would *not* need to bear it.

"You have all my friends. Now they are yours, too, you know. They will care for you."

"Will they? But do I want them to . . . ?"

Miles's brows arched. *"I* want them to. I need to know you have protection, that they will be there for you."

Thérèse swallowed hard. Very gently she released herself from his grip. Straightening, she nodded. "Because you will worry if I do not allow this thing, then I will let your friends see that I am safe." There was tension around her eyes as she stared into his. Then, nodding, she moved to where Prince Ravi was describing the celebrations, which would be held when he returned to his home.

"Will Aaron and Beth be housed in the palace?" asked Lady Renwick.

"My tutor has asked that a house be given them for their use. He says that they will want privacy and—" the prince grinned "—that there may be times when I wish to consult him where we will not be overheard. Aaron McMurrey is a very intelligent man to think of that. It had not occurred to me that there might be some wishing me harm. But he is correct. There are those who objected to my father sending me far away for my education, who thought it wrong that I be exposed to the evil notions of those who did not understand our ways, our beliefs. So my father sent Bahadur—to see that, while I learned your ways, I did not stray from ours. And I have not. I *could* not. And yet—" he frowned and looked much more adult "—there *are* things I learned which are important but which the old-fashioned will disapprove."

"The world is changing," said Miles. "One cannot return to the old ways no matter how one might wish to do so. One must be able to meet strangers on their own terms."

"Yes, that is what I meant," said Prince Ravi. "Will you remain in my country for a time?" His eyes twinkled and he added, "To talk to some of the old men and explain that?"

Miles smiled a tight smile. "I will see you safely home,

Prince, and I will stay for a few weeks, but I will not talk to your old men. They would not believe me and—" Miles sobered. "—they might think that the fact I attempt to persuade them merely proves they are right to be suspicious of you, of what you learned while here."

Ravi nodded. "Again I would not have thought of that. I still have a very great deal to learn, do I not?" he finished in a much more humble tone than that in which he usually spoke.

"We will discuss such things on board ship," said Miles. "Now is not the time for serious thoughts. We must not spend our last hours in England in sober discussion!"

The company laughed, but was at the same time reminded that they were all together for the last time in what could stretch to years. Miles, when he left England the first time, had not returned for over a decade. The thought, crossing Ian's mind, propelled him to Miles's side.

"Miles, when my brother and new sister are ready to return to England, will you bring them back?"

"I cannot promise, Ian. I don't know where I'll be."

Ian sighed. "Well, that didn't work."

Miles tipped his head. "What didn't work?"

Ian's deep voice rumbled his response. "My plan to make certain you return to England more quickly than when last you left it on your adventuring!"

Miles smiled. "I think I can promise to return far more quickly than *that.*"

Lady Serena and the new bride were standing in the front window, talking, when they saw a carriage come up the drive. "Jason," called Serena, "you've company coming. Were you expecting someone?"

"No. Eustacia?"

"I can think of no one."

Silence blanketed the room while they waited to see who had come. The job carriage pulled to a stop and one of the Renwick footmen descended the steps. He opened the carriage door. Several soft gasps could be heard.

And one, "Oh, no."

Miles swore softly. Suddenly, he grasped Thérèse's arm. "Everyone!" He instantly had everyone's attention. "We are not here. We have not been here. You don't know where we are!" Still holding Thérèse's arm, almost as if he believed she'd not come if he did not, Miles headed for the door.

"Very well, Miles, but where will you be?"

"If you do not know, then you cannot say, can you?"

Sahib roared. There was an element of approval in the sound.

"Well," said Eustacia after a long moment, "I think we've a bit of playacting to do. Everyone? Do we know our lines?"

"I am not good at charades," said Beth softly. "Aaron? Shall we go up to our rooms? I believe you said you had one more box to pack with books, did you not?"

"Yes. Thank you, my love, for remind—"

The door closed on the words. The remainder of the party sorted themselves out into several groups around the room and, hesitantly, began conversations. And that is what Jean-Paul Laurent, Comte de Saint Omer, and René Laurent saw when the Renwick butler announced them.

Sahib at his side, Lord Renwick advanced toward the newcomers. "Is there something we can do for you?" he asked politely once the conventions had been obeyed.

"You can tell us where my cousin's daughter is to be found!"

"The *comte's* daughter? But do I know the *comte's* daughter?"

"She was stolen away by your friend. We are informed that what one of you who are called the Six does, the rest know it instantly."

"Not," rumbled Ian's deep voice, "when the one is Miles Seward. That is the one to whom you refer? He is the only one of us to have been in France recently, so I think it must be he."

"When did you last see him?"

"Not long ago," said Ian. "My brother was married in London a week ago. Miles attended the wedding."

"And my daughter?" asked the *comte,* who was becoming more than a trifle concerned about Thérèse. An unaccountable girl in many ways, but she had never before disappeared for so long.

"Your daughter?" asked Ian.

"Sometimes she calls herself Mademoiselle Antoine-Clair," suggested René.

"Ah! Mademoiselle! Yes, she was here, oh—" Jason pretended to think. "—it must have been something over a month ago when she was our guest, was it not?"

Lady Renwick, remembering when Miles had brought Thérèse and her crew to Tiger's Lair as prisoners, nodded. "About that, I think."

Ian spoke before René Laurent could ask the question hovering on his tongue. "If you are searching for her, you will have to look elsewhere. She is not here."

The Frenchmen apologized for their intrusion, said goodbye, and left. "René, I swear," said the *comte* in rapid French, "if anything has happened to Thérèse, I will have your—" The rest, providentially, was cut off by the closing of the door. No one wished to know exactly what it was Jean-Paul would have!

No one spoke until they heard the carriage rolling back down the drive. In fact it was much as if they were playing a game of statues and the cue had been given for everyone to remain absolutely still. When the crunch of wheels on gravel faded, it was as if everyone could breathe again. Eustacia moved to the bell pull and yanked it.

"Reeves," she said when the butler entered the room, "you may tell Mademoiselle and Miles that it is safe to return."

Reeves blinked. "But, my lady!"

"Just tell them."

"My lady, I cannot."

"Why can you not?"

"They are not here."

"Not here!"

A babble of voices, questioning and exclaiming, rose only to be silenced by Ian's deep voice asking, "You would say they have left Tiger's Lair?"

"Yes sir. They exited through the kitchen, very nearly running. Shall I determine where they have gone?"

"Please."

Once again silence descended on the salon. Gradually, here and there, low-voiced conversations started up, but when the door opened once again, everyone broke off what they were saying to turn to Reeves.

"Well, man?"

"They took horses. The animals will be returned."

"Oh dear. Thérèse Marie was not dressed for riding!"

"They did not say where they were going?"

"No, my lord," Reeves answered Lord Renwick.

Sahib roared an exultant sort of roar and the kitten, Sahib's friend, stood on the tiger's back, his back arched, and mewed loudly.

"Lady Renwick," said Prince Ravi, a smile playing about his lips, "I think you should pack up what Mademoiselle Laurent has and send it with our last bags to the *Nemesis*."

"Out of the mouths of babes," muttered Ian. "A very good notion, Prince. You have, I think, guessed it. Miles has taken Mademoiselle to the *Nemesis*!"

"He will sail with her?"

"He did not leave word that she would return!"

"Serena," said Eustacia, with decision, "come. We must work quickly if her trunk is to be added to those last bits carted to the cove! It is to leave before we sit down to eat."

"Then you all think I have guessed correctly?" asked Prince Ravi, who had made his comment more in the way of a jest than seriously.

"We do. Come, Prince, I will beat you once more at billiards before you leave," said Ian.

"You will *not* then," said the prince and the two exited the room, going to the game room.

Lord Renwick was left with Sahib and David, the kitten. "Well, Sahib? You too believe that is where Miles has taken Mademoiselle?"

Sahib roared one of his almost silent roars. The sound, which Jason had long before decided meant agreement, was followed by the odd chuffing sound that was the tiger's purr.

"You think all will be well?"

Sahib rubbed against Jason's leg, the purr louder.

"In that case I will not worry," decided Jason. "Take me to my study, Sahib. I seem to have gotten turned around."

Sahib gently nudged Jason until he faced the door and then took up his usual position so that Jason's fingertips touched his head. They walked to the door, stopping so that Lord Renwick reached out and opened it without fumbling, and then crossed the entryway to the hall to Lord Renwick's private wing.

Thérèse stood in the middle of Miles's cramped cabin and looked around. There was a wide bunk beside her with storage bins built in both below and above. There was a hinged table attached to one wall. When it was down, one could sit on the bunk and use it as a desk. Or one could stand at the end and use it for a washstand. Or, if one wished to dine *tête-à-tête,* chairs could be brought in and put at either end. There were pegs along the end of the cabin from which clothing hung, and on a chain, a lamp that moved gently to and fro as the *Nemesis* rocked to the gentle waves rolling into the small cove.

Miles had practically carried her from Lord Renwick's salon, rushing her out to the stables and then across country all the way to the coast. When she'd attempted to suggest she wasn't exactly dressed for riding, he'd put his hand over her mouth and told her that there were times when one didn't wait for proper dress and this was one of them—and had fixed it so she could ride. Beyond that he refused to speak.

"May we talk now?" she asked, turning to where he lounged in the open door.

He nodded.

"Why are we here, Miles?"

"You couldn't stay there."

"Your friends will not lie for me?"

"Perhaps, but they'd not like it. That is why we had to leave. With us gone they can speak the truth. You are not there."

"But if they are asked more particular questions?"

"Ian is very good at saying no more than he wishes to say. Your relatives will go away believing you have never been there."

"Then I can return when the carriages arrive bringing the Prince and the McMurreys."

"No."

Thérèse blinked. Her heart pounded. Was it to be so easy? Was it unnecessary for her to become a stowaway as she'd planned. "No?"

"I have decided I cannot leave you in England."

She was silent for a moment, working that out. "You will return me to France?"

"No." He unfolded his arms and straightened away from the door. "I have discovered I do not trust anyone but myself to keep you safe. You will go with us."

He turned away and strode off before Thérèse could close her mouth, decide what to say, and get it said. For a long moment she stared out the open door toward the Channel, facing into the breeze that, with luck, would turn with the tide and help take them away from land. The clean air of open water filled her lungs and, gradually, cleared her head. And then a smile formed, spread.

All my plans to stow away were for nothing! He is taking me with him!

Thérèse was still floating on the happiness of knowing he was not leaving her behind when, as she smoothed down her skirts, she realized her only clothing was what was on her back. She looked down. Because Miles was leaving, she had donned the most attractive of the gowns Lady Renwick had given her. It had been a lovely dress, made of an overdress of sprigged muslin worn over an undergown of plain muslin.

Had been.

Miles had pulled up the spring muslin and had grasped the hem of the undergown. He'd ripped it well up the seam, allowing her to sit astride her horse. The muslin had become badly crushed and everything smelled of horse! Was she to sail off to India with nothing else to wear?

Her chin rose and she turned to the door . . . only to pause. She reached down and attempted to hold closed the torn seam. And then she sighed, plopped down on the bunk, and leaned back, her arms extended behind her and holding her.

Something over half an hour later Miles returned. She scowled. His brows arched. "You don't wish to go to India?" he asked.

"Of course I wish to go. I had planned to go, if I could manage it! But I *cannot* go with nothing to my name but a torn gown!"

"Planned . . ."

Thérèse bit her lip. "I meant to stow away."

Miles's eyes lit up. He nodded. "I am glad." He turned to a cupboard she had not noticed in her original perusal of the cabin and dug around the shelves until he found a small box. He turned, tossing it in one hand and catching it and then suddenly tossing it to her.

Thérèse caught it easily and looked down at it. "What is this?"

"A sewing kit."

"A . . ." She tossed it back and Miles caught is just as easily. "There is a small problem."

"You can't sew."

She grinned. "You will admit it is a problem?" Then she eyed him. "Can you?"

"Sew?" His eyes twinkled and a smile teased the corners of his mouth. "Do you want the truth?"

"Of course."

"No."

"No, I do not want the truth?"

"No, I cannot sew. But," he added when she'd have said something, "Toby sews a fine seam. Take it off and hand it out the door. You can wear the robe folded under my pillow." He left, pulling the door shut and the room dimmed, the only light entering by way of a small window high in the wall beside the door.

Thérèse opened the door a smidgeon and handed out the under gown. Twenty minutes later Miles knocked and handed it back. Thérèse was soon dressed and again opened the door. "That helps, but I cannot see me doing much work dressed like this!"

"The cart arrived." He pointed.

Sitting next to the railing across from the door was the trunk she'd used when they'd gone to London for the wedding. She moved across the deck and ran her fingers along the top. "My clothes?"

Miles nodded.

"They knew what you meant to do when I did not?"

"They *guessed* what I meant to do." More gently, he added, "They know me well, Thérèse."

"So." She eyed him. "Is there room?"

"You'll have my cabin."

"And you?"

He shrugged. "There'll be room in Toby's cabin."

"Toby has his own cabin?"

"The *Nemesis* is a much larger ship than your *Ange Blanc*, Thérèse."

"I am beginning to know you, Miles Seward, and that does not answer my question!"

He grinned. "He has, in the past, shared with his son. Now he and I will share it and Johnny will hang a hammock with his mates."

"Where they'll not be able to move unless they perform a dance as does a *corps de ballet!*"

"They'll manage. They'll be less crowded than Prince Ravi's men."

Thérèse frowned. "Miles, have you a good-sized tarp that can be strung over the deck somewhere where they can live outside in good weather?"

"An excellent notion. I believe we do, but if not we'll buy one in Gibraltar."

"Our first stop?"

"Our first stop."

Miles took her arm and led her to the salon, where he laid charts on the table and discussed with her the route around the Cape of Good Hope and up the east side of Africa to India.

"Toby spent time with several captains familiar with the journey who were in port in London." He pointed. "Here. Here and here. You see that he's marked every spot where one may find water and food, marked where there are dangerous tribes or the coast is unsuitable for putting ashore and . . ."

An hour later they were still talking when the rest of the party were rowed out and came aboard. There were two small cabins on the port side, one of which would be the McMurreys' and the other Prince Ravi had himself suggested he share with Bahadur.

"You cannot believe how shocked we all were," said Miles softly to Thérèse. "If you had known the lad when he first arrived in England!" He shook his head. "Spoiled! Arrogant! Our Prinny is nothing next to the Prince Ravi that was!"

"He has changed so much?"

"Well, that is why we were surprised, you see. We had not thought the change had gone so far!"

Thérèse laughed. Once again dressed in male clothing, she felt at ease and comfortable and could not restrain her impatience that the tide had yet to turn. She wanted, so badly, to be away. Gone. Far from René's machinations, yes, but still more importantly, out on the water where she was free as a bird, where she felt she could *breathe*.

She said as much to Miles. "Yes," he responded as he glanced at the position of the sun. "I feel exactly the same. It won't be long now. Perhaps you would go see that Mrs. McMurrey is settling in. Toby saw that the trunk she wanted for the journey was set outside their cabin, but it is my guess she hasn't a notion how to stow everything away."

Thérèse grinned. "Very likely she has brought far too much and we will have to pick and choose and repack some to go below decks."

Thérèse and Beth were still deciding exactly what was needed and what was not when Thérèse felt the ship come alive. She stilled for a long moment, staring at nothing at all.

India, she thought. *I am off to India!* Another thought slipped in under that one. "With Miles."

"What did you say?" asked Beth, folding a chemise and then rolling it tightly as Thérèse had shown her so it would take very little space.

"What? Oh. Nothing. I was unaware I spoke aloud. Do you think you will need this *pelisse?* In bad weather it would be better if you remained in your cabin or in the salon. And in good weather you will not need it. And, as we go farther south, it will become very warm indeed."

"Yes. India, I have read is unbelievably hot, but Prince Ravi said that up in the hills where his father's kingdom is it can be quite cool . . ."

Thérèse, with a patience she had not known she possessed, continued to help Beth until everything was either stowed or repacked. And only then did she feel free to go out on deck and look about.

As she had expected, the *Nemesis* was not only in perfect

condition, it was a truly beautiful ship. Somewhere during her perambulations about the deck, Thérèse felt a tiny hot little spot of jealousy eat into her. Miles possessed just the sort of ship she had always dreamed of owning!

"Mademoiselle," said Aaron McMurrey when they gathered for dinner in the salon.

There were eight of them and the room was a trifle crowded and the talk and laughter made speaking privately very nearly impossible. "Let us go out on deck," suggested Thérèse, leading the way.

"First I wish to thank you for the aid you gave my wife, earlier."

Thérèse shrugged. "It was nothing."

"But you are a woman and it was much easier for her to learn what she must do from a female than if the captain or his mate had had to teach her. It was not nothing, and I am grateful. However," he continued, when she would have, again, demurred, "that is not the important thing. You know that your father and his cousin arrived at Tiger's Lair, but did anyone tell you what occurred while they were there?"

Thérèse tipped her head and wondered that she had not thought to ask. "I have not been informed."

"I will tell you what my brother told me. He, too, found your cousin a miserable excuse for a man."

Thérèse grinned and nodded.

"Your father, however," Aaron continued, "is a different kettle of fish."

"A . . . ?"

"An expression. It means they are unalike."

Thérèse nodded, remembering that Miles had used the expression.

"Ian thinks your father is truly concerned for you. Not merely that he wishes to know your whereabouts, but wishes to know you are safe and unharmed." When Thérèse didn't respond, he added, "You, of course, know him far better than Ian could, but that is what he thinks."

Thérèse's lips compressed and a rather stony look hardened her features. "He listened to René. He would sacrifice *me* for his own selfish concerns. I cannot forget that." The grim expression softened. "On the other hand, I will be gone for a very long time and very far away. I will send a letter from Gibraltar."

Aaron breathed a silent sigh of relief. For a moment, he had thought she would not suggest doing so and that he must interfere still further by suggesting it himself as Ian had ordered him to do! Aaron looked back toward the *Nemesis*'s salon, saw his new wife laughing at something Miles Seward said to her and, not jealous precisely, nevertheless felt a sudden urge to return to Beth's side. He excused himself and Thérèse nodded. He went back into the salon and she moved nearer the rail, where she leaned, looking out over the water.

Miles soon joined her. "Thinking deep thoughts, Thérèse?"

"Hmm? Oh. No. For the first time since I learned of René's plans for me, I am relaxed and at peace. And I am at sea. The two, together, make me feel as good—perhaps better—than ever before in my life."

That there was a third element, she dared not add. Not only was she away, but she was with Miles. That was the icing that made her cake of happiness complete!

"I too am feeling on top of the world. I have felt stifled, unsettled, penned in, irritable . . . all those things I dislike, but now I am at sea it is as if all that were someone else, not me at all."

She nodded. "It is strange, is it not? This love affair we have with the sea?"

He laughed. "Love affair . . . I would never have called it that, but it is as good a name as any." He carried the metaphor farther. "Perhaps the storms are like lovers' quarrels—quick and dirty and soon over, even when they seem to go on forever."

They were silent then, standing there side by side. So deep was each in his and her own thoughts that they had to be called twice when dinner was served.

Even the Bay of Biscay, notorious for its bad weather and huge seas, behaved itself, and changing his mind, Miles made course for Lisbon, where he meant to acquire more clothing for Thérèse. Thérèse refused to sit with Beth twiddling her thumbs, and instead made of herself another sailor, following orders with alacrity and dexterity. Miles could not help but admire her for it, but obviously if she would not act the passenger, then one suit of male clothing was not going to survive all the way to India!

Thérèse stood beside Miles as he eased through the busy port. "It must be one of the most beautiful harbors in the world," she breathed.

"One of them. A good port is almost by definition beautiful. Or, they begin that way! Then wharves, storehouses, and shipyards are built—all necessary to keeping commerce going—and then the rot sets in. But a huge harbor such as this one is less damaged by it than a deep cove which is smaller, one where the whole of the shoreline must be used for seagoing business."

"You are a cynic, Miles Seward!"

"Very likely. Are you ready to go shopping?"

"I don't know that I am. It occurred to me I haven't any credentials. Any papers."

"No papers?" Miles blinked. Then he swore softly.

"Hadn't thought of that, had you?"

"No. Now what do I do?"

"What had you meant to do?"

He grinned down at her. "Add to your working wardrobe so that you'll not be working in rags long before we reach India!"

She laughed. "There is a solution. One of Prince Ravi's cook's helpers is my height and very nearly my size. Try things on him, but allow a little extra room. Not only will things shrink, but I am a trifle larger"—she blushed—"in a couple of areas."

Miles's grin turned to laughter. "Very well. That is what I will do. I am sorry, however, that I cannot show you Lisbon."

"You know it well?"

His grin turned more than a trifle sardonic. "Let us say I know *parts* of it well. *Very* well. Still—" his look turned to one of innocence—"there are many areas to which I might, with propriety, introduce you and a few families, as well."

Prince Ravi also went ashore. He and his people had spent one winter at an estate Miles owned in southern Portugal and he hoped to find friends he'd made at that time. When he and Miles returned, they were followed by a couple of men carrying far more than Thérèse thought necessary, but Miles was so pleased with himself she merely said thank you, stowed her new clothes away, and changed into a Portuguese-made ankle-length riding skirt for dinner. She had discovered it was made with wide-legged trouser legs which, when she stood still, looked like a skirt. It pleased her a great deal and she wondered why all women's skirts were not made in such a way.

They ate early since the tide would turn at an inconvenient hour and had nearly finished, when Miles cleared his throat. "I've something to say."

Everyone stopped talking and the sounds of eating stilled.

"I went to the embassy today, to see about getting Thérèse proper papers so she would not need to keep aboard all the way to India and back."

"Well?" asked Toby when Miles's lips compressed and he stared over their heads.

"We've a problem. It was lucky I saw a friend there, someone who knows me and owes me a favor."

"Miles!" said Toby. "You are worrying us."

Miles grinned a wolfish grin. "Well I might. They are looking for Thérèse. It seems René sent out letters before he and the *comte* ever left France. He was convinced, despite what Armand must have told him, that I kidnapped Thérèse and ran off with her. I am to be apprehended and Thérèse returned to them instantly."

Thérèse blinked rapidly several times. "But he *wants* you to marry me."

"Perhaps. Or perhaps he has a new plan. Perhaps he thinks he sees a way to force me to *cede* the estate to him."

"To my father, you mean?"

"I meant exactly what I said. To *him*."

"But it would never have been *his*."

"Never? To whom would it go if your father died?"

"To me," she said promptly. "That is, it would if Father owned it at the time of his death."

"So, if it were ceded to *René* now, then it could not pass from your father to you and, besides, René could manage it as he pleased with no interference, and we can make a good guess that that would not be along modern lines!"

"No. He would turn back the clock to before the revolution. It cannot be done, but he is not quite sane on the subject, I think," mused Thérèse. "Well, then, it is obvious. We are careful what ports we enter and Miles and I *both* must stay aboard!"

"Must we?" asked Miles, eyeing her.

"Have you a better solution?"

He was silent for a moment, eyeing her. "I might," he said softly—and would say no more.

Twenty-one

Again, the winds were favorable and they reached Gibraltar expeditiously. Miles went ashore the instant they were given permission and disappeared into the citadel. Two hours later he returned with two gentlemen, one wearing clerical garb. They went directly to the salon, where they were closeted for some time.

Finally, Miles stuck his head out the door, looked around, and beckoned to the nearest man. "Find Mademoiselle for me, and send her here."

Thérèse, dressed in male attire, entered the salon after a brief knock. "You sent for me?"

"Thérèse, I'd like you to meet an old friend, John Moore, and also Frère Pierre. They have been kind enough to join us here for . . . for . . ."

"My dear child," said the shocked cleric, interrupting, "you will not wish to be married dressed like that!"

Thérèse's eyes narrowed. "Married."

The single word had a flat, unemotive element that sent a *frisson* up Miles's spine. "It is the only solution, Thérèse," he said on a wary note. "If we are wed, that makes you an English citizen. Not only will no one arrest an eloping couple, but I can get papers for you.

"You do not wish to wed."

Again that frighteningly unemotional tone. "If I ever actually *said* that," said Miles, his pitch changing to one of exasperation, "I wish you would forget it. Or perhaps it was so when we did not know each other so well."

"You said marriage would ruin friendship."

"You have seen my friends. Has friendship ruined their marriages?"

Thérèse felt her lips twitching at the corners and immediately controlled them. "I wondered if you had noticed that."

The cleric had followed their conversation, confusion clear to be read on his features. "If," he now said, "the mademoiselle does not wish for this marriage, then I will not perform a ceremony!"

"I do not believe I have ever heard Mademoiselle say she does not wish to wed. Her only comment on the subject is that no one would wish to wed such as she."

"Which is still true. You do not wish to wed me. You only suggest this because you are a good man and you would protect me in any way you can find to do so."

Miles turned away. "Would you find it terrible to be married to me?"

"No woman would find it terrible. No one could."

He turned back, his eyes wide with shock. "Do not lie to me."

"Have I ever? Miles," she began . . . and then turned to Mr. Moore and the priest. "Gentlemen, would you leave us for a little? I believe we need to speak in private."

They nodded. "We will go out on deck," said John Moore. "I have had few opportunities to explore such a ship as this."

Miles went with them, found Toby, and set Toby to entertaining the embassy man and the priest until he and Thérèse had sorted out their problems.

"I should not have surprised you in such a way," he said, closing the salon door behind him as he entered.

She nodded.

He sighed. "I did not know how to suggest that we wed.

And we haven't much time here, so I guess I thought perhaps if I just . . ."

"Just thrust a *fait accompli* on me that I would agree?"

"It is a good plan," he said a trifle defensively.

"Miles . . ."

"You would say that marriage is forever," he quickly added. "But we like each other. We work well together. We . . ."

"I love you," she said, interrupting. It was Thérèse's turn to turn away. "There. It is said."

"Love me," he repeated, his voice soft, wondering.

She turned back. "I would marry you in a trice if I did not fear that you would come to regret it, that this is the impulse of the moment."

He smiled. The smile widened. In two strides he was before her, reaching for her hands. He stared down at her. "You *love* me? But how is it possible."

He sobered and she felt his hands trembling.

Shaking his head sadly, he said, "It is not me you love, but an imaginary man you have set about me like the clothes I wear."

"They said you had this ridiculous notion in your head that you were unlovable," she said in a grouchy voice. But then she smiled mistily up at him. "How *could* one such as you possibly be unlovable?"

Miles's hands tightened around hers until the pressure verged on pain. He looked over her head. "But it is true. You will discover the real me and you will wonder that you ever thought you loved me."

"Nonsense."

"It isn't."

"How long have your friends known you?" she demanded.

He blinked, returning his gaze to meet hers. "Since we were children."

"And in all that time they have discovered no reason to stop loving you?"

"Well . . ."

"I think, Miles, I would like the opportunity to see if I discover whatever it is you think is in you that is so awful."

"I didn't say it was awful!" he said, defensively.

She laughed. "Miles, will you marry me? Will you take a chance that you'll not regret it?"

"I don't know how I could ever regret it, Thérèse—unless you come to do so."

"We do seem to need to reassure each other a great deal, do we not?"

They stared at each other. And then, gently, Miles drew Thérèse into his arms. She came trustingly and, for another long moment, their gazes mingled. Then he lowered his face to hers and awkwardly their lips met. But only that first time. With a groan, he pulled her closer, tilted his head slightly, and kissed her as he'd wanted to kiss her for what seemed like forever.

Some minutes later they looked at each other, something like shock visible in both expressions.

"I didn't know it could be like that," said Thérèse.

Miles drew in a deep breath and let it out in a whoosh. "Neither," he said, "did I."

Beth helped Thérèse dress in the best of the three gowns she owned and then seated the bride so that she could dress her hair. "You have lovely hair. Why do you never allow it to show?"

Thérèse shrugged. "It is a nuisance. I saw cropped heads in London and thought it was by far the most sensible way of wearing one's hair I'd ever seen. I think I will cut mine."

Beth chuckled. "Had you not better ask Miles about that? For some reason men like long hair." She blushed. "My Aaron says they like to play with it."

"Play with . . . Oh." Thérèse blushed. "You mean when you make love." She drew in a deep breath. "Beth, would you tell me . . ."

Beth did. Gently but completely. She was glad that Thérèse merely nodded. "It is wonderfully nice once you get used to it," she finished.

"Yes. I felt amazing things when Miles kissed me. I cannot believe I'll not feel more when we are free to . . . to be together as man and wife." She twisted her head and tried to see what Beth had done to her hair, but unable to do more than see a part of it at a time in Miles's small shaving mirror, gave it up, pushed away from the table, and stood. "I suspect they are waiting for us."

They were. Somehow the salon had been transformed into a bower, flowers stood everywhere in large makeshift vases. A small table, replacing the dining table, was covered with a shawl. On it rested a cross and a Bible and the sacraments. The priest stood behind it and Miles paced before it. He stopped when Beth opened the door and held it wide. Thérèse stepped into the opening and was backlit by sunlight streaming down over her. Miles stilled.

"Beautiful," he breathed. "You are so beautiful."

"Nonsense," said Thérèse. "But, my love, *you* are."

Red touched Miles's cheeks. "Men are not beautiful." He strode toward her and reached for her hands. "Handsome perhaps," he said, smiling, but tipping his head in a self-deprecating manner. "And do not contradict me. You, my lady, are beautiful." He turned and led the way to the altar. Their friends and as many of the crew as could manage to squeeze in, found places. Miles heard grumbles from outside and, as the priest was about to speak, held up his hand. "This will not do."

Fifteen minutes later the flowers and altar had been moved out on deck. Again everyone found places and, this time, all were able to do so. Prince Ravi was happy because now his men, dressed in their best, could form an honor guard on either side of the bride and groom. If the priest looked at them a trifle askance, he said nothing about it, but turned to the couple before him and smiled.

"I can see in your faces," he said, "that there is no question of either of you marrying the other for any reason than that you wish to do so."

Miles and Thérèse looked at each other. Thérèse lifted her hand and Miles took it between both of his. "We wish to be wed," he said. Some minutes later they were married.

Miles invited the priest and his friend to stay for the celebratory dinner Piggy was, even then, overseeing. The men shook their heads, thanked Miles for the invitation, but Mr. Moore, speaking for both of them, said they must return to their duties, that he, at least, had been away far longer than he should have been.

"You will come to the embassy tomorrow to attest to our marriage?" Miles asked the priest. "Your signature will be required on the legal papers, I am sure." They agreed on a time, and Miles ordered a sailor to row the two men ashore.

The feast topped Piggy's former best efforts. He had arranged for the use of the kitchens on the ships to either side of the *Nemesis*, and cooked enough for several courses. Miles and Thérèse managed to stay for two of them, but as the table was cleared for the next course, he stood up and tugged her to her feet. He nodded toward the door, and without a word to anyone, they slipped away.

Thérèse had not been wrong that the sensations his single kiss had roused in her were only the beginning of what he would teach her to feel. The night was long and her desire for new lessons unending so that, come morning, Miles, a very happy man, left her sleeping and warned everyone that she was not to be bothered. He himself went to the embassy, where he was to meet with the priest and the English legate.

When he returned to the *Nemesis*, he not only carried papers for Thérèse, but letters that were to be sent to his London solicitor containing orders for his French estate. Several more letters were added to the pouch before it was transferred to a ship sailing that evening for London. Among them were the following two.

Dear father, wrote Thérèse.

    You may cease to concern yourself about me—assuming you ever did in the first place, of course. I am no longer your concern, you see, but my husband's. We were married by a Spanish cleric aboard the Nemesis *yesterday and will set sail for India within a few days. My husband is also writing you concerning Saint Omer, which he has deeded to me. Arrangements are in train for an English agent who will oversee Armand Mouton who, at my request, will replace Rabaut as my land agent.*

    I do not add that you give René my best because I do not wish him my best. He very nearly ruined my life and I cannot forgive him. You will say that I am wed to the man he wished me to wed, but I am certain you will agree that it is different that we have agreed to be man and wife and were not forced to be man and wife. I do send you my best wishes. We will visit you when we return from India in a year or so.

Your undutiful daughter,
Mrs. Miles Seward

Monsieur le Comte de Saint Omer.

    Official papers will be brought to you detailing what you may and may not do concerning the Saint Omer estate. As a beginning, however, you may move at once into the chateau if you so wish. I have ordered suites prepared for you and for your cousin. In general, what you may not do, now or in the future, is give orders concerning estate business. In no way whatsoever have you or your cousin the authority to interfere.

    I love your daughter and will care for her to the best of my ability. I apologize that I was unable to ask your permission to wed her, but our situation, forced on us by your cousin, made it necessary for us to wed at once

*rather than take the time to know each other better
before making this great change in our circumstances.
We will visit you when we return from India.*

Sincerely,

Your son-in-law, Miles Seward

off his back and pushed to place his paws under it he
hoped—

—Me and that wouldn't dare I'm not sure but now it would be
enough.

Epilogue

"Jason," said Eustacia, bursting in on the five friends sitting around the Renwicks' study, "we've a message from Miles!"

Sahib raised his head.

"Well? Read it, my dear. At once."

"They are wed! They wed when they reached Gibraltar!"

"Excellent news. Why are you surprised?"

Eustacia chuckled. "I am, am I not? I suppose because I thought them both so stubborn they would never get around to admitting they loved each other."

Sahib chuffed happily and Jason dropped his hand to scratch him behind the ears, jerked it away when small claws scratched him, and more carefully maneuvered his fingers into the tiger's fur.

"Sahib is content with your news. I think he too feared those two too stubborn to come to terms."

All the Six were wed and Sahib, his work done, chuffed contentedly, uncaring that his humans didn't always understand him. Sahib liked caring for those about him, seeing that everyone was happy.

At the moment all was well.

For the near future—

Sahib made a special sound and the kitten crawled down

off his back and around to where his paws made a safe haven.

—he had this youngster to care for. For now it would be enough . . .

Dear Friends,

SMUGGLER'S HEART is the last of the books about the Six. Sahib goes into contented retirement, but I admit I'll miss him. And his friends. Perhaps someday I'll come up with a way of meeting up with all of them once again.

MISS SELDON'S SUITORS is the title of my next book. Miss Matilda Seldon's mother died when she was quite young, so Matty did her best to care for her absent-minded father, the much beloved but overly erudite vicar of their small village. Then, once she was firmly on the shelf, her father died, leaving her destitute—except for a few insignificant pieces of her mother's jewelry and her father's extensive library. A villainous cousin in need of money comes to her aid. Except he doesn't of course. He tells her he'll put her on a stagecoach, which will take her to his family where she'll have a home—and then puts her on a stagecoach to nowhere-in-particular before he goes off to sell the library and her jewelry for himself.

Luckily there is a kindly vicar on the coach who takes Matty to his patron's wife. Her ladyship, however, is a suspicious soul and doesn't believe our heroine's story. The village's elderly mystery lady is taking tea with her ladyship. She does believe and takes our heroine into her home, much to the smitten vicar's concern. There is that mystery, after all.

And then the wooing begins. The mysterious lady has a number of young males visiting with great regularity—

which is only one reason she is a mystery to those who know her. One is a barrister, one a rake, another a young man-about-town not long down from university—and, of course, the middle-aged vicar who rescued her.

Having too many suitors is quite a coup for a spinster lady long on the shelf! Of course, Matty isn't quite certain exactly what sort of proposal each offers, which does cause her a few pangs here and there. Life would be far simpler if only her head didn't tell her one thing and her heart another!

Cheerfully,
Jeanne Savery

I enjoy hearing from my readers. E-mail reaches me at: JeanneSavery@yahoo.com. Snail mail may be sent to: Jeanne Savery, P.O. Box 833, Greenacres, WA 99016.

More Zebra Regency Romances

__A Taste for Love by Donna Bell $4.99US/$6.50CAN
    0-8217-6104-8

__An Unlikely Father by Lynn Collum $4.99US/$6.99CAN
    0-8217-6418-7

__An Unexpected Husband by Jo Ann Ferguson $4.99US/$6.99CAN
    0-8217-6481-0

__Wedding Ghost by Cindy Holbrook $4.99US/$6.50CAN
    0-8217-6217-6

__Lady Diana's Darlings by Kate Huntington $4.99US/$6.99CAN
    0-8217-6655-4

__A London Flirtation by Valerie King $4.99US/$6.99CAN
    0-8217-6535-3

__Lord Langdon's Tutor by Laura Paquet $4.99US/$6.99CAN
    0-8217-6675-9

__Lord Mumford's Minx by Debbie Raleigh $4.99US/$6.99CAN
    0-8217-6673-2

__Lady Serena's Surrender by Jeanne Savery $4.99US/$6.99CAN
    0-8217-6607-4

__A Dangerous Dalliance by Regina Scott $4.99US/$6.99CAN
    0-8217-6609-0

__Lady May's Folly by Donna Simpson $4.99US/$6.99CAN
    0-8217-6805-0

Call toll free **1-888-345-BOOK** to order by phone or use this coupon to order by mail.

Name_____

Address_____

City_____ State_____ Zip_____

Please send me the books I have checked above.

I am enclosing	$_____
Plus postage and handling*	$_____
Sales tax (in New York and Tennessee only)	$_____
Total amount enclosed	$_____

*Add $2.50 for the first book and $.50 for each additional book.

Send check or money order (no cash or CODs) to:

Kensington Publishing Corp., 850 Third Avenue, New York, NY 10022

Prices and numbers subject to change without notice.

All orders subject to availability.

Check out our website at **www.kensingtonbooks.com**.